I0550021

# Shrink

*An Abby Chilton Novel*

By Doug Romig

Copyright 2014 Doug Romig
All Rights Reserved
Second Edition 2016

# Dedication

To all of you who support my
dream of being a writer

# About the Author

DOUG ROMIG lives in Knoxville, Tennessee where he enjoys the writing, hiking and spending time with his sons. Doug's first book was *The Spiritscape Chronicles Book One: Angelcide*. Other mystery titles from Doug include *The Spiritscape Chronicles Book Two: New Fallen, Reunion: An Abby Chilton Novel, Interpol,* and *Cryptos: ICE.*

Keep up to day with Doug at **http://www.dougromig. com**, see what's happening on Twitter **@DougRomigWriter**, follow on his Facebook page at **DougRomigWriter** or just send him an email at **dougromig68@gmail.com**.

# Table of Contents

# Chapter One

For two weeks the Observer watched Will. Habits were noted. Personality traits were glaringly obvious to the Observer's nimble mind. Will was a simple man with no close family and few associates. He had no girlfriend, as long as you didn't count the inflatable toy under his bed. Being currently unemployed, there would be no employer to miss him. Any friends had not made contact with their comrade in the week the bug had been on his phone. He rarely used his flip phone for calls and never sent any texts. Online friends would notice if anything happened to him but gamers come and go. His Facebook status was never updated. Even Will's sense of humor – such as it was – had been written out in painstaking detail. Nothing was left to chance. The profile had to be perfect or this could be disastrous.

Will's home was a simple bungalow-style cottage with the stereotypical retired, nosy neighbor sitting on her front porch across the street. The backyard had a nice garden with a very handy tool shed where Will spent his offline time. The Observer had explored the shed, discovering many helpful items for his plan. He chose the two which would work the best.

The forecast was for rain tonight. Rain was a double-edged sword, it had been both an ally and an enemy in the past. Tonight it would serve as his ally. Since it was a Friday night, Will would be on his way home from job hunting to spend the evening playing a massively multiplayer online role-playing game with fellow cyber geeks who had no real life outside of the computer. The Observer arrived an hour before Will was due. He took his time preparing everything in the home from setting up in the kitchen to unscrewing the light bulbs in the hallway. He sat on a wooden chair in the spare bedroom and sipped from the tube coming from his backpack. It would only be a short wait. The Observer knew his target all too well.

Ten minutes later, he heard the garage door raise and lower, then the soft shuffle of Will as he entered through the kitchen. The Observer quietly got up from his seat, noiselessly crossing to the hallway. There was a crinkling sound which was not made by the hunter, but the hunted.

"What the hell is this doing here?" asked Will. The Observer smiled as he moved like a specter in the shadows of the hall. "Bobby? Is this a joke? I don't get it." It was not Bobby moving swiftly and silently into the room. All Will saw was a figure dressed in black from the top of its head to the tips of its toes, seeming to fly at him. An instant too late, Will saw the metallic glint crashing down as his own screwdriver pierced his heart.

The lips of the dying man moved making the word "why" even though the only sound was the gurgling of blood from his mouth. The last thing he saw were two of the bluest eyes he had ever seen staring into his as life dripped away like the blood leaking from his body. The Observer breathed a sigh. His fun was over.

"It's all in the cleanup," said the killer, with neither sorrow nor remorse in his voice. There was an eerie happiness as he began to whistle a lively tune, wrapped the body in its own tarp and took it to the victim's waiting car.

"Who was the idiot who came up with the idea of making one cup of coffee at a time? If you're only going to drink one cup, why bother?" asked Abby Chilton to no one in particular. She was glaring at the new coffee maker in the break room.

"Don't ask me, Tiny," said Marcus Shon. "I just work here." Both shared a laugh, even though neither one thought it was really funny. It was why they got along so well in this high stress environment. They were two of the few who knew how to laugh. "Time to make the doughnuts," sighed the Korean American. "Later, Tiny."

Abby gave him a casual wave as she ignored the new single cup coffee maker with its prepackaged coffee, grabbing a filter out of the cabinet. She poured coffee grounds into the waiting paper, not measuring the amount. She had two simple rules about coffee. Rule One: If it is called something you cannot pronounce without sounding like a total douche, it's not coffee. Rule Two: If you can float a horseshoe in it, it's about ready.

Needless to say, hardly anyone else ever drank the coffee she made. Abby suspected this was part of the reason there was a new coffee maker in the room. *What a bunch of pussies. No. Wait. I can't call them female genitals. They are merely intimidated by my ability to digest vast amounts of caffeine, and this particular neurosis led to the purchase of a new device which would allow them to maintain a level of self-esteem elusive in their personal lives so much so they needed to control this situation at work to maintain their illusion of stability.* Smiling to herself, she thought, *Pussies would work fine on their psych profiles and save a lot of time.*

"I know that smile," stated a tall, lanky blonde. "What are you calling them today? Neurotic? Sociopathic? Bed wetter's?"

"Pussies," said Abby.

"Accurate. Not very PC, but accurate," said Barbara Johnson. Looking at the new coffee maker, she taunted, "I knew you'd hate it. That was one of the biggest selling points to Jeremy. Jeff loves ours at home."

Abby had to smile. "Glad I could help." Jeremy was her boss who did not think she was needed most of the time and made every effort to make her life a living hell. It was hard enough being a woman in the Federal Bureau of Investigations without others going out of their way to make it harder. Abby also had two other strikes against her from Jeremy's point of view. She had given up something the bureaucrat had always wanted, but never achieved. Abby had been one of the finest field agents, doing some of the most detailed profiling many had seen. She was very good in the field and had a knack for sensing a situation, being able to tell what to do and when to do it. Pure instinct. She was on her way to working with some of the greatest minds of the Bureau at the Behavior Analysis Units. She voluntarily walked away to use her talents internally. As talented as Jeremy had been, he knew he was not on the level of the BAU, but Abby could have been.

This led to the other reason her boss tormented her. Abby had a PhD in psychology. That meant all the type-A alpha males and females hated being sent to see her. She was the shrink. They had to jump through her hoops to be unshackled from their desks. She was notorious for making them feel small doing it. It was how she got the nickname from Marcus: Tiny. Only she, Marcus and Tina got the joke. Everyone else thought it was because she was not overly tall. *Let 'em think what they want. If any of those assholes try to call me Tiny, I'll hand them their balls.*

Agents and analysts tended to steer clear of her as Abby stared at the coffee maker, waiting for her witch's brew of caffeine to be completed. As the coffee maker beeped, causing the pleasure center in her brain to create a rush of anticipation, a voice blasted away all those good feelings.

"Good morning, Chilton," said Jeremy Mathis. "How are you today?" The question was merely an empty gesture intended to open a dialogue. Abby wasn't one for idle chit-chat, but she always made an exception for Jeremy. She knew he really didn't care how she was so she made an extra effort to tell him all her joys and woes.

"This PMS is a bitch, Jeremy," she began and kept going. "I'm feeling a little bloated. Other than the female stuff, I'm feeling happy with my life. The new apartment is really starting to feel like home. Now if I can lose these last nine pounds to get back into the size four dress I wore last year, I'll be great. I looked good in it if I do say so myself. That dress got me laid!" She always found ways to make the Special Agent in Charge of the Knoxville Field office feel uncomfortable. He made her life hell; she made him blush. She considered it a win-win.

"Thanks for the over-share, Chilton," he replied, trying to be funny. "You always know what not to say. But you say it anyway."

"It's my gift," she retorted.

The boss got down to business. "As much as I love our verbal sparring matches, we have a situation and both of us need to get to work." Taking a mug, he went to the single cup machine to make himself some kind of cappuccino which would have turned Abby's stomach. He watched her pouring her coffee. "How do you drink that shit? At least put some cream or sugar in there?"

Abby took a long, slow sip of her coffee. It was bitter and strong. "Coffee is an art. It takes time and effort to create the right taste and combination of flavors to sooth the troubled soul one must conquer each morning before the day can be faced with sufficient stamina."

"Psychobabble?"

"Colombian coffee commercial," smiled Abby. "I saw it one morning while checking YouTube for coffee references to throw at you."

Jeremy sighed. "Grab your battery acid and come with me. You really need a life."

"Tell me about it. But as long as I have you to torment, I'm good." Getting serious, she asked, "So what's going on? And why are you asking me? Your ass must really be in a sling if you need my help."

Walking through the cubicles to the end of the hall, the pair turned a few heads. It was infrequent for them to have more than the most perfunctory conversations. Seeing the two walking to the conference room was a rarity. Abby was accustomed to looks from men. Anyone would describe her as pretty without being strikingly beautiful. Her hair was in a constant state of flux. This month it was nearly shoulder length brown with blonde highlights with the barest traces of red. Abby knew she looked good and took pride in her appearance while trying not to obsess over it. She had a figure which was well proportioned to her five foot five frame. She had breasts which were big enough to be noticed, not so big they got in the way. Abby liked her behind which she resisted referring to as her best asset. Too puny for her sense of humor. The hours in the gym had worked well to avoid the thirty-something softening she had seen in so many happy, suburbanite soccer moms. Neither the softening nor the soccer mom lifestyle were in the cards for her. This was her life.

Entering the room, Abby left her smartass attitude for professional mode. There was someone she did not know standing there. One of Abby's greatest strengths was also one of her greatest weaknesses. While she had been bantering with her coworkers, she had been adding to their profiles. She could see things in people others missed. On the flip side, she could not stop seeing things in people others missed.

Marcus, she noticed, was wearing the same pants he had worn the day before. His normally pressed dress shirt had been folded as could be told from the sleeves. It was from the go-bag he kept in his car. He had left on time yesterday while avoiding a long conversation with her or prolonged eye contact. Conclusion: Marcus finally got past second base with the woman he had met at Starbucks two weeks ago.

Barbara tried to sound casual this morning. As the office manager, she always looked professional. Her clothing was immaculate and makeup was perfect. Hair was well coiffed. She looked to the world to be ready to face any kind of bureaucratic bungle which came her way. However, she was not carrying herself as confidently as usual. Her shoulders were slightly slumped. The sound of her heals on the tile floor of the break room told Abby her normal gait was less crisp than usual. No known work issues. She had mentioned her husband, Jeff, but not her daughter, Rachel. No mention of the report card from two days ago or bragging about all the A's. Conclusion: the report card was not filled with A's as she had expected.

Jeremy was less cruel in his wit this morning. There was something going on. He was never nice to her; however, he knew she had some skills he needed from time to time. When he did not use sarcasm to an extreme, he needed her to get in the head of someone else. Escorting her to the conference room meant this was the man behind the less-rude boss.

She looked over the newcomer. Tall. Six feet. Between two hundred and two-ten. Short, blonde hair with traces of gray on the temples. In good shape. No facial hair. Intelligent, striking green eyes. No real facial expression yet. Poker face. Charcoal gray, two-piece Brooks Brother's suit. Not tailored. Royal blue dress shirt sans a tie. Black Kenneth Cole shoes. Nice, but not too expensive. Lapel pin from the University of Tennessee. College grad. Holding himself with a level of confidence you do not normally see in a visitor to an FBI building. No weapons under his suit coat. No badge on his belt or pocket. Unlikely LEO. Law enforcement officers like to show their badges so others know they are on the job, too. A good Seiko watch. No wedding ring, but there is a mark on the finger. No tan line. Divorced. More than a year. Less than five since the muscle has not grown back. Making an effort to look middle class. Something is not quite right. There is more to him than this.

"Abby Chilton. Allow me to introduce Michael Sims. Mr. Sims has an issue he wanted to share with the Feds." The way Jeremy said the last part told her those were Sims' words and not his. He hated it when people referred to them as "Feds" and knew Abby would catch it.

"Ms. Chilton. A pleasure." Sims' voice was somewhere between tenor and baritone. Nothing uncommon. There was a subtle twang to his voice which sounded native east Tennessee.

"Mr. Sims. It's Agent Chilton," corrected Abby. "What seems to be on your mind?"

"My apologies, ma'am. I meant no disrespect. Mr. Mathis told me you were the local psychologist. I didn't know you were an agent, too."

"Long story. Let's make this easy. I'm Abby. Do you prefer Mike or Michael?"

He smiled a very disarming smile, totally throwing her off. "It's Mick."

*Damn! The smile and the name are too cute. Focus Abby. He's not that cute.* "So tell me, Mick, what brings you here and got you all the way up to the top floor?"

For the first time, he looked unsure. "I don't think you'll believe this; but I think there is a problem in Oak Ridge." Oak Ridge captured Abby's attention. She looked at Jeremy, who nodded.

"Really, Mick? And why would a nice Knoxville boy like you be worried about Oak Ridge?" asked Abby, trying her best to sound charming.

"Miss Abby, are you making fun of me?" asked Sims. He was not sure how to take her and it showed.

"Not at all, Mick," replied Abby. "It simply seems like something unusual to say." *Don't call me Miss Abby! That is way too distracting!*

"The father of one of my students works at Y-12. Robbie has been out of school for a week and no one can get in touch with him," Mick explained. "I even went by their home; but no one is there."

*A teacher. Makes sense. But where?*

"Are you a professor at UT?" asked Abby, but instantly knew she was wrong by the chuckle.

"Not my kind of teaching. Too much politics. I'm one of the technology teachers at the STEM Academy. It's the downtown high school for..," began the teacher.

"For science, technology, engineering and mathematics. STEM. It's a public school with a private school curriculum. Very progressive." said Abby while thinking, *Impressive. A technology teacher. Cute and a good heart. Time for a background check on Michael Sims. Focus, Abby. You really need to get laid.*

Both men in the room looked impressed. Jeremy raised an eyebrow. "I read a lot," she said in explanation. She had read everything she could about east Tennessee when she had gotten the assignment to Knoxville. Knowing the schools was only part of the research.

"You don't have a student there?" asked the impressed Mick.

"No kids. Just a career," replied Abby. "Now about Robbie?" She could see Mick was giving her the once over. Twice. *Stop looking at me and get to the point. Well, you can look a little; but not too long because there is work to do. I really need to show more cleavage. Note to self: hit the gym at lunch.*

"Robbie is a great kid. Very smart." Sims sounded worried by his tone. "He built his own notebook computer first semester. His parents are very involved. It makes absolutely no sense they would disappear without a trace. No word to the school. No nothin'!" That was the first time his grammar slipped into Tennessee slang.

Jeremy had enough. "Mr. Sims, thank you for bringing this to our attention. I will ask someone to look into this and, if there is anything to tell you, I will make sure someone gets back to you. Agent Chilton, will you please get Mr. Sims contact details?" Jeremy left the room, obviously not impressed.

*Bless your heart, Jeremy!* It was one of the few southern phrases she had adopted into her vocabulary. She was certain she had used it wrong, but didn't care.

"Why do I get the feeling I was brushed off?" asked a slightly annoyed Sims.

"Don't let it bother you. He brushes me off all the time," said Abby, in a placating tone. "I'll make you a deal. Why don't I do a little bit of checking and get back to you? If you'll give me your number, I'll let you know what I find."

A card appeared in his hand. "I'm in school until about five. After that is good, or before 8:30 in the mornin'."

Abby removed a card from her card case. She turned it over and wrote her cell number on the back. "This is my cell. If you hear anything else, please call," she shared, trying to remain professional.

Mick smiled again. "I will definitely call if I hear anything. How do I get out of here? I'm going to be late for my first class."

"You must be escorted at all times," replied the psychologist. "I'll take you down." *I hope he didn't hear the double entendre.* The sparkle in his green eyes told her he may be thinking about something more salacious than an elevator ride as well. When they reached the lobby, Abby held out her hand. "Thank you for stopping by Mr. Sims. We will keep you informed." She sounded overly-professional.

"Thank you very much, Agent Chilton," replied Mick, with equal over-formality. "I appreciate you taking the time to talk to me." Abby felt a tingle as he shook her hand and retreated through the security checkpoint.

*I hate suit coats. It is totally impossible to check out a cute butt when they wear those!*

# Chapter Two

The Observer was dressed in an unremarkable t-shirt and jeans. On his kitchen table were the remains of his breakfast. It was the most important meal of the day. In high spirits after his Friday night's exploits, he treated himself to his favorite morning meal – Eggs Benedict. There was something about the Hollandaise sauce over the soft poached eggs that made them taste phenomenal.

Now, sitting before him, were several dice which would make his Monday even better. A roll of a twenty-sided die came up with the number fourteen. It was a number that had not come up in quite a while. Why couldn't he ever get the elusive eight? The next dice to be cast were five six-sided dice totaling nine. Two coins were flipped. Both heads. The penultimate die was six-sided which came up three. On his last throw, an eight-sided die with eight colors was tossed onto the table with pink being the color of the day.

Time to go. The fates had given him direction to his next target.


Abby stayed in the lobby, staring after the man she had just met. There was something going on with Michael Sims, but she couldn't put her finger on it. Was he as nice as he appeared? Was there something darker going on behind those gorgeous, green eyes? Or was it that it had been over a year since anyone had caught her attention? Was she being paranoid? *Maybe he is a very nice psychopath who has caught my attention, thus answering all my questions at once. Who says, 'thus'? You really need to tone down the vocabulary a little bit.*

Turning to the bank of elevators, she continued her inner musings. *Why does something have to be wrong with him? Well, there are the last three relationships which ended in disasters. Could they have something to do with it? While I'm talking to the voices in my head, why are you asking yourself questions to which you already know the answers?*

The elevator opened to the investigations unit of the Knoxville field office. It was nine and the office was starting to show the barest signs of life. Abby tried to make it through the office with a minimal amount of conversation. She knew most people were put off or intimidated by her and she didn't really care. There were some things more important than being Miss Congeniality. Besides, if she didn't talk to them she wouldn't profile them.

As she passed the desk of Special Agent Rupert Michaelson, he called to her. "Hey Abs. How did it go with the paranoid teacher? Is he a little nuts or a real head case?" Rupert was fresh out of the academy on his first field assignment. He was eight years younger than Abby, but never missed a chance to flirt with her or check out her chest. He was about five feet, nine and in great shape, but that was to be expected since he was still in his twenties. Michaelson would be a good middle of the road agent, he would never be great. It was sad Rupert thought he stood a chance with her.

She barely broke stride, smiled, and said, "Jury's still out, Rupert; but, if he is a head case, I'll give him your number so he can join your support group." Walking toward Jeremy's office, feeling his eyes checking her out, she called loudly without looking back. "And call me 'Abs' again and I'll tell everyone the reason behind your bed wetting issues."

Rupert laughed, noticing others were looking at him. "She was joking," he said, more defensively than he intended. "Tell them you're joking, Abby!" She didn't even look back.

At the end of the row was the door of the triple sized, corner office of the Special Agent in Charge. As the SAC, Jeremy had an open door policy. By "open door" he meant his door was open but if you walked in you better have something worth his time or he would hand you your head. Abby didn't care, she always walked in. The office showed much about the man to Abby's well-trained brain. The first time she walked in fifteen months ago, she knew he was going to be a pain in her ass; but he was going to be easy to torment and manipulate.

Their first meeting could have been much better. She had left her last posting at the San Antonio Field Office and had completed the testing with certifications to become a "Traumatic Incident and Grief Support Specialist." It was the Bureau's fancy name for "The Bitch Who Will Listen to You Whine and Tell You How Long You Will Be Shackled to Your Damned Desk Before You're Allowed to

Go Out and Shoot Someone Else." She really preferred the honest title. It was so much more graphically descriptive. The instructor teaching the course offered a courtesy laugh when she suggested it but said the original title was fine. Some people can be such bureaucratic assholes with hardly any sense of humor. Oddly, Jeremy and the instructor had that in common.

The field office SAC had greeted her with the warmth of a polar bear who had been stuck on an iceberg for a couple decades. "Based on the picture in your file you are Abby Chilton," said Mathis. No chit chat. No hello. No kiss my ring. You are Abby Chilton. It told her he was not one accustomed to being questioned. He made statements. Everyone said, "Yes, sir!" and did their Nazi boot click. She hated Nazis.

Making a show of looking down at her badge, she replied, "Why, yes I am, sir." She had a way of saying "sir" which made most men think she had called them an asshole. "You are Special Agent in Charge Jeremy Mathis." Two could play this game. Now, what could she profile? He was five foot, eleven and about two-hundred pounds. A little soft in the middle, but not fat. The diploma said he graduated from the University of Chicago with a Criminology bachelors in 1987. Very cliché for the FBI. No law degree. His academy certificate was in 1989. Two year gap means he may have washed out of law school. It would make him in his mid to late-forties. He had a slightly receding hairline with plenty of gray. Jeremy had the gaze she had seen countless times in the FBI. The look on his face said, "Get the hell away from me! If you try any of your mind shit on me, I'll shoot you." It was the standard look she expected to see as a new counselor.

Looking him in the eye, she said, "You also have no desire to put up with a shrink on your floor, in your office, or at your building. I also suspect you would prefer not having any in the Bureau at all."

Mathis raised an eyebrow. He was better than most who usually told her off. He was smarter. "At least we're beginning with a clear understanding of where we both stand," he said with a little less liquid nitrogen in his voice. "You laid my cards on the table for me. What else can you deduce – other than the blatantly obvious?"

A challenge? This would be fun. What was the easy stuff beyond the physical? He was married with three kids. The wife looked pleasant enough; but nothing to get excited about. He likes red heads. Mental note: change hair color to red in six months to see how it messes with his head. Two kids were grown or in college and one was in high school. The oldest was a son. He is likely Jeremy, Jr. based on the initials JR on the base of the fairly happy family portrait. The second oldest was a daughter – Rebecca. Prettier than either parent. Adopted? No. She has mom's ears. Not much of dad in her. Good for her. The youngest was the jock - Robert. Cute kid playing soccer.

Office décor often told more than most people realized. First thing was the color. It was a standard light brown, but not the same as everywhere else. He had some individuality, but did not vary too far from the standard. The desk was larger than most SAC desks and looked to be non-government issue. It was a deep, dark mahogany with about an extra six inches in width. Several compensation jokes came to mind, but she let them pass. On closer examination, there was a large, hidden flat screen on the right side of the desk built into the desktop allowing him to examine her file while seeming to not look at a screen. There was a wireless mouse on the left side of the desk as were several pens. Left handed. His papers were in neat piles. Organized. There were three chairs in front of the desk which were nowhere near as comfortable as the luxurious chair from where he ruled his tiny dukedom. A separate area with a couch and two larger chairs around a coffee table was situated so the three desk chairs could be moved to be part of the more intimate setting. These chairs were given to the less important individuals when the more relaxed location was used. Why did she suspect she would never be offered any of the comfy spots?

"Are you sure you want me to do this? It makes people uncomfortable." Abby knew his answer before he said it. She was tempting him in the only way she would ever tempt him.

Jeremy took the bait, the hook, the line, the sinker and part of the fishing pole. "Please, Agent Chilton. Indulge me," he said with a trace of condescension. He would pay for that.

"You asked for it, sir," she rejoined. "You are in your late forties. You are happily married. Same wife for more than twenty-four, but less than twenty-eight years. Three children. One is still in high school. You have a degree in criminology and considered getting a law degree. You show some subtle narcissistic tendencies. You are left handed and like having information nearby without others knowing. You know your job and are very efficient as an administrator. While you have no problem using intimidation when you need to, you also know when to create a more casual atmosphere while still keeping others in their place and on the defensive." The repeated "you" was part of her mind game.

To his credit, Jeremy never showed any sign she had gotten anything right or wrong. He would be a badass at poker if he ever loosened his tie. After considering her for some time, he said, "You may be somewhat useful. You see much others miss, but I need to tell you I'm not..."

"A narcissistic asshole? I know. I wanted to see your reaction when I called you one," said the psychologist with a smile. "Nice poker face, by the way."

"I heard about poker," said the SAC, with a smile. "Maybe I should study it."

Abby had been surprised to hear the man make a joke. "I can teach you some of the basics, Jeremy. But I don't gamble. It is not any fun when you always know what the other person has in their hand."

Thus, the complicated relationship between the SAC and the woman who could ground his agents had begun. Today's meeting was not much different than the first. Abby sat down without waiting for an invitation. Jeremy, knowing she was there, continued typing something on his hidden computer. She could wait, too. There weren't any appointments on her schedule until ten.

"So what did you see in there?" asked the boss, without stopping his work. "Anything untoward?"

"'Untoward'? Word a day calendar?" asked Abby, trying not to sound impressed. He didn't even look up, so she answered his question. "He appears genuinely concerned about his student. I didn't see anything that makes me think he is anything more than a teacher wondering about what the hell is going on at Y-12. Except..."

The "except" made him look up from what he was doing. "Yes?" he asked, crinkling his forehead. He looked at her a long time and asked, "Is your radar jammed by a cute guy?" Even if he hid it on his face, she could hear the smile in his voice.

"No. My radar is not jammed by a 'cute guy'," she replied, perhaps a fraction of a second too quickly. "There is something he is not telling us. I'm going to get Marcus to dig into the internet and see what we can find without a warrant."

Mathis slid a manila folder across the desk to her. The tab had a typed label: Sims, Michael "Mick" Arthur. His middle name was Arthur? He did not look like an Arthur to Abby. Adonis was a better middle name for him. *FOCUS!* It was thicker than she expected. The folder that is.

"When did you do this?" asked an impressed Abby.

Mathis had a well-earned, smug look on his face. "Yesterday, when he called for an appointment. Marcus is very thorough. But you already knew that." Jeremy was referring to the occasions she had Marcus do some snooping on agents who were having some issues.

"All part of my job, sir." *Asshole.* Abby hated it when he looked smug.

"I need a profile on him. I called Walker. He'll stop by the kid's house and look around. Let's see how long it takes Wilson at Y-12 to e-mail me back about the dad. This is a local matter unless something is related to Oak Ridge." Apparently, Jeremy had not totally blown him off after all. Detective Walker was their Knoxville Police contact and Wilson was head of security at Y-12. Was there something to this?

"I have three agent interviews today, but I'll make some time between them. Are you worried about this, Jeremy?" Abby was curious. It could be he was being his usual over-efficient self.

"I'm hedging my bets, Chilton. I'll worry when there is something to worry about." With those words the impromptu meeting was concluded. Abby rose to leave when he asked, "What does your gut tell you?" He had never asked her that question; but this was the first time he had really used her talents other than internally.

"My gut tells me I need to know more about Mick before I jump to conclusions," she replied cautiously. "But there is something going on."

"I agree," said Mathis. He was beginning to look worried.

# Chapter Three

The Observer left his car parked in the public parking lot. He was always careful to pay the full-day's amount in case things took longer than expected. A ticket is a good way to get noticed. The stroll to the main bus terminal was a short walk past the Knoxville Coliseum, onto the bridge where the bus for line fourteen was waiting. The dice always found the right line to ride. Paying cash, the Observer took a seat in the middle of the bus. Out the window, the faintest outline of the Smoky Mountains could be seen. The air quality in the Tennessee Valley made a clear view of the mountains an uncommon occurrence.

Many people found riding the bus an uncomfortable and boring affair. The Observer was not like most people. He sat down and relaxed as the first three stops allowed many more patrons to board. These buses always brought in interesting faces. There was one man who chose to sit in the seat right in front of the Observer. The obscene body odor of the man made the killer consider breaking all his rules. Killing him wouldn't be any fun. Plus, it would take soaking his kill suit in bleach to get rid of the odor.

The first eight stops were uneventful. Thanks to the roll of the dice, the ninth stop found the Observer rising from his seat and disembarking with two other riders. Turning right thanks to the first coin flip, he stayed on this side of the road thanks to the second coin. Taking a few steps he found a chair where he could sit and close his eyes for three minutes. The World's Fair Park on such a nice day would be a great place to relax to wait for his new pink wearing observee to cross his path.

Abby went through the central bullpen to the far end of the open floor. Among the rooms along the walls was her double sized office. It was nowhere as luxurious as the SAC's office; however, the profiler had made this space her own with a modicum of modesty. Abby knew others would be in there, trying to decipher more about her as she mentally dissected them.

The desk was a standard issue oak with the requisite drawers. She had her locked filing cabinet, but had very little to lock up. The computer desk was perpendicular to her main desk serving two purposes. It created an open space without a flat screen getting between her and whomever was sitting in the two matching chairs. This made others feel like there was less getting between them, other than the huge desk. The second purpose was to allow her to work at her computer and still see through the glass wall into the bullpen. She could observe how others were interacting and make notes if needed.

The double sized office gave Abby an area which was a smaller version of the casual space of Jeremy's office. She didn't need the same amount of area. Her relaxed lounge had two chairs and a love seat. She couldn't bring herself to have the cliché couch that is supposed to be in the shrink's office. The art on the walls was what truly made the office hers. She loved the surrealists. While others were fans of Dali and Magritte, Abby found the art of Yves Tanguy more her taste. His use of a limited number of colors with few accents on bizarre landscapes appealed to her. She had never been able to explain the attraction. Maybe it was his odd hairdo. She had framed prints of *Indefinite Divisibility*, *The Great Mutation*, and *Day of Inertia* placed in strategic spots guaranteed to capture the attention of anyone who sat on the love seat. It was all part of her technique to get the agent to talk about something they believed to be unrelated to the reason they were in the office. Often their thoughts on the paintings told her more than their thoughts on the supposed issues.

The clock told her she had thirty-five minutes before her first appointment. It was enough time to get an initial picture of Sims, Michael "Mick" Arthur. Her ten and eleven o'clock appointments would take her conscious concentration, it would be good to get something for her background processing. All through school she had been able to multi-process. Several friends had tried to get her to tell them the secret. There wasn't one. It was simply how she was wired. She could be totally absorbed in counseling a troubled soul while her mind worked out a solution to some problem of which she was only peripherally aware. It came in handy.

"This is going to take more coffee," she said aloud. Grabbing her University of Tennessee mug, the one concession in her office to her temporary home town of Knoxville, she took the two page summary of Marcus' internet search and headed for the break room. The first day she had been in the Knoxville field office, she had walked around to every desk and introduced herself. It served the dual purpose of meeting the people she would be working with while allowing her to memorize the layout of each of the floors. She walked to the break room without needing to look up from the notes, using peripheral vision to make sure she was not about to plow into anyone.

"Hey, Abby. How's the psycho world today?" asked a voice with a distinct New England accent. Abby looked up to keep from running into Tina Jacobs. The diminutive brunette analyst had the girl next door looks with a porn star physique. There were other women who had a more refined beauty; but Tina was one of those who looked great naturally and would age gracefully. Every guy in the office was constantly at risk for sexual harassment charges when they were around her, especially when she wore anything showing her ample cleavage. Fortunately for every man in the building, she was one to coyly flirt back without giving them any real hope. Tina was one of the few people who was not intimidated by Abby. This made her one of the two friends Abby had made at work. The profiler liked her in spite of the annoyance that she was prettier.

"Hey, Tina. How's tricks?" asked Abby, knowing the answer. The running joke around the office said Tina was an analyst because if she were an agent the bad guys would try to make moves on her while she cuffed them.

"S.S.D.D." laughed Tina, as she joined Abby on her walk to get coffee. The idea they dealt with the "same shit, different day" mentality around there truly was laughable. Nothing was ever the same from day to day. Tina looked at her more closely. "Abby, what's different?" It was a simple question. Abby's instincts kicked in as she pondered the real question behind the question.

"What do you mean?" asked the counselor, fearing she knew the answer. Her friend was always trying to get Abby to go out with her to meet men. The one time they had gone to the comedy club, Tina had been asked out for drinks afterward, but the guy did not have a wing man for Abby. Tina turned him down and told the profiler he wasn't her type. Abby was very proficient at detecting lies. She had resisted other invitations, knowing the time was coming when her ferociously persistent friend would wear her down.

The smile on Tina's face showed the kind of mischief every man on the floor would sell a kidney to see. "You are glowing. Did we get laid last night?" asked the dark haired pixy.

"I didn't. Did you?" asked Abby, trying to turn the tables on her friend and distract her from whatever she was thinking.

"Bobby is still out of town. I'm still virtuous until Thursday," replied the undeterred Tina. "Give. What has you looking like you met a guy who actually may be able to sandblast your thighs apart? Rumor has it Mathis had you meet a civilian. Could he be the cause of your blush?" Abby knew better than to let her win this.

"You and I both know I don't blush," stated the therapist. A compact mirror was thrust in her face to reveal she had more red in her cheeks than simple rouge could explain. "You are a pain in the ass, you know."

The pleasure in Tina's Vermont voice spoke more than her words. "It is part of my charm. Lunch is on Marcus today. The story is on you. Don't worry. I'll text Marcus and let him know you have a crush to tell us about." She waved as she continued past the break room, laughing her very unladylike laughter.

"You can be a real bitch sometimes," Abby called after her.

"Takes one to know one," retorted Tina.

After filling her mug and returning to her office without being accosted by any other coworkers, Abby began to look at the file Marcus had created. What had her favorite hacker hacked on Mr. Perfect? *Please, don't let it be an addiction to midget porn.*

The data said everything was as it appeared. They had much in common. *Dammit, Abigail! This is not the Dating Game.* He was two years her junior at thirty-four. Not part of any watched groups. He was on a kickball team which played on weeknights. *Kickball? Do adults play kickball? I think I was in sixth grade gym class the last time I played.* He was a well-liked teacher based on the blogs about him. Some of the little girls had crushes on the cute teacher. *What a shock?*

Abby continued to read about this man who had captured her attention. Something was not sitting right with her. She made a couple of notes on the file to mention to Marcus when they went to lunch. A knock at the door announced her first appointment for the day had arrived. Mick had to be moved to the background of her mind while she worked with the soon-to-be-ex Mrs. Seymour concerning her resentment toward a cheating husband and the consequences of using Bureau resources to make his life miserable.

As the lunch hour rolled around, Abby was more than ready to take a break from her latest counselee. He spent more time trying to look down her shirt than actually listening to her questions. It was going to take a while with this one. As Tina showed up at her door, the agent who had been hitting on Abby changed the target of his leers. *No, he will not be going into the field any time soon with that attitude toward women.*

The two women met the Korean computer guru at the elevator. Pushing the down button, he greeted them. "Hey, Tiny and Teeny. How are my two favorite Feebs? And why do I have to find out from Tina you have a crush on some guy you met today, Tiny?"

The "I'm-gonna-kill-you" glare Abby shot Tina did nothing to wipe the shit-eating grin off her face. "It's not a crush. It is someone I met who did not make me want to run screaming into the hills."

Tina chimed in. "He came in this morning to report a missing student. What is his name, Abby?"

"It's not Sims, is it?" asked Marcus, with the same grin which had not left Tina's face.

"You two need to grow up!" said Abby with no conviction. "Yes, I met him. Yes, he is Michael Sims. No, I don't know anything about him."

Abby stepped out of the elevator and began walking to the exit. She noticed her friends had not followed. She turned and looked back to see both of her friends standing in the elevator with shocked looks on their faces. Neither moved as the door began to close. If Abby hadn't put her hand in the way to keep it from closing, they would have ended up on a different floor. Abby motioned for them to come as they followed her out of the building.

Tina spoke first. "What do you mean you don't know anything about him? You know everything about everyone as soon as you meet them."

"Tiny is in love!" joked Marcus.

"I am not!" laughed Abby.

"Tiny is in lust!" retorted Marcus.

"That may be true," said the still laughing Abby.

As they piled into Marcus' car, Tina joined in. "'May be true'? Give me a break. You've needed to get laid since you got here! Now, where are we going to lunch, Marcus?"

"I know this little cafe down on World's Fair Park..." began the computer genius.

"NO!" shouted Abby. She knew exactly what Marcus was up to. World's Fair Park was in the middle of Knoxville, the Sunsphere was its centerpiece. There was also the art museum, the convention center, several hotels and the old L & N train station. The old train station was also the location of the STEM Academy. "We're not going there!"

The car pulled out of the parking lot, through the security checkpoint and headed toward the skyline of Knoxville. "Hey Teeny. Tiny thinks she is driving!"

"Don't worry, Abby. We won't embarrass you too much." Tina chanted those last two words.

As they parked, Abby considered remaining in the car in protest, but knew it would be worse if she didn't go with them. Tina would be down at the school, flashing her FBI I.D. and asking to speak to Michael Sims on a matter of national security and the desirability of her friend who he had met earlier that day.

The cafe overlooked the central area of the park with the art museum on one side, the outdoor amphitheater on the far end, and the STEM Academy on the near end. High school students were all milling around doing the things high school kids do after they inhale their lunches and are looking for a little bit of trouble before their next class. Sitting on the outside, the trio of FBI personnel could hear more than they really wanted. It wasn't until they saw a group of students playing Frisbee on the lawn they were able to distinguish a particular phrase. "Good catch, Mr. Sims!"

Marcus and Tina's heads both moved so quickly Abby worried about whiplash. They peered at the group of four students and one adult throwing a disc around. The teacher had his back to the trio for which Abby was grateful.

"Okay. You've seen him. Now can we go?" pleaded the profiler.

"I want to see his face," stated Tina. Her tone of voice clearly communicated she was not going to move from her spot until she got to see him. Abby moved her chair so her back was to the lawn, he would not see her if he looked her way. "Hmmm. He's okay. Is he really your type, Abby?"

The Korean added, "Now, I'm not one to be judgmental, but even I can tell he's not all that and a bag of chips, Abby." He had called her Abby instead of Tiny. That was odd for him.

She turned as she said, "What do you mean? Look at those..." Words died in the air.

Mr. Sims was about five foot, eight with dark hair and brown eyes behind thick glasses. He wore jeans and a golf shirt. As the bell rang, the students and teachers all headed back into the school.

Abby beckoned as she opened her FBI I.D. "Mr. Sims?" The man looked at them, pointed to himself, and slowly walked over to them, eyeing Abby's credentials.

"Yes, Agent..." he looked at the name on her I.D. "Chilton? Is something wrong?"

Abby did her best to maintain her professional voice. "Not at all, sir. One of my friends has a son who attends the STEM Academy and was going on and on about Mr. Sims. Are you that Mr. Sims, or is there more than one of you?"

The look on the man's face went from concern to pleasure. "I'm the only one. I'm Mickey Sims. I teach some of the technology classes. Thanks for the kudos. It is nice when people say good things behind my back. I'm really sorry, but I've got to get inside before they try to hack into NORAD," laughed Sims as he walked away.

All three FBI employees were wondering the same thing. *Who had been in the office if it wasn't Michael Sims?*

# Chapter Four

The Observer opened his eyes after three minutes. He never needed a timer. His internal clock worked perfectly. With eyes behind dark sunglasses he wondered who would be wearing pink today. Since it was lunch time, there were quite a few people on the park. The Observer was the epitome of patience. He could wait all day for the right person. A granola bar was taken from his pocket and unwrapped. As he was about to take a bite, he froze. A flash of pink appeared in the distance.

The jogger was wearing a pink tank top and a pair of white shorts covering the essentials, but leaving little to the imagination. She was out getting some exercise and hoping to be seen. The Observer watched as she passed without even moving his head. A flick of his wrist and a small device landed lightly on the back of her colorful running shoe. The killer smiled as he took a long walk back to his car, gazing at his smart phone which showed a dot jogging away.


Tina looked at Abby. "I'm guessing he was not the man who had your panties on fire this morning?" Tina was trying to ease the tension she saw in her friend's face with humor while still asking the pressing question.

Abby was still staring after the man who was heading into the school. "No. Definitely not. Eat. I need to know for sure." She rose and began to move toward the school office.

Marcus was on his feet in an instant. "If you think I'm going to let you go over there by yourself, you're wrong, Tiny." The lovable Korean was trying his best to be macho. It would have worked if not for the detail that he was the same height as Abby, but not as toned. He had what he called "cyber-muscle". As a computer geek he hardly ever found time to work out. He often joked how his mom and dad had come to America to have an American family so he was Korean only in blood. He didn't even know Taekwondo, much to his father's shame.

"And you are going to do what?" asked an amused Abby. "Slash someone's credit rating?"

"Only if they piss me off," said a defensive Marcus. "Seriously, what do you think you are doing, Abby?"

She gave him her best withering psychologist look. It never worked on him or Tina. It was why she liked them. They didn't let her use her psyche-bullshit on them. "I am going to the office. I'll flash my credentials and make sure this guy is the real Sims before I call Mathis and get everyone excited," said Abby. What she said made perfect sense, was totally logical, and was a complete lie. Her friends knew it too.

"Are you sure this is a good idea?" asked Tina. She knew Abby as well as anyone.

"Of course not," smiled Abby. "But I need to know what the hell is going on and I can't do it while eating a grilled chicken and raspberry salad. You two stay here. This is not official and you aren't agents anyway. You two eat and keep an eye out for a tall, cute, blonde guy following me." Abby moved away, ending the discussion. Her friends watched her walking away.

"She is such a pain in the ass sometimes," said Marcus.

"Yes she is," agreed Tina.

"I heard you," shouted Abby over her shoulder.

"You were supposed to!" Marcus shouted back.

Walking across the open area, Abby couldn't shake the feeling she was being watched. Her training and instincts had her staying close to the buildings, using the trees as a small bit of natural cover. She picked up a piece of litter and used that an excuse to look around. There was no one following her. The only eyes she could see were those of her friends who, both tried to hide their concern behind smiles. It was so cute when they tried to fool her. Seeing no one, she went to the main structure of the old L & N Station and found signs taking her to the far side of the building for the office. She took one last look behind at her friends before turning the corner out of their view.

The office had the tall ceiling of the old train station with the requisite posters, warnings that students could not be released into the custody of anyone without proper documentation. It was nice to see some things had changed since the days when she could leave with anyone she wanted. She smiled at a couple of memories of her bad girl years in high school. This office even had the requisite matronly secretary, ready to greet a guest or fire a cold blooded stare at an interloper. Abby smiled.

"Good afternoon," said the matron, with a small amount of warmth. Abby's smile worked better on men. "Can I help you?" she said, giving her best totally fake grin.

Abby decided to cut through all the bullshit and went for the professional approach. Flipping open her FBI ID she said, "I am Special Agent Abby Chilton, FBI. I am doing a routine check on one of your teachers." In a conspiratorial tone she whispered, "The parent of one of your students has a high security clearance."

Practically jumping to her feet, the air of indifference immediately changed to one of total deference at the sight of the letters FBI on the ID. On the outside, Abby gave her the "I'm an agent doing my job stare", while on the inside she jumped up, clicked her heels together and wished this were Ms. Hunsacker who had always made her life difficult when she came back late from lunch that Junior year she had a "real" boyfriend.

"Yes, m-m-ma'am," stammered the matron. "I'm only filling in for today but I'll do all I can to help you?" This poor woman was about to have a coronary. Abby had let her stutter and sputter for long enough. *Take that Ms. Hunsacker!*

Abby smiled her warmest, counselor smile. "Relax, Ms...?" asked the counselor.

"Davis, ma'am. Rita Davis," said the quickly jabbering matron.

"Please relax, Ms. Davis. I'm making a preliminary inquiry. This is a verification of employment in the event we need to do further background checks." She lowered her voice to a conspirator whisper as she leaned closer to the matron. "You understand, don't you? With all the hush-hush things happening in Oak Ridge, we can never be too careful with technology teachers."

Unconsciously lowering her voice as well, Ms. Davis replied, "I totally understand. This whole technology curriculum could be a powder keg. Which one of the teachers are you wondering about? It is Mr. Ortega or Mr. Sims? It's Ortega, isn't it?" She had the "good ol' boy" attitude about her which really pissed Abby off.

*Just because he was Hispanic, he was suspicious? What an idiot.* Hiding her anger, she said, "Actually Mr. Ortega already has a security clearance. He was recruited to work at K-19, but declined preferring to help the young minds of Knoxville." The look of shock and awe on the face of Ms. Davis was priceless. It was all a complete lie. Abby didn't show her anger but liked to mess with idiots. *I really need to stop doing that. But it's so much fun to watch them squirm.* Continuing after a moment of enjoyment, "I need to verify Michael Arthur Sims. His name came up as we were doing preliminary checks. It's probably nothing."

The shock of the Ortega security clearance was wiped away by a look of confusion on the matronly face. "Mick is well liked by all the student and faculty. I can't imagine him being involved in anything that would make the FBI want him."

Abby really hated dealing with idiots. Smiling and putting a trace of a laugh in her voice, she said, "He is not wanted, Ms. Davis. In fact, you can save me having to talk to him and causing any embarrassment. Can you verify his address for me? I have an address in Fountain City."

She pulled up a file on the flat screen in front of her. "Yes, he lives on Cedar Lane." Abby leaned in slightly. Ms. Davis unconsciously moved the screen so she could see more clearly. Abby loved the trick. She scanned the screen, hoping to see a blonde man looking back at her. The face of the Frisbee playing Sims smiled back at her. *Damn!*

Trying to extricate herself as quickly as possible, the FBI psychologist said, "Ms. Davis, thank you very much for verifying the information. I doubt anything will come of this. If you do not mind, please keep our conversation about Mr. Sims confidential. If I need your assistance, may I ask for you if I need more information?" Abby was playing to her ego.

Beaming, the matron exclaimed, "Of course, Agent Colton! I'll be glad to help in any way I can!" She had gotten her name wrong, Abby didn't mind. When she told everyone she knew how she was helping the FBI with an investigation into someone at the school, she could use any name she wanted. At least Ortega would get a boost in reputation.

As Abby walked out of the office, her phone rang. Typically, she looked at the number before answering, but she already knew it was Tina. "I'm good, Tina. But guess what I discovered?"

"Let me guess. You figured out I'm not Mick? I can't throw a Frisbee as good as he does either. But do you have to call me Tina? It is a little insulting?" The voice was the same one which had come out of the blonde-haired, fake Sims this morning, but with a change. Gone was the subtle trace of East Tennessee to be replaced by a pure neutral American accent.

Abby immediately scanned her surroundings. "If I can't call you Tina, what shall I call you? Mick doesn't seem right." She was not scared. It was exhilarating being in the field again with so many things to process. *Where is this bastard?* He was watching because he knew about the Frisbee playing Sims.

The voice laughed. "I wasn't a fan of his name. You can call me Jonas. So Abby, how much of my profile did you toss in the trash?"

Abby put in her Bluetooth earpiece as she picked up her pace. "Pretty much all of the personality profile. I am working on a new one as we speak." Turning the corner, she saw Tina and Marcus were still at the same table, chatting amicably over their lunches. Abby tried to get Tina's attention and failed. She started texting as fast as her fingers would move. To Marcus and Tina, {He is here! Watching us! He is not Sims!}

"Really? So soon? That is impressive. Watch out for the tree. You really should stop walking to text. Please don't tell me you text and drive, too." There was a playfulness in the voice which she both liked and hated at the same time. She stopped and looked around. He was here. Somehow he knew she would check him out and had waited for her. *Who the hell is this guy?*

"Why don't you come out and see me, Jonas? Let's chat about who the hell you are?" asked Abby, trying the tactic of pretending to be angry. Abby never got angry in situations like this. The higher stress the situation, the calmer she became. It's what made her so good in the field.

"Seeing you again would give me great pleasure, Agent Chilton. Shall I come to you or do you want to come to me? The view from my perspective is awe-inspiring!" hinted her nemesis.

Both Marcus and Tina were looking around after getting her text. Marcus was on the phone to the office calling for backup. Tina looked genuinely scared. She was a forensic accountant and not trained for field work. There were no numbers to crunch here.

Abby smiled. "I'm sure it is. I haven't been up there in a few weeks. I'll be right there. If you are holding anything in your hand, I will blow you through the window. See you in a minute." He was in the Sunsphere! It was one of the few things that remained from the World's Fair in 1982. It had been many things over the years since the end of the fair. Currently the golden globe atop the metal stand was offices, a restaurant and a public observation deck. The offices were closed to the public. The restaurant didn't open until four. The deck was the only real option.

She stopped at the table. "He is in the Sunsphere. Marcus, is Mathis sending backup?"

He held his hand over the mouth-piece. "Yeah. They'll be here in fifteen minutes. Mathis says to stay put." Abby drew her Glock 23, moving toward the base of the Sunsphere. "Abby?" called Marcus.

"I'm simply going to secure the elevator," fibbed Abby.

"Abby, please wait!" begged Tina. The fear in her voice made Abby slow her pace.

Abby smiled her best comforting smile as she glanced back. "Relax. I'm not going to do anything stupid." All three of them knew she was lying through her pretty teeth.

Tina glared daggers at her. "You know for someone with a great bullshit detector you aren't a very good liar!"

Abby walked at a brisk pace toward the elevator which would take her to the Observation Deck. She knew he could see everything she was doing so she made no effort at sticking to cover. If he wanted to shoot her from there, he would have by now. This was some kind of game. She could play, too. As she passed under the bridge which bisected the park, she saw exactly what she needed.

There were a select few reserved parking places and one of them had a car pulling in. Holstering her weapon, she pulled out her ID. A young man in his mid-twenties was getting out of his car. She approached him with her most serious look.

"Special Agent Chilton. FBI," she said in her most no-nonsense agent voice. "You are going up to the fifth floor. Correct?" The young man was stunned. He tried to speak but no words came out. All he could do was nod. *Lovely, he's a mute.*

"Relax. I need to get to the Observation Deck from your restaurant. You need to take me up the service elevator so I can take the stairs down." Her instructions were clear, concise and served to scare the kid even more. *What about relax does the kid not get?* Abby tried to be firm but comforting. "I will make sure you're safe, but I need to go now." She grabbed the kid by the arm and led him along the underside of the bridge so they could not be seen from above. They reached the service elevator without seeing the glass of the sphere above them. Abby reasoned that the mysterious Jonas could not see them either.

Her phone buzzed. It was Mathis. She let it ring. Hitting ignore would piss him off more than he already was. They went up to what was the fifth floor of the Sunsphere. The still silent young man led her to the back stairs. Breaking his silence he handed her a set of keys. "This one will turn off the alarm."

She smiled at him as she pulled her Glock. "Thanks. Please go call the elevator and send it to the Observation Deck. I want to surprise this unsub." She threw out a term everyone thought the FBI used these days. The young man went to call the main elevator.

Plan in place, Abby went down the stairs to the doorway to the Observation Deck. She could hear the elevator approaching. She put the key in the door to deactivate the alarm. The elevator had arrived above and was now coming down to her level. Abby opened the door, prepared to sneak around and surprise Jonas. He was standing in front of the door with nothing in his hand but an ID.

Agent Jonas Lange. Interpol.

# Chapter Five

Arriving at his car, the Observer put away his phone as he climbed behind the wheel. The woman in pink was running a course through the park. If only she had an inkling of the attention she would soon receive. He was pleased to see it was only half past twelve, leaving him plenty of time to get some work done. A small aftermarket screen rose in the mid-section of the console to show his favorite jogger still jogging. Seeing her in that outfit would make many of the high school boys have nice dreams tonight.

Pulling into his drive on the north side of Knoxville, he took one last look at the screen. She had stopped running and seemed to be inside one of the taller buildings in the heart of downtown. The Observer had not been able to discern much: she had a very well-toned and nicely proportioned body, didn't mind being watched, and was disciplined enough to workout instead of having lunch with peers. She was definitely going to be fun to kill.

Getting out of his car, he called out to his elderly neighbor. "Hey, Bea. That was some party you threw last night," the Observer laughed. "I almost called the cops. Make sure you clean up all those beer cans." He continued up the walk and unlocked the front door.

The elderly woman hobbled toward the mail box with the aid of her walker while laughing at him. "When are you going to let me introduce you to my niece? She would be perfect for you."

Opening the door, he called, "When are you going to take me up on going out for martinis? I want to see you dancing on the tables." Without looking back, he entered his sanctum, turned on his computer, and got to work.

"Before you say anything unladylike, let me say: good job," began Jonas as he slowly put away his ID. He was smiling his most disarming smile with the hope he would not need to disarm Abby before she tried to shoot him.

"Fuck you!" retorted Abby. She was seriously contemplating the amount of paperwork involved in shooting an Interpol agent.

Jonas smiled. "So much for not saying anything unladylike. Plus, I'm not so easy. You'll need to buy me dinner and at least three cocktails." The steely look in her eyes was not softened by his attempt at humor. "In case you are wondering, there is a shit-load of red tape to deal with if you actually shoot me. As much as you don't want to, I'd appreciate it if you would put down the gun. It always makes me jittery when I'm on this side of a barrel."

"I was thinking of paperwork – not red tape," retorted Abby, her Glock remained steady. "It would be a hell of a lot easier to shoot you instead of having to make a whole new profile. I think I like being in the power position."

Jonas was so fast Abby never even saw the move. There was a blur on her left, pain on the back of her hand, and her pistol flipping through the air between them. Suddenly her pistol was in the hand of the Interpol agent and her hand would not obey her orders. He calmly removed the clip, emptied the chamber, caught the bullet, and placed all three at their feet.

"Now we can see who can get to your Glock first or we can talk. I really prefer talking about things like this; but I can also make your other hand uncooperative if it will help with the decision making process," joked Jonas. Reflexively, Abby moved her left hand out of his reach as she tried her best to stay angry at the charming agent. His smile made it difficult to stay mad at him.

"What is wrong with you? Have you ever considered therapy for your obsessive need to play games that can get you shot?" asked Abby, finally finding the words which had eluded her. He was not going to win this game.

"Let's see. I watched you order your salad, find Sims, go to the office, walk over here, waited for you at the staircase, and disarmed you. Checkmate." The smile on his face was one of confidence, just short of arrogance. It was the kind of smile that always worked on Abby.

"I still don't like you," responded Abby. It was as close to admitting defeat as he was going to get out of her.

"Yes, you do. But let's stick to business for now." There was a mischievous glint in Lange's eyes that defied definition. It was bothering Abby that she could not read what it meant. She had some thoughts, but she did not trust herself with this man. He was something she rarely met – an enigma. "Shall we go down and check on Tina and Marcus before they both stroke out? You may not want to work with me if they die because of our little game." Jonas began the short walk to the elevator. Abby picked up her weapon and followed behind.

As Jonas reached for the button, he felt the barrel of the Glock on the back of his head. Even though she could not see his face, Abby could hear the smile in his voice. "Are you really going to shoot me? There is so much to do and we need your help." Jonas began to turn around.

"Stay put, Agent Lange." Abby was using her best FBI voice. "I still don't know for sure who you are. You will wear these nice little bracelets before we go any further."

Continuing to turn around as if she had said nothing, Jonas responded to her threat, "Abby, if you pull the trigger, I'll be fine but your very nice pistol will be ruined by the block I put in the barrel." The smug look on his face was mirrored by Abby causing Lange to show the first hesitation she had seen. He looked directly into the barrel of the Glock and she could tell he was seeing the device he had slipped in there. His confidence returned and he smiled even bigger, then grunted and grimaced as the barrel of Abby's .22 Beretta pressed hard into his crotch.

"Oops. Sorry about that, Jonas. I hope I didn't damage anything precious down there," said a cocky Abby. "Now, the cuffs please." She handed him handcuffs and stepped back as he put them on while simultaneously protecting the spot where her Beretta had been moments before. "Good boy. Now, let's go down to the park. Button, please." Jonas turned and faced the elevator doors as he pressed the button.

"Mental note: she carries a Beretta for a backup," said Lange to himself. "Our files didn't have that bit of trivia." The doors opened and the pair entered. Abby would be concerned being in such tight confines with this man if he weren't cuffed. When they reached the bottom, the Interpol agent asked, "By the way, do you like magic?" He calmly handed her the restraints, strolling out the doors to be met by Marcus, Tina, Mathis and four FBI agents with guns raised to greet him. "Hi, guys. How ya doing? Special Agent in Charge Mathis, please call this number before any of you shoot me." A card had appeared in Jonas' hand as if also by magic. He looked back at Abby and said, "Admit it. You're a little impressed."

*I'll be damned if I'm going to give him the satisfaction.* She smiled at him and said, "Yes I am." Turning to the other agents, she continued, "Good work boys. I'm impressed you got here so quickly!" Lange gave her a smirk as he watched Mathis dial the number he had been given. The conversation was short, sweet and made Mathis' face a shade of red Abby had never been able to get him to turn. *Shit! This can't be good.*

After saying "yes sir" several times, Mathis ended the call, glared at Lange and said, "We are to give Agent Lange every courtesy and escort him back to our office for a vid-conference." There was venom in his voice and daggers in his stare, Jonas didn't seem to notice. He smiled at all the agents who were reluctantly lowering their weapons. Abby was certain he had noticed.

"Thank you, Special Agent in Charge Mathis. I appreciate not being shot," jested the Interpol agent.

"The day is still young," taunted Abby.

"I told you, dinner and drinks before anything fun," retorted Jonas. All eyes went from him to Abby as if they were all synchronized.

Abby was frustrated and flustered. "Will you all please grow up?" She turned and walked away, Tina and Marcus falling in step with her. Without looking to either side of her, she growled to her friends, "Don't say a word."

Tina was not intimidated. "About what, Abby? The minor detail that you got beat by an Interpol agent? Or that you think he really is impressive?" The joy in her voice was exactly what Abby needed to cool her temper and allow her to verbally joust with her friend. It was safer than sending a real lance through her heart.

"Have I told you lately you can be a real bitch?" asked Abby, a smile tugged at the corners of her mouth.

"Have I told you lately it takes one to know one?" replied the accountant.

The office was abuzz with chatter as the trio exited the elevator only to be replaced with an unstable silence when all saw who had arrived. Abby, Marcus and Tina looked around at the eyes upon them. Marcus broke the silence. "I knew I shouldn't have worn these pants today. Everyone always stares at my package when I do and then they are stunned into silence since no one thinks Koreans have dicks this big." Laughter broke the silence, the normal sound of voices and the tap of keyboards slowly resumed.

Abby turned to Marcus. "Thanks, dude. That was awkward even by my standards." It was so unusual for Abby to say thank you the gratitude left Marcus momentarily speechless. Abby added, "But honestly, your gray pinstripes show off your package better."

"I disagree, Abby. His navy blue Dockers are better," added Tina.

Not to be outdone by either of his friends, Marcus retorted, "And I thought neither of you had noticed." He headed down the hall to his domain of CPUs and flat screens with a wave. "Let me know how much trouble you get in. We still on for dinner, ladies? I'll wear the Dockers."

"Yes. My place at seven. I'll give you all the details," replied Abby. Looking at Tina she said, "Go back to your world of numbers. I'm sure there is some crooked lawyer you need to stop from sending ill-gotten booty to the Caymans."

"I'll see you tonight. Let me know if you need me to pick up anything," smiled Tina. "What color of wine will we need? And shall I bring enough for three or four?" The hint was there and Abby was not about to let her get away with it.

"A blush and three. Don't even think it," challenged the therapist.

"Four it is. See you later," giggled Tina in a way that caused several male agents to look her way longingly. Sometimes Tina could be so annoying when she was right.

No sooner had her friends departed than the doors opened with Lange and Mathis emerging in deep conversation. "What can you possibly know about baseball? You're European!" demanded Mathis.

"You assume since I didn't happen to grow up in America I can't appreciate the American pastime," replied a passionate Jonas. "Besides, when was the last time you saw them play? A month ago? I was there three days ago watching them beat Chattanooga. There will be at least three of those young guys called up within a year."

Mathis was not backing down. "The Smokies don't have the same depth since Johnson got called up last year. These new kids don't know what it takes to play in the majors."

"You two are arguing baseball? Really guys? Could you possibly be more stereotypical alpha males?" asked Abby trying to get a response.

"Jeremy, do you want to share a beer and fart to make it more testosterone drenched in here?" asked a chuckling Lange.

"Somehow I don't think Chilton would appreciate it too much. And she can ground my agents so I will play nice," replied Mathis.

Abby was torn between being surprised she was still not reading much from Jonas, or that Jeremy had made a joke which was halfway funny. "The past fifteen months were your version of playing nice? I don't want to see your bitchy side." She gave him an opening to see what he would do with it.

The old Mathis snapped back into place. "No, you don't, Chilton." Looking from the psychologist to the Interpol agent, he said, "We are late for a vid-conference. Shall we?" He began walking to the same conference room they had shared earlier in the day.

Slowly following the SAC, Jonas stage whispered to Abby, "Does he always ask questions that are really orders?"

Abby mimicked Lange, "Usually. Sometimes, he really doesn't know something and asks a question that is more like a demand for an answer." She hated that she really liked him. He was almost as good at messing with Jeremy as she was.

"Doesn't he know you can catch more flies with honey than vinegar?" bantered Jonas. He was enjoying this which also concerned her. It would be much easier if he wasn't so damned likeable.

"Jeremy eats too many pickles to even remember how honey tastes anymore." Abby was certain she heard a sigh coming from her boss as they entered the room. The door was closed and the privacy button was pressed. Sound dampening blinds were lowered between the layers of glass in all windows of the room, creating a softer light and deadening any sounds. The only door was sealed by noise absorbing foam pads between the door frame and the floor creating a sound barrier. The room was as sound proof as possible for the call.

Mathis sat at the head of the table and pressed a series of buttons on a hidden keyboard causing a large screen to lower from the ceiling and smaller screens to rise in front of the SAC and two other places on either side of him. Abby chose the one which would allow her to see into the bullpen if the windows had not been blocked.

Once all three were seated, the large screen flashed to life, filled with the desk and face of Deputy Director Michael Billingsly. The Deputy Director was a man in his early sixties with a mane of white hair much longer than the standard bureau style. He had dark brown eyes which many agents found unnerving in their intensity. He was always able to see right through the bullshit, calling out anyone who tried to fool him. Few people tried to lie to him and no one ever tried twice. Behind his back he was called the Whale, he would swallow you and spit you back out if you crossed him.

"Well it looks like we're all here," began the Deputy Director. "I'm glad Agent Chilton chose not to shoot you, Lange. I am supposed to play golf with our Interpol liaison next week and I would have had to let him win."

"I'm glad I didn't mess up your record against LeBou, Mike." Abby noticed the use of the first name as did Jeremy. Neither allowed it to show other than a quick glance at each other to make sure the other had caught it. "You did sucker me on Abby here, though. A Beretta? It would have been nice to know."

As the face filling the screen boomed with laughter, the director continued, "Jonas, I can't tell you everything. How am I supposed to see how good you really are if I give you too much of an advantage? Agent Chilton, I'm assuming, met your challenge and surpassed your expectations?"

Those green eyes gave Abby an appraising look. "She will work quite well. Now if she can see through my masks and figure me out, then I'll be impressed."

Billingsly looked surprised. "Agent Chilton, that is the first time I ever heard Lange say anyone would 'work quite well'. Take it as a compliment. Jeremy, I need to borrow your counselor for a while. I am reassigning Agent Chilton to a special joint task force which will be working out of your office for the time being. Before you say anything, yes this is unusual; but this is an unusual case.

You and I can discuss this in depth after this meeting. Can I count on your support?"

Always the politician, Mathis replied, "Of course, sir. Can I assume this will be something that will need our logistical support as well? And how much space will this task force need?"

Billingsly replied. "We will need a place for Agent Lange to work. The rest of the task force is Agent Chilton and whomever she needs from your team." Seeing the look on his face, the Director responded before the questions could be asked. "You are still in charge, Jeremy. Chilton and Lange will be working independently, but will need your help to track this one. He is... unique. You and I will talk about your role in private. Any other questions?"

Jeremy was placated for the moment. "No, sir. I look forward to the briefing." Abby didn't believe him.

"Now, gentlemen. I require this room for a private discussion with Agent Chilton. Thank you." It was clear to the men in the room they were no longer needed for the discussion; both left grudgingly. Once the room was secured again, Abby took the seat vacated by Mathis. The Deputy Director looked her in the eye and asked, "Okay Abby. Are you ready to get back into the field? I gave you the year you wanted. But I need you back out there."

# Chapter Six

The Observer was content. He had located his latest observee and flirted with a blue-haired lady. Now, he was sitting down at his bank of four monitors getting some work done. He was paid very good money by companies to try to break into their own networks. As a white hat hacker, he was skilled at finding ways around network security systems. The most impenetrable firewalls were always penetrable with enough care, caution and patience. Those were three traits the Observer had in copious quantities.

Today, he was testing a Canadian law firm's intranet security. With less than twenty keystrokes and one of his favorite programs, he discovered their intranet had no security to speak of. It was laughable they thought they could go down to the local Best Buy to find a program which could keep out hackers. Out of curiosity, once he was past the joke of a firewall, he found their purchase orders to locate the invoice for the security program. *They actually went to the mall to buy their security software? How embarrassing!*

After downloading a few incriminating files, noting the obscene amount of porn on the hard drives of three of the five partners, he turned his attention to the one monitor he kept free from work. This was his game monitor. His new playmate had not moved since the end of lunch. The pink jogger had put away her workout, stripper outfit and was undoubtedly sitting at a desk. He thought of her working without the slightest hint of who would soon be coming for her.

The ping from the minimized window made him smile. His friend was online.


"Well, I think I'm about ready. I did have fun tracking down Lange today. Although, it wasn't really too much of a challenge," boasted Abby. They both knew she was lying. Lange was Abby's equal in many ways and superior in others. *I've really got to find out how he did the move with my pistol.*

The Deputy Director raised an eye brow. "Really? Why do I have the sneaking suspicion you are not telling me something? Did you try to cuff him?" There was a sly smile on the face of the Whale. He was staring straight through her. Chuckling, he continued. "I tried it once, too. He still won't tell me how the hell he does that."

"If I discover the secret, I'll let you know, sir," smiled Abby. The change of expression on Billingsly's face caused her smile to slowly fade. *Here we go.*

"Are you done blaming yourself, Abby?" The concerned look on his face was something few ever saw. "You didn't know and couldn't do anything to prevent it."

Abby's hand moved on its own to her stomach, over the scar of a wound that had long since healed. With wide, watering eyes, she looked at her mentor. "I should have known, Mike." Few knew Abby was on a first name bases with the Deputy Director. She intended to keep it that way.

Billingsly did not waver in his scrutiny of his protégée. "Philip is gone, Abby. You couldn't know the bastard would be waiting. Your profile was perfect. Phil made a mistake and you both paid for it."

A tear slipped from the corner of her eye and down her cheek. "We all three did," came a whisper of a voice from Abby. "I still can't believe I didn't know."

Eighteen months ago, Abby and Phillip Robbins, her partner in the FBI and her partner away from the office, had been on the trail of a child molester. He had taken and killed two young boys and hid a third somewhere nearby. Through Phil's leads and Abby's profile, they had discovered the degenerate in a small town southwest of San Antonio. Everything in his actions indicated he would have the boy somewhere other than his home. The profile was right but the lead to the house in the small town was off. The house was not his home but his killing cottage. The asshole lived in downtown Austin.

The two were going to interview the man who was currently their most likely suspect. They knocked on the door of the house Phil had discovered through a confidential informant. When the man opened the door to see two FBI IDs in his face, he panicked. The door was slammed. Weapons were drawn. The door was kicked open to face the pedophile over the body of the third boy. In his hands were the twin dark chasms of a double-barrel twelve gauge pointed at the agents. Three shots rang at the same time. The blast from both barrels of the shotgun caught Robbins full in the abdomen and legs as his shot went wide of the target. Abby's Glock found its mark as a single bullet traveled through the heart – ending the life of the man who had taken three boys long before their time. It wasn't until she lunged to cradle her lover she felt the pain. Even though Phil's body had taken the brunt of the attack, Abby did not escape unscathed. Her blood flowed as she called 911. She passed out holding her dying partner.

When she awoke in the Hospital forty-eight hours later, she was met by the same eyes she was now staring at on a computer screen. It had been Michael Billingsly who had told her of the surgery she had undergone. It was one operation which led to losses she never anticipated. As they were trying to repair her wounds, they discovered she had lost a baby she didn't know she was carrying. She had lost her partner and lover. She had lost her unborn child. To add insult to injury, the shot from the shotgun had severed the uterine artery, leaving the organ without blood flow for far too long. Now, she would never be able to have a child.

The tears were still rolling down her face as the Deputy Director asked, "Are you ready, Abby? I need to know. You don't have to do this. But you are the best person for the job."

Trying to pull herself together, she asked, "Why me, Mike? You know plenty of agents who are as good as I am in the field and are even better profilers. Plus, they are not as damaged as I am."

Billingsly gave her a fatherly smile. "I've got agents who are better in the field. I have better profilers, too. But there aren't any who are as good at both as you. Most of them are damaged, too. Abby, this is your chance to make a difference. And Jonas has something that will challenge even your profiling abilities. If he is right, this is a career making case for both of you. Please get out from behind a desk and get back out in the field where you belong."

The profiler wiped the tears from her eyes before giving a smile. "You were supposed to say I'm the best at all of those things, sir." Her "sir" definitely sounded like she was saying "asshole". "So what is happening that you need my skill set?"

The smile on the Deputy Director's face was genuine. "I think I'll let Jonas tell you. And Abby," he paused giving her a semi-serious look, "do not underestimate him. Jonas Lange is one of the best investigators at Interpol and has a very different skill set than you. You will complement each other well."

Abby didn't like the sound of this. "What aren't you telling me, Mike? You are up to something. Your devious Machiavellian mind has something planned that you aren't telling me or Lange."

"Why Agent Chilton, I have no idea what you are talking about," said Billingsly with an evil chuckle, ending the call.

Staring at the blank screen, Abby thought to herself, *I hate it when he does that. Now I need to make sure I don't look like a black-eyed clown with tears before I go back out there.* Moving to the small restroom, Abby repaired the damage to her makeup and gathered herself together before pressing the privacy button, releasing the door. Jonas was leaning against a desk holding up his Interpol ID as he had done in the Sunsphere. He appeared totally unaware of the distraction sitting on the secretary's desk caused the poor woman.

Trying not to smile, Abby said, "It's getting old already. You think you're so cute, don't you?"

Smiling the smile which made Abby have butterflies in her stomach, he replied, the Tennessee twang back in his voice. "Why Miss Abby, I don't know what you're talkin' 'bout." Switching back to a normal Midwest American accent he continued. "But you think I'm cute. I call tell those kinds of things. Don't you think so, Sherry?" He hit the bespectacled secretary with his gorgeous green eyes. Her mouth moved making noise without words. "See? Even Sherry thinks that you think I'm cute."

"Sherry thinks that Sherry thinks you're cute," retorted Abby. "Let's go. I need to know what's going on if I'm going to be strong-armed into working with a raging egomaniac." She headed back to her office without waiting for him to reply.

Falling in beside her instead of behind her, Jonas countered, "I don't think Mathis is a raging egomaniac. He's very confident." There was a lilting tone to his teasing which Abby tried hard not to like. Sherry, the secretary, sighed watching him go. She tried hard not to like him, too; but quickly decided she would be first in line if Abby let him slip through her fingers.

Not willing to back down, the profiler continued, "Well, he does have some redeeming qualities. He doesn't annoy the shit out of me every time he's around."

"Yes he does," came Jonas' verbal repose. "Whereas, I have the bad habit of getting you all hot and bothered." She gave him a sideways glance which he noticed and reciprocated with a sideways wink. She really hated herself for liking him.

Abby wondered how many people heard this flirtation as they traveled through the cubical jungle, trying to avoid the many caged animals who would love to find something on Abby. Rupert looked up as they passed by and was about to say something which one of them would regret. A quick, ice-cold look from the psychologist froze the words before he could say them.

"Cool trick," said Jonas, as he noticed the young agent backing down. "I wonder if your look would work on me. Hit me with your best shot." The gauntlet had been thrown down.

Abby picked up the gauntlet as they walked into her office and shut the door. Looking at him with all the ice she could muster, she said, "Enough of the playful banter. You lied to me, played me, followed me, and almost got shot by me. Why the hell would I think you're cute?"

Lange had a look on his face which resembled fear. Abby was mildly shocked he had backed down. The shock was replaced by annoyance when Jonas' look of fear morphed into a mischievous grin. "You were really intimidating. Well done. But you know if you really wanted to make it believable, you shouldn't have been trying to check out my ass as I was leaving this morning."

Abby's shock made her defensive. "I did not..."

"Think I could see you in the reflection of the package scanner?" explained the Interpol agent. "I need to compliment your maintenance department on how shiny they keep the metal. Is there a form for 'complimenting maintenance so that you can see someone trying to check out your ass'? This is the FBI. There must be a form for that somewhere."

"Shut up and tell me why you want my help." Abby wanted to change the subject. She knew he was right. She wanted to get away from this topic because she was still having a hard time reading him. Jonas portrayed abnormally high confidence levels and self-awareness. He knew the effect his looks and demeanor had on others. It was impressive the way he had turned Mathis around in a car ride by debating baseball. Turning on Sherry by sitting on her desk and probably chatting with her while waiting was a cute trick, too. *It will take more than a cute smile and green eyes which make you want to dive in and get lost for hours to make me want to... Where was I going with that thought? Dammit!*

"Before I tell you too much, let me ask you a question. Who is the most terrifying serial killer in your opinion?" The question changed Lange from a smartass flirt to a hardened investigator without passing through the expressions in between. There was a cold side to this man who had the personality of an entertainer. Abby could tell Lange had seen some things no one should ever see. There was something which was both sad and dangerous about this man, making him even more attractive to Abby.

"The Killer Clown," said Abby, testing the agent. She wondered if he knew the nickname.

"John Wayne Gacy? Good choice. The whole entertaining children as a clown while killing the teenage boys and young men makes him quite the sick sociopath." Abby was impressed by his knowledge and the use of the word "sociopath" instead of "psychopath". She was unsure what it said about her when she found his use of proper psychological terminology a turn on. "But for me, it's Karl Denke. Someone who targets the tourists and eats them pisses me off. He makes all of us Germans look bad. Efficient, but bad."

Abby knew the story of the early Twentieth Century cannibal. It made sense he would choose someone from his own country. Serial killers, though a fascination to the populous, had never been one of her obsessions. "Where are you going with this, Lange? Are we hunting a cannibal? You know those are very rare."

The look in the eyes of the usually jovial Interpol agent exuded intensity and a level of animosity which was beyond the norm for an investigator on a normal case. "What would you say if I told you we have the opposite of Denke? We need to find a serial killer who does not target the tourists, he is one."

Abby could not believe her ears. A tourist who is a serial killer? That was new. She asked the first questions which came to her mind. "How do you know this guy even exists? What's his MO? Why would he do it?"

"Why don't you ask him yourself?" replied Jonas, as he sat down without asking and opened up a chat window on Abby's computer.

# Chapter Seven

The Observer was overjoyed his latest playmate was in the custom chat room he had created. He had made it so he could have conversations with anyone, anywhere, at any time without being traced. Being a computer genius was definitely an advantage. This particular chat room was one of the slowest on the internet. The killer was proud of this sluggishness in an otherwise rapid-paced world. It sent the chat through fifty proxy servers from his side before reaching the chat room and would go through fifty more before reaching the other side. Those servers would change every seventy-two seconds to make tracking through all of them as close to impossible as anyone could make it.

He had only used this room with two people. The first had been a member of the British Security Service known as MI5. She had been trying to track down someone who had killed four different people in Scotland over a two year period. She was good. Very good. But the Observer had only been responsible for three of the four deaths. Once he learned there was someone looking into them, the killer contacted her with a link to this chat room. They had bantered for thirteen weeks before he had the chance to make it to her side of the pond. She died well. The shocked look in her eyes was one of the best he had ever seen.

A light flashed on his chat room control panel. His playmate was not at his usual IP address. Where was his favorite Interpol agent today? Shock was not unknown to the Observer; however, it was not a common feeling. When he tracked the IP address to the FBI field office less than ten miles from his home, he did something he rarely did. The Observer began to worry.

Abby watched as Jonas logged in to an unusual web site. *Please don't let it be porn. Marcus will never let me hear the end of that.* As she continued to gaze over Jonas' shoulder, the screen which had originally been a custom curry creating website faded into a chat room.

"Welcome to my day-mare," said Lange, with less humor than usual. "This is why I need your help. I'm not sure how many people he's killed but I do know of two in Germany and possibly four in Scotland. It takes a second if he is online." Jonas typed, {*Guten tag, Klaus.*}

Abby stared at the screen still trying to take in that they were chatting with the killer. Suddenly, the screen had a smiley face with the phrase, {*Guten tag, Jonas.* Or should I say good morning since you are in the colonies?}

Jonas shook his head with an annoyed look. "I have no idea how he does it. None of my computer geeks can track down his real IP address, but he can always find mine no matter how I tried to hide it." Jonas began to type again, {I hate it when you do that.}

After what felt like an ungodly pause to Abby, another series of words appeared on the screen. {I know. That's why I do it? What are you doing in Tennessee? Still think I'm on that side of the pond?} replied the Observer.

Abby spoke up, "He's a game player. He is trying to make you think he's British, isn't he?" Abby recognized his use of British phraseology, but also detected something was not quite right.

Jonas raised an eyebrow. "You don't?" There was a hint of a smile on the face of the German. As he spoke, he typed, {For all I know you are in Brunei. So who did you kill lately?} The matter-of-fact way Jonas typed the question surprised Abby.

She gazed at the screen and at the unusual man at her computer desk. "If you want my help then nothing should be taken at face value. I doubt he's British. Some of his phrases don't seem right. British would be too easy and you would be sitting with someone from MI5 right now instead of me."

The screen showed another set of words. {Only one since we last spoke. It was a pleasant enough kill. Don't worry. It wasn't anyone from Hamburg this time. But you would be surprised what kinds of dangerous things people keep around their homes.}

"You are right. He has killed in Europe, but I'm pretty sure he is American." Jonas looked away from the screen for the first time since he started typing. "If you want to know the truth, I think he lives in Tennessee." He typed as he stared at the pretty profiler.

{And what kind of dangerous object did you use this time? A knife? A chainsaw? A melon baller?}

Normally Abby would be uncomfortable with his amazing green eyes looking into hers. This situation was too intense for that. *Why was Jonas jumping in like this? What was he doing by tossing her into this strange world of his?* Thinking about his statement, she asked, "Why do you think that?"

The killer's words appeared on the screen. {It was a screwdriver. But it was very effective. Well, since you found my proxy server in Knoxville, it's time to reprogram again. You are getting better. Have a great day. Make sure you go to the Sunsphere. I hear it's really boring.} With those words, the window closed on its own and the conversation was over.

The Observer hit three keys on his keyboard in rapid succession. The first accessed the computer Lange was using, searching for the owner's identity while deleting any traces of the conversation. The second shut down his proxy server in Knoxville which was one of many bouncing his chat all around the world several times. The third key set up a decoy in case Lange was as good as the Observer feared. *This guy is way too close for comfort. I think it's time for him to go.*

"*Scheiße*," said Jonas under his breath. "Well, it was worth a try." Closing the browser he spun in his chair to face Abby. "Welcome to my world." There was no real humor in his voice even though a casual onlooker would think so.

"Is this for real or are you playing another game with me, Lange?" Abby asked the question, knowing the answer. Gone was the playfulness in Jonas' eyes, his demeanor changed while chatting with this killer.

His voice took on a tone she had not yet heard. "No jokes. No games from me, at least. Klaus – or whatever his name really is – wants someone to taunt and he has chosen me. A friend of mine in MI5 also had contact with him. She died in southern England about two years ago. I'm sure she got too close to Klaus and he killed her."

Abby was unsure. "All this sounds like some kind of setup. Are you sure he is what he says he is and not some crackpot?"

"I'm sure there are elements of truth in some of the things he says; but he's also claimed to have killed more than two-hundred people and never been caught. He knows details about three 'accidental' deaths that he says were not accidents. They were in my home town. An autopsy report says what he claims could be true. He kills and makes it look like something else. Somewhere today there is a car wreck or some other casual-appearing accident where a man or woman has a wound caused by a screwdriver. I want this animal. He kills for the joy of killing. Nothing more. He's a predator, pure and simple." There was a hardness and strong resolve in his voice which told her this was beyond a professional tracking a killer. This was personal.

Hitting the speaker phone, the profiler speed dialed Marcus. "Information Counter-Espionage, Marcus here," came the voice.

"It's me. I like the new name but the ICE acronym is already taken," bantered Abby.

"I'll come up with something better. I was thinking about Computer Logistical Information Technology Operations Research Investigative Systems," joked the lovable Korean.

The flippant Jonas was back as he spoke up, "I'd gladly call CLITORIS for all my needs." Abby was impressed and a little nervous how he could replace his mask of casual humor so quickly and effortlessly.

"Shit, Abby. Tell me when you have someone there!" said a startled Marcus. "We haven't been formally introduced since you had guns pointed at you the last time I saw you. I'm Marcus Shon, computer god extraordinaire. And you must be the elusive Jonas Lange."

"Nice to meet your voice, Marcus. And I really do like the idea of calling CLITORIS," he said with a wink to Abby.

"Really?" said Abby. She was trying for exasperated but only managed to sound amused. She heard Marcus taking a breath to say something which would embarrass her, she beat him to the first word. "Marcus, I need to check the activity on my computer for the past ten minutes. We were in a chat room with the person Lange is trying to find. Do that voodoo that you do so well and tell us where he is."

"Gladly. Remote accessing now." The cursor moved on the screen of its own accord. Several windows popped up as if by magic as the tapping of a keyboard could be heard over the phone. "Looks like you were shopping for custom curry. Are we having Tai tonight?"

Jonas raised eyebrow with a mischievous smile. "It's not like that. Marcus and Tina are coming to my place for dinner." Still watching the computer screen, Abby asked, "Can you track the chat room down?"

"What chat room? All I can find is a Kashmir curry site. Checking the keystroke log." Tapping could be heard and another screen popped up. "This is strange. No keystrokes logged today. No clicks. No boot logs. That's not possible."

Lange shook his head. "Yet, he does that every time. I can even do a screen capture and it is gone when the chat is done. The only proof I have is when someone else sees the chat or the pics I've taken of my screen with my phone." He removed his smartphone from his jacket pocket, pulling up an image.

The windows on Abby's computer were flying with pages and pages of code flowing as the machine gun sound of keys tapping came through the phone. Several inaudible swears could be heard under Marcus's breath. Screen after screen scrolled past. Finally Marcus' angry, curt voice said, "Be right there." The sound of the phone slamming came right through the speaker.

"Am I about to get a lecture about letting people sneak through firewalls and infiltrating the FBI network?" asked a smiling Lange.

"Oh yeah," snickered Abby.

"Let's go get some coffee," said Jonas heading for the door.

"Oh yeah," repeated Abby, starting to laugh. Grabbing his arm, she warned, "We'd better take the long way around. There is a slightly built Korean bulldozer coming from that direction."

As they turned the corner, they could hear Marcus' voice coming down the hall, "Get away from the computer before I take that keyboard and stick it..." Fortunately his voice was muffled by the slamming of Abby's office door as he went to work.

"What am I going to need to do to make up for this faux pas?" asked a smirking Interpol agent.

Laughing, Abby said, "It was not simply a false step. And you may want to buy Marcus a really good bottle of wine or at least a twelve-pack of microbrew."

Turning the last corner into the break room, the eyes of the three people in the room turned to face them and abruptly stopped talking. For the second time in one day Abby could feel people staring at her because of who she was with.

Barbara and Sherry were both leering at the Interpol agent while Brenda was more subtle in her observations. *I guess you really don't need a water cooler to gossip.* Abby handled the introductions. "Hello, ladies. This is Agent Jonas Lange of Interpol. Jonas, you already met Sherry – who is looking at your crotch. The one on her left is Barbara Johnson, happily married with two kids. The one on her right, trying to be subtle except for the drool, is Special Agent Brenda Nevins, who is currently seeing a guy in accounting and a girl in reception." Brenda's hand reflexively shot to her mouth only to discover Abby had been tormenting her.

Brenda glared at Abby, "You can be a real bitch sometimes, Chilton." Moving deliberately between Abby and Jonas, she greeted the handsome agent, "Abby is joking. I understand you are putting together a task force for a special project. If there is anything you need, please feel free to ask. We can meet after work if you prefer."

Lange smiled his best smile at his three admirers. "Thank you so much, Brenda. If there is anything you can do I will let you know. Sadly, I already made dinner plans. Now, Abby," he moved around the flirtatious agent, "about the coffee?" All three women rolled their eyes as they walked out of the break room. Almost in perfect synchronicity, they all looked back at Lange only to see him chatting amicably with the profiler. The three women began talking amongst themselves with the word "bitch" being the only one reaching Abby's ears.

Abby reached for two cups and poured both of them tall, strong cups of her notorious java. She handed the agent a steaming, if somewhat old, cup of coffee and she indelicately took a greedy gulp of hers. Without looking at what was offered, Jonas took a sip of his. The psychologist watched the blonde-haired man carefully, hoping for a reaction. Lange gagged, choked, tried to take a breath and discovered her coffee was not something intended for inhalation. Stumbling to the sink, he coughed up the coffee and what felt like his right lung.

"You... are... vindictive," gasped Jonas, still trying to breathe. "What the hell was that?" he asked and then broke down into a coughing fit.

"Payback's a bitch," said Abby. Taking his face in her right hand, she stared into his gorgeous, watering green eyes. "And so am I when you piss me off. So I take it you're not really a coffee drinker?"

Lange regained his composure and waved off the agent who had entered the room to make sure everything was all right. "I love coffee. But my question remains, what the hell was that?"

Moving to the single cup coffee maker, she found the least coffee sounding packet and tossed it to Jonas. "Here, have a decaf vanilla-nut, weeny-ass special."

"Thanks. No Frappuccino? How disappointing," said Lange replacing the frilly coffee to choose a simple Colombian medium roast. Tossing a casual glance down the hall where the women had traveled, Jonas asked Abby, "Unless you want to make me into a liar, what time is dinner?"

# Chapter Eight

The Observer was pleased. Lange was turning out to be a worthwhile playmate. Not only had he tracked one of his deep proxy servers, he had also made it to Tennessee. This was truly unexpected. Ms. Pink would be getting a reprieve for the moment. Well, somewhat of a reprieve. His tracker would automatically send a signal at four AM. It should tell him where she is spending her nights. That would be enough for him to begin profiling her. By morning her name, phone number and contents of her trash can would give him ample information.

A file was blinking on his game screen. This was the data on the person who had loaned Agent Lange a computer. Who would it be? FBI undoubtedly. A click and the file opened with a cacophony of raw data to an untrained eye. The Observer had a gift with both computers and people. He could manipulate either with equal ease. This was where both of his passions intersected in a symphony of information. He sifted through the information his worm had mined from the computer. A smile showing equal parts pleasure and malevolence crept across his visage as he trimmed the data into something usable.

The new file read:

Name: Abigail Renee Chilton

Federal Bureau of Investigations – Knoxville, Tennessee, United States

Agent, Psychologist, Profiler, Therapist

PHD in Psychology from The University of Texas - Austin

Residence: 9880 Middlebrook Pike #44

Phone: 865-555-4367 (cell only)

Calendar appointments of significance: Tonight – Dinner with Tina and Marcus @ home.

Favorite stores: Kroger, Fresh Market, Walmart, Forever 21.

The data list continued for two pages with several pics of Abby and two others. A quick sift through the data revealed the names of her FBI friends. *Dinner tonight? I think I need a few things from the store.* The Observer's smile became even lustier. *Dinner for friends means Fresh Market. I hope Abby doesn't get the cheap stuff.*

Walking through the Fresh Market, the sights, sounds and scent permeated Abby's senses. She loved shopping there with the array of aromas feeding her desire to cook. She went straight for the produce section to begin collecting her ingredients. Abby had taken several cooking classes in the past few months and had transformed from a 'can-opener' kind of cook to a 'make-it-from-scratch' kind of girl. She had several new recipes she was dying to try out on her friends. Well, her friends and Lange. She was still not sure why she had let him invite himself over. *Sure you do. You think he's almost as cute as he thinks he is.* She pondered the thought. *No. He is as cute as he thinks he is, dammit.*

The acorn squash looked perfect. She found two large, ideal specimens. Adding to her cart a quart of raspberries and a lime, she moved on to the bread section. She loved bread. As she was looking at a wheat version of a French loaf, a stranger was helping himself to another kind. He noticed her looking and said with a Tennessee twang, "If you haven't tried the multi-grain artisan you are missing out, sugar." She loved the friendliness of this town. Many women from other parts of the country found the terms of endearment offensive. Abby subscribed to the philosophy which stated others could not offend her; only she could chose to take offense. She made an effort to choose not to. Taking the rounded loaf, she moved on to the butcher shop.

The man behind the counter knew her well. "Hey, Abby. What ya need today? I've got some stuffed chicken breasts y'all haven't tried yet."

"Thanks, Billy. But tonight I want to make my own. Give me four of the regular breasts and two of the turkey bratwurst." Abby smiled thinking of the twist she was adding for her uninvited guest. Her smile faded as the hairs on the back of her neck prickled. Someone was watching her. She looked around to see her friend from the bread section trying to look inconspicuous by the olive bar. He knew he was caught and did something which was too cute: he blushed. *Abigail, you need to stop being so paranoid.* Her inner

voice often chided her. *He's kind of cute, in a stalker kind of way.*
She waved at her admirer and headed up an aisle, grabbed some
couscous, and headed for the checkout. The profiler paid for her
groceries and headed to her Accord.

As she pulled away, the Observer watched from a safe distance
inside the store. Noting her plate number, he complimented himself
on his ability to blush on command. *This is going to be all kinds of
fun. Now I have two playmates. Abby will be much more fun than
Jonas.*

Arriving home none the worse for the wear after a long day,
Abby tossed her keys in the basket on the island which divided the
kitchen from the living room. After setting down her two bags, she
walked over to something resembling a breadbox on the kitchen
counter. Abby flipped open a hidden latch and pressed her thumb to
the scanner. With a beep, the side opened to reveal it as a small gun
safe. Placing both her weapons inside with her badge and cuffs, she
closed it.

She glanced at the clock on the stove. 5:55pm. Abby had
enough time for a quick shower before everyone started arriving.
She got out several items from her refrigerator to warm to room
temperature then headed to her bedroom. She stripped down to her
birthday suit and was more careful than usual to put her clothes in
the hamper. *Don't even think about it, Abby. No one is coming in
your bedroom tonight.* She answered herself. *Too late. I thought. But
there is no harm in thinking, is there?*

Shaking her head at her own internal voice, she headed into the
bathroom and turned on the shower. The water was scalding, steam
filled the room. Abby stepped into the shower and let the water rain
down on her. The hot drops warmed her skin and loosened the
tension in her muscles. She stood in the shower for longer than she
should; but the water was cleansing her body and clearing her mind.
Using one of her few luxuries, she put a quarter-sized bit of Sisley
Eau Du Soir Shower Gel on her loofah and scrubbed herself clean,
the moss and woods scent of the expensive body wash filling the
room. Rinsing the suds she glanced down at her legs. *Do not shave
your legs! No one will be touching them.* She toweled off with her

over-sized, over-fluffy towel. Some luxuries were really necessities in disguise. Good body wash and fluffy towels were two of them.

Dressing in denim shorts and a v-cut t-shirt, she went back to her kitchen. *I'll be damned if I'm going to get dressed up for Lange.* Looking in the hallway mirror, she noticed the v-cut showed off her cleavage nicely. *But I like looking good for me.*

Heading to the kitchen, it was time to get the appetizer ready. Spreading Neufchatel cheese on a plate, she covered it with cocktail sauce and tiny shrimp. The doorbell rang as she was shredding parmigiano-romano cheese on top of it. Abby was torn between hoping it wasn't Jonas arriving first and hoping it was. Tina bounced in, bottle in hand.

"Hey, Abby. I don't smell anything cooking," teased the New Englander. "And I see you got all dressed up for your date." She always managed to look better than Abby. Tina was wearing beige capris and a striped halter top which looked trashy on most women. Tina could pull it off. She had good fashion sense for an accountant.

"Shut up and give me the damn wine," said the profiler. Grabbing the bottle, she led the way to the kitchen. Four glasses were placed on the bar side of the island as Tina seated herself on the center stool. Abby placed the shrimp dip in front of her friend and passed a bowl of gourmet sesame crackers. The dark haired damsel wasted no time in digging into her favorite appetizer as Abby removed the cork with a pop. The California blush went well with the crackers and dip. The first sip of wine had barely passed their lips when a double ring of the doorbell told them it was Marcus.

Tina went to the door as the cook spread out ingredients on her workspace. Marcus strolled into the kitchen with two boxes. One contained dessert with over thirty mini cream puffs. The other had a spigot and white paper covering it with the words "red wine" in black letters on the box. He made it into generic wine. It was a running joke. None of them were wine snobs by any stretch of the imagination so they enjoyed a variety of less expensive wines. Marcus, who was more comfortable with Apple computers than apple wine, always insisted on bringing quantity over quality. He had once explained, "I'm a Korean, born and raised in Boise to be a computer savant. None of those things makes me any good at choosing a great wine." He was right, too.

He sat down and made a show of looking around. "I don't see your new boy toy, Tiny. Do you think he got lost?" Grinning like the cat who swallowed the canary, he turned to Tina. "Should we call him? Me and him still need to chat about letting people hack into my network."

Abby stopped in mid-slice of the raw chicken breast. "You will not call him and you will not ruin my evening by yelling at Lange. No harm was done. It's all cool." Abby began to stuff the chicken breasts with the contents of the turkey brats. "If he makes it, he makes it. If he doesn't, he doesn't and we have someone to talk about." There was an evil smile on the face of the cook as she added feta cheese to the interior of the chicken.

Tina noticed the smile. "What?" She knew Abby had that look when she found something amusing. It was usually present when she had a misogynistic agent on her list of those to be counseled before they would be allowed back into the field. Seeing Mathis trip over a computer cable or Brenda getting shot down by her latest potential conquest also brought the smile to her face.

Adding several sprigs of fresh herbs which only she recognized, Abby chortled, "It's not my fault if he invited himself over and didn't even ask where he was supposed to be. I've been waiting for him to call so I can make a big deal over..." The doorbell rang. Abby visibly deflated.

Tina nearly bounced to the door to let Jonas in. "I'm sorry, Abby. Did you want to finish your sentence?" asked Marcus. "You were saying something about making a big deal that he already had your address. He has your federally protected home address. How do you supposed that happened?" The computer tech was laughing at his own joke.

"Fuck you," said Abby, as Tina and Jonas entered the room.

Jonas raised an eyebrow. "I'm glad she says that to you, too," he said to Marcus, offering his free hand. "Sorry about the whole computer thing." What had looked like a handshake turned out to be an exchange of alcohol. Marcus looked in his hand as he read the label. His eyes widened. In his hand was a Westvleteren 12 Belgian Quadrupel ale.

Going from confusion to shock to awe, Marcus finally spoke. "You're forgiven. I've only heard about this. How did you find it?" It was rare to see the Korean change his tone so quickly. Usually an agent was on his shit list for weeks – sometimes months – for the kind of computer iniquity Jonas had committed.

Jonas smiled his winning smile. "I did a favor for the Trappist monks who brew this amazing elixir. They save a case for me every time they brew it. Being Interpol does give me a few perks now and then. Sip it. Don't gulp. It's about the same alcohol as the," he looked at the box labeled red wine and raised an eyebrow at Marcus, "wine?"

"Shut up and let's drink some beer," laughed Marcus. As Abby rolled the chicken in Italian bread crumbs with other special spices, the computer guru went to the cabinet and got out two tall glasses for the beer. The rich, dark brew was slowly and lovingly poured into the glasses as two men toasted one another and bonded over priceless ale. Some things were universal.

Abby continued her show of cooking as all watched and asked about the various dishes while enjoying the shrimp dip. The chicken was placed in the lower oven as brown sugar and raspberry stuffed acorn squash was placed in the upper. Snow peas with a lemon-honey glaze were prepared alongside a couscous dish with red bell peppers and mushrooms. Jonas kept the three FBI employees entertained with stories of Interpol exploits as the meal was prepared.

Marcus excused himself to the balcony for a cigarette and a second beer as Tina excused herself to answer the call of nature. This left Abby and Jonas alone while the plates were being heated in preparation for the food. The psychologist had been watching Jonas all night trying to profile this enigmatic man. Each time she thought she had something figured out, he threw a monkey wrench into the gears of her profile.

"Tell me, Jonas. What's your deal?" asked Abby without even a hint of subtlety.

"My deal? I like women. Not into men. Sorry if it gets you all hot and bothered but it's not my thing," replied the German. It both amused and pissed Abby off how he could make a joke out of anything. She was pretty sure it was a defense mechanism to keep people off guard and at a distance.

"You know what I mean, kraut," replied Abby, trying to get a rise out of him.

"There are actually eight of us Germans who don't really care for sauerkraut all that much. It tastes like spoiled cabbage to me." Making of show of thinking about it, Lange added, "If you want to get a rise out of me, try calling me a Germ. It gets to some of us."

Tina had returned. "Did I miss any sexual tension? Was there flirting? Did you do it on the counter?" She was trying to embarrass the profiler. Abby turned the tables on her friend.

"No. I flashed my tits and he did me on the coffee table. Was it good for you?" she asked Jonas.

"The earth moved," said Jonas, gazing longingly at Abby with enough false sincerity Tina actually had a moment where she considered the possibility. "I needed a cigarette but I think it'd be too odd to smoke with Marcus after sexing Abby."

They all laughed as Marcus came in from outside. "What's so funny? Did I miss something good?"

Tina chimed in. "We were talking about Jonas smoking with you after wild sex with Abby on the coffee table."

Not one to miss a straight line, Marcus looked at his watch and asked, "How long was I out there?" The laughter resumed as the meal was plated. All sat around the island enjoying the food. The meal was devoured, compliments given to the chef, and all helped with the dishes. The cleanup was also a water fight as Tina "accidentally" got Jonas with the spray and Abby dropped a dish rag on Marcus. When everything was clean, they moved to the living room.

Marcus, on his fourth beer, began the interrogation of Lange. "So, Jonas. How many languages do you speak? German and English and what else?" There was a slight slurring to his speech.

"Only five fluently. But I can do different accents in each of them. I'm known at Interpol as The Chameleon. Blending in is my specialty. It is why Abby is having a hard time profiling me." He looked Abby right in the eye and winked as a battle of wills began.


From a distance, the Observer watched the meal preparation. The telephoto lens on his Cannon digital camera had caught Abby returning from her bedroom through the open blinds on her patio door. The short, busty brunette had arrived a few moments later. "Hello, Tina. You look well tonight." An Asian man arrived next. "Why Marcus, that is an interesting name for someone with origins in the East. You must have parents who wanted an American son." A smile crossed the Observer's face as his nemesis arrived last. "*Guten aben, Jonas.*" Nothing was missed as the Observer observed every aspect of the dinner and dish washing. When Marcus stepped outside for a cigarette he made a careful examination the computer tech. He could be the most dangerous of this quartet. If Marcus could track him down, an accident may need to be arranged. Time would tell. The hunter watched his prey of three Americans trying to understand the Interpol agent who had been on his radar for a few months. *I wonder if he'll tell them about Kristin.*

# Chapter Nine

The Observer had been watching Abby's dinner party for four hours now. Play time was over. It was time to get back to work. The trees where he had perched offered an excellent vantage point. He placed a bird house there which looked old and weathered. It was both. This was one of the many he had placed around his targets. The wireless camera within was activated. The bottom was filled with batteries so he would only need to return once a month to replace them. Using his tablet, he found a strong WIFI signal and tapped into it, sending his video feed around the world and back to his home across town.

Walking casually back to his vehicle, he placed bugs on Tina's car, Jonas' BMW and Marcus' SUV while removing the one from Abby's. It is always good to know where your playmates spend their time. He smiled, as he got into the Prius parked next to Abby's Honda. His silent car moved away, making one last pass of Abby's apartment to savor the anticipation of what was to come.


"All right, Abby. You've had all day and four hours this evening to profile me. What have you figured out?" asked Jonas. He was genuinely curious to see how much she had seen and how much he had been able to keep from her.

"Yea, Tiny. Tell us all about the Germ." Marcus had adopted the nickname as soon as he heard about the joke. It didn't seem to bother Jonas, plus it was a sign Marcus had forgiven him for the network fiasco. The computer guru had the recliner all to himself. He liked being able to swivel, he was always moving. If his fingers weren't dancing across a keyboard, feet were moving or hands were twitching. It was one of his annoyingly endearing qualities.

Tina was on the opposite end of the couch from Abby. She was sipping her wine and watching both Abby and Jonas. She was nowhere near the reader of people as Abby; but she could detect a few things when she tried. So far, he had given away nothing to her.

Jonas had taken a spot on the love seat, sitting with one leg on the unused part of the two person couch looking as casual as anyone could possibly look. To Abby it seemed to be a practiced casual. Truth be told, it looked like a very familiar way of relaxing.

"All right, Jonas. You said yourself that you're a chameleon. There's very little I can take at face value. Right now you are doing you're very best to look casual in a very American kind of way. Yet the seat you chose allows you to see the front door and patio door where you seem to glance at every thirty to forty-five seconds. Since you are on alert, you suspect there is someone watching you. It makes you either hyper-vigilant or paranoid. Maybe a little bit of both." Abby was watching his reactions to her analysis, he wasn't showing anything at all. "Even with your watchfulness there are no obvious signs you saw anything. Your accent has not slipped in the slightest even though you are on your third glass of wine after having one of your uber-beers with Marcus. You're European so a high tolerance for alcohol is not surprising. Beer in the baby bottle?"

Jonas smiled his best smile as he said, "It was my sippy cup. Go on. This is interesting." Although impressed she had caught him checking the doors, there was no way he would let her see that.

"Humor is one of your greatest weapons. Since you understand American humor I deduce you truly are a chameleon. From the broken Spanish I learned, I know humor is the most difficult concept of any culture. Still you are as comfortable making jokes in American English as if you were born here." A smiling Abby went in for the kill. "It tells me that humor is also one of your greatest defense mechanisms. You are hiding something behind the jokes and the flirting which you do not want anyone to see. My guess would be the loss of someone very close to you. Using all of your humor and charm, you make everyone think you're their best friend while really keeping them at a distance. All of this, with your linguistic ability, tells me your I.Q. is above average. I suspect your university degree is in some kind of international studies."

Keeping his poker face was a challenge for Jonas with the last bit of Abby's profile. She was right on target with many of her thoughts. Attempting to distract the Americans, he faked a thoughtful look and said in a perfect English resonance, "You should hear my British humor some time. I watched Monty Python to get it right. On the other parts you are way off. My degree is in linguistics with a masters in criminology and a doctorate in law." With a twinkle in his eye, he sounded American again. "But it is a doctorate in international law so I suppose you were close."

The jaws of Tina and Marcus dropped in unison. Abby maintained her composure but was obviously impressed. "Now for the sixty-four-thousand-dollar question. Anyone can tell you are good at what you do. You are smart and don't look like Quasimodo." It was as close as Abby was willing to give him even though everyone in the room knew he looked like an Adonis. Jonas laughed at the contrast. "What do you want with me?"

All eyes turned to bore into Jonas, trying to see anything revelatory. The casual slouch slowly morphed into something which was both appealing and frightening. The smile on Jonas' face melted into a wicked smile, showing there was much more to this man than even Abby had deduced. The chameleon has transformed into a panther, ready to spring at helpless prey. Both Abby and Tina had the same thought. *DAMN! That's hot!*

His voice sounded like it dropped an octave and was soft, but still crystal clear. "I can do and have done many things. But the one thing I know I cannot do well is where you excel. I need a profiler. Abby, you and I are going to find this son of a bitch and I will do whatever it takes to stop him." Turning to Tina, he said in the same low, smoldering voice, "I'm not available for marriage. Sorry." Then, with a wink, the Jonas they thought they knew was back as his casual persona slouched back on the couch. "More wine anyone?"

"Dude, you are one scary bastard," said Marcus.

"You should see me when I'm trying to ski. That really is scary," joked Jonas, refilling his wineglass.

Abby had missed nothing. Her profile on Jonas had taken a whole new, exciting direction. There was something personal about this case for the German. What had Klaus done to make him so... passionate? Jonas was a dangerous man. With his ability to take her pistol, get out of the cuffs and the ice cold side she had glimpsed; the Chameleon was showing many of his hidden colors. *But what was going on in his head?* Would she ever see? *And why the hell did it make him even more attractive?* The logical part of her brain spoke up. *Abby, it's the classic attraction to the bad boy like Jason Aluna in high school. He was hot shit but Jonas makes him look like cold crap.* Her libido was also curious. *I wonder if his passion translates to other areas.*

Tina finally regained her voice. "I need some more wine. Abby, want to help?" The ladies left the men and went to the relative privacy of the kitchen. "Oh my God!" whispered Tina, trying to pour the wine. "If you don't hit that, I will. Damn! What is it with him?"

Abby was equally impressed. "He has the bad boy side. It gets me every time. But there is something wrong. Something we're missing. He has some kind of pain that I can't see. Not yet, at least."

Tina looked at her friend in disbelief. "No wonder you never get laid. Stop thinking so damn much and at least have some great, tension relieving, hot, sweaty, tearing the sheets off the bed, sex. It's not that hard. Well, it's not so complicated. Hopefully it's hard."

Picking up the full glasses, Abby said with a laugh, "You're impossible."

"No. I'm very possible," taking the glasses which were for she and Marcus, Tina poured them in the sink. "Hey, Marcus, let's head out. They have a case to discuss." The way she said "case" sounded scandalous, her smile telling Marcus it was time to get out of the way.

"Now you kids behave yourself. Don't do anything I wouldn't do," said a mischievous Marcus.

"Really? How was your date with the Starbucks girl last night?" asked Abby with a knowing grin.

Marcus blushed while heading out the door. "I hate it when you do that."

After the two analysts had left, Jonas spoke up. "Alone at last. Starbucks girl?"

"Marcus has been trying to get past second base with a woman he met at Starbucks a couple weeks ago. He got lucky last night. It was all over his face this morning."

"Perhaps he needs to shower better," joked Jonas. "Now, about the sexual tension between us. What are we going to do about it?"

Abby was momentarily surprised by his forward style. Then again, why would he be any different than what he always portrayed himself to be? "What makes you think there is sexual tension?" asked Abby trying too hard to sound innocent.

"There isn't? Oh, sorry. My mistake. I told you I'm a terrible profiler." Jonas tone was one which Abby could not identify. He was either mocking her or was backing off.

*Please let him be mocking me.* Abby was not sure what to say. "No harm done."

Rising, Jonas said, "Well, I'd better get going. I'll be at the office by eight. My files have already been sent to your e-mail so we can start trying to figure out Klaus first thing in the morning." Abby walked him to the door. "It's too bad about the absence of sexual tension. I know where to find two g-spots and have a Gene Simmons tongue. See you tomorrow." He stuck out his tongue which touched underneath his chin as he waved good-bye and headed to his car.

Abby closed the door and slid down to the floor. "Holy shit! I need another shower." She eventually got up, stripped off her clothes on the way to her bedroom, and stood under an ice cold shower until her skin began to turn a light shade of blue. *Cold showers work well at making a hot and sweating horny person into a cold and clammy horny person. Damn you, Jonas.*


The Observer watched the feed from his new camera peeking in at Abby's home while driving to his house. He was surprised to see Jonas leaving so soon after her coworkers. *So Jonas is not getting lucky tonight. That is unusual for him. Could this one be a challenge to his charms?* Watching Abby crossing the room, removing her shirt, he chuckled. *Never mind. He is playing hard to get and she is hitting the shower. That's how my buddy works.*

When he got home the Observer went to his bank of computer screens to see he had an e-mail waiting for him. The Toronto law firm wanted to meet with him on Wednesday. It would give him tomorrow to set up his surveillance and begin profiles on all his new playmates. The pink girl would have to wait. So sad. But he did have several targets ready to go in Toronto from his last meeting. This would be fun. He turned to his game screen and typed series of keyboard strokes which didn't seem to do anything until a window popped up. The blank screen was waiting for a passcode. Twenty-five keystrokes later, most of which were not even letters, the screen revealed his wish list.

Typing in the words {Toronto, Canada} in the location bar, a list of eight names appeared. Each was color-coded. Two were green, one was yellow, two were blue, and three were red. One of the greens would be his new target. Staying in Toronto for ten days, he would be able to update the status of several of the others. It was so sad seeing such unhappy colors on the list. If there was time, maybe he would add some new people to research.

Each person on the list was selected and new files were created. Internet searches began. By morning, his search bots would discover all kinds of new information about all eight of his Toronto targets. Turning to his other screen, he sent similar bots into the Toronto internet to find some new clients who would need the services of a white hat hacker. *I may was well make this a profitable trip in every sense of the word.*


When he left, Jonas' had a feeling something was wrong. His training had given him heightened awareness of his surroundings which led to strange feelings once in a while. He was right sixty-five to seventy-five percent of the time. The percentage increased if he could discern why he was having the feeling. Though he was staying near the airport, he felt a scenic route through the countryside was needed. As he drove he began to move his subconscious concerns into his conscious mind.

He had long since given up trying to keep up with all the detail his mind was continuously accumulating. His instructors had tried to discover the secret to his intuition but only Jonas knew. His mind kept information he may need in his short term memory, his subconscious would nudge him when it saw something. This time it was a missing car. When he had arrived he saw eight vehicles in the parking area. Three had belonged to his new associates, five belonged to others. Thinking back, six were local and the other two were from Michigan and Virginia. Out of town visitors were common enough, not suspicious. When he had left there had been six other cars. One had been a loud pickup he had heard leaving an hour and ten minutes after arriving. Not subtle. Not the killer's style.

The missing car was a hybrid. The Prius had left after they had finished eating. About four hours into the evening, if he remembered correctly. He had heard nothing but saw it leaving. A leaving car should not send up red flags. Why had this one? *It went past the door. The parking lot exit was the other direction. Could Klaus have been watching them?*

One of his coolest toys was his mobile phone. This phone, which could use any tower it found, could also link to satellites when no towers were available. It was getting harder and harder to find places with no cell towers, but it did happen. After driving for almost an hour, he was in place with no cell signal at all. Shutting off his BMW, he got out and disconnected the battery to remove all electronic signals from the car.

With the press of an app, he began scanning for anything searching for cell towers. Nothing. He used the same app to search for anything trying to find a WIFI signal. Again, nothing. One more scan and he would call it a night. This last time searched for any electronic signals at all. He went around the car to learn there were several battery backups. Many capacitors still had power and so did one of the tail lights. *Tail light?* With his flashlight in hand, he lay down in the gravel and looked under the bumper. Behind the light was a small metal disc unlike anything Jonas had ever seen.

Getting back up, he opened the rear hatch and dug into a knapsack he affectionately referred to as his goody bag. Inside were several devices which would have made the Observer drool. The one he removed had wheels. Placing it on the ground, it went back and forth under the BMW. On his phone he watched the results of the mobile scanner. Just the one unknown device was found. No explosives. No electronic interference. Only the device on the back bumper using GPS but not sending the information anywhere.

Jonas put his toys away and headed back to his hotel. His phone remained in WIFI and cell scanning mode, still it detected nothing. When he arrived back at his room, there was a beep on his phone. The device had found and used the open WIFI at his hotel and uploaded something. Most likely, all the GPS information had been sent somewhere special. Now someone knew where he had been tonight.

Abby's phone rang. In a groggy voice, she answered. "It's 12:45. This better be important," grumbled the profiler.

"Abby, wake up. It's Jonas. I'm coming over. Don't get any ideas. We have a problem." There was an urgency in Jonas' voice which Abby caught right away.

"All right. I'll put on a pot of coffee. Are you all right?" Abby's concern was genuine.

"I'm good. Be there in twenty minutes. And Abby," he tried not to sound melodramatic, "keep the lights off."

# Chapter Ten

The Observer left home. It was 1:00am and it was time to retrieve his trackers. Placing the one on Abby's car before entering the Fresh Market was easy. Retrieving it was a safety countermeasure. He had no idea what scanners were around the FBI field office. It was too risky to take a chance. Now he needed to get to the other three devices.

Jonas' would be the easiest. That one would be last. He drove through the west end of Knoxville to discover Tina had half of a duplex with an attached garage. This was not a problem for the very resourceful Observer. Parking three doors down, he sent a focused signal to her garage door. The device sat on the dash of his car, sending code after code. After ten minutes, the garage door opened, lighting up the driveway. The code was saved in the device in case he needed it in the future.

The light went off and no one had come out to investigate. After another ten minutes with no security or a police cruiser, he got out of his hybrid and began walking along the edge of the street. He carried a leash, looking around with a slightly frantic look on his face. He even stage whispered the name of his imaginary dog: Bongo. When he reached the open garage door, he made a show of looking under the car from the street, softly calling the dog's name. His approach would look to anyone checking to be a man searching for his lost dog. As he knelt down and pretended to look for Bongo, he removed the tracker and walked on down the street.

After making a lap around the block, the Observer returned to his car and quietly drove away. Not only was his car eco-friendly and great on gas mileage, it also made leaving a neighborhood a silent affair. One down. Two to go.

Abby was waiting in her darkened living room when there was a soft knock. She walked to the door, Glock in hand. Looking through the peep hole, she could make out the outline of Lange in the darkness. Jonas was in her apartment as soon as her door was opened. He latched it back and made a quick survey of the room. Abby knew he would find nothing to complain about. She had drawn the drapes and left the lights off.

"This better not be a booty call, Lange," she began. "If this is some kind of play to get in my panties..."

"I hate to burst your bubble, but your panties are way down on my list of things to worry about. Third. Maybe even forth." Abby could almost hear him smirking in the dark. "Make it third."

Abby chuckled, the joke relieving some of the tension. "Let's hit the couch. So, what's so important it couldn't wait seven more hours? I am a delicate flower. I need my beauty rest." The soft sigh of the cushions of her sofa as she sat was echoed by the silhouetted form of Jonas on the opposite end.

"First, there is nothing delicate about you. Second, I'm sure you look great even with no sleep." Jonas' tone changed to the soft, serious sound Abby had heard earlier. "And third, there's a tracker on my car." She could picture the panther sitting across from her.

"Are you bullshitting me?" Abby asked. "People do not track cops. Cops track people." Jonas had to be joking or making one of the strangest moves she had ever seen. His face was lit by the glow of his cell phone. She could see the serious, dangerous side of the Interpol agent in the harsh light. "OK. You're not bullshitting me. What did you find?"

As he finished telling Abby of his adventure, Jonas handed his phone to the profiler. Abby saw the gray disc in the photo. It was something his rover had taken and sent to his phone.

Jonas explained, "I'm sure whoever put it on my car knows I was here. You're not safe, Abby."

She returned the phone to its owner and chambered a round in her Glock. The sound of the bullet being prepared for firing broke the near silence of her apartment with a crack. Jonas moved from the edge of the couch to a defensive stance before the sound died away. "Relax, Jonas. I can take care of myself."

"There is something you need to know I was waiting until tomorrow to tell you." He took a breath and sat back down. "I know Klaus lives here in Knoxville."

The Observer found the next bug without any problem. Marcus lived in a townhouse in the Fountain City area. There were no garage doors, but there were other concerns. With townhouses there tended to be dogs. Dogs would bark at anything they sensed outside their homes. The Observer chose to hide in plain sight, again. Using the leash, he parked a block away and went through the parking lot of a different apartment complex before entering the one where Marcus resided. At 2:00am, looking for a missing dog was one of the more believable scenarios he could use.

Walking through the grass, he saw something coming. Instead of hiding, he waved the pickup down. "Have you seen a medium sized black dog?" he asked the man. The Observer knew right away this man would never remember him. His tired eyes told it all. He was off work and all he wanted was sleep.

"Sorry, dude. Ain't seen no black dogs, but we got a hell of a time with all the stray cats 'round here. Don't s'pose your dog'll chase 'em off will he?" replied the man in the Braves baseball cap.

Smiling but looking like an owner worried about his dog, he said, "He might. I gotta find him. Night, bud."

"Good luck. If I see him I'll holler." The truck pulled away and the hunter continued to his target's car. Kneeling down, he surreptitiously removed the tracker. Mission accomplished, he continued on a circular route back to his waiting car. Two down. One to go.

Abby waited for Jonas to continue. The photo didn't lie; yet she wondered if Jonas was being paranoid. It could be anything.

"Jonas, did you consider this could be a device from the rental company to keep track of their car?" Though she was being pragmatic, her instincts told her Jonas knew something she didn't.

"That's good thinking, Abby. But there is one problem. It's my car." The soft, serious tone of Lange made her shiver for multiple reasons.

"Your car? You brought your car from Germany?" She was confused.

"Of course not. I bought it when I got here. I don't like renting." The casual way he said it made her more curious.

---

"You don't like renting so you bought a car? How long are you staying in America?" asked the profiler.

"You're missing the point, Chilton. I've had the car for two days and there's a tracker on it." The Interpol agent took a deep breath. "Who do you think is interested in me? You know the only people I know in Knoxville. The only one who would care where I am is Klaus. I made sure he knows I'm here."

Abby had enough. "OK. Give. Why do you think this sick bastard is in my city?"

"Klaus is amazing on computers. He hides his trail better than the most devious hacker I know. But I know a hacker who knows a hacker who knows a few other hackers. I had seven of the best hackers in Europe on his cyber-trail. They each took a leg of his trail and kept finding a common thread leading to the proxy server in Knoxville." He looked at the pretty agent across from him in the darkness. "And then there were the tickets."

Abby was intrigued. "Tickets? Like parking tickets?"

Jonas took a steadying breath. "I know many of the most notorious killers in history were caught by stupid mistakes like speeding tickets; but I'm talking about plane tickets. There has been a man who has passed through customs on multiple occasions using different passports and different aliases. He looks slightly different, but our analysts in Lyon found it is the same man based on some facial recognition software which is barely legal. When he has been places, people disappear and a few are found dead. Yet, he keeps coming back here."

"Let me get this straight," began Abby. "You have hackers and analysts who tracked some serial killer to Knoxville, Tennessee? And you think he has killed over two-hundred people? You do know we're talking about an area of the U.S. that is best known for hillbillies, moonshine and *Breaking Bad* wannbes making meth, right?"

"And it has a major university, the most dangerous nuclear facility in the world, and the electrical power base for a huge section of the south-eastern part of the country." Jonas Lange was not one to take kindly to condescension or being underestimated. "Abby, don't treat me like I'm an idiot. I know your I.Q. is in the 150s, but mine is only slightly lower. Plus, I have more field experience than most men twice my age." The tone of voice Jonas used pissed her off until she realized he had perfectly mimicked the tone she had used on him.

"Point taken. My apologies." Seeing his head nod in the dark, Abby continued, "Do you really think Klaus has been watching us?"

"I will tell you in a few minutes." His cell phone once again lit up his scowling face. Jonas moved so Abby could see what he was doing. A small picture was showing heat signatures. "This is you and that is me." Panning around the camera showed the apartment next door had a couple who was so close together it looked like they were one large person. The angle shifted dramatically. The overhead view caused Abby to look from the screen to the man sitting next to her. Jonas saw her observation out of the corner of his eye. "Outside is a very quiet drone that we can watch from here. It has an infrared camera and is on a search pattern trying to find heat sources."

"Interpol has some really expensive toys," said Abby. "I need to tell Jeremy about this. Marcus will want three of them for God only knows what. Probably something to do with Starbucks girl."

Jonas laughed. "I'm sure he would. But this is not standard Interpol issue. This is mine." Abby turned back to the small phone screen as she added to the profile of this man. This man who was far too close to her for comfort. Sensing her thoughts, Jonas said, "Yes, I'm loaded. Dad made good money with medical tech. I can buy any toys I want thanks to a generous trust fund and a few lucrative investments." He squinted at the screen. "Looks like someone's in trouble." A one bedroom apartment had one person in the bedroom and another on a couch. "And someone else is busy," said the agent as another apartment showed two people obviously enjoying themselves in their bedroom. "Moving on."

It wasn't until the roving camera began scanning the trees around the apartment that something caught Jonas' eye. "What is this?" asked the German, curiosity and concern were in his voice. It found a birdhouse which was way too warm to have simple birds within. Jonas took control of the drone from his phone and moved it for a side approach. The batteries of the camera left by the Observer were giving off too much heat, the infrared had found it. With a tap of a button on his phone, Jonas and Abby were looking through the wall of the birdhouse to see a camera pointed directly at the apartment of the profiler.

"I really hate being right all time," said Jonas.


The Observer was on his way to take the bug off Jonas' BMW when he received an upload to the screen in his car. Jonas' tracking information had been sent and his computer had noticed an unusual route. The screen showed a time stamped route showing where Lange had traveled after leaving Abby's.

"Where did you go, Jonas? Did you have a booty call lined up?" asked the killer. As he looked, a satellite view was superimposed over the route. He had stopped in the middle of nowhere. "What are you up to, Agent Lange?" This place had nothing special. There were no towns and very few houses in that area. No cell service but surely Lange had satellite access. The Observer stopped his car and considered a multitude of options.

Lange had met a contact who could know something about disappearances around east Tennessee. *Possible.*

Lange had met up with someone for some kind of social interaction since he struck out with Abby. *Unlikely.*

Lange had gone for a drive and stopped to look at the scenery in the middle of the night. *Very unlikely.*

Lange had gone somewhere to check his new car for tampering. *Possible and not out of character.*

Lange thought there was a connection out there to him. *Possible.*

Lange had discovered all his hackers had freak accidents and one of them was actually able to trace him to Knoxville. *Dangerous situation if true.*

There were too many variables and the Observer did not take chances. For all he knew, Jonas Lange was sitting at his hotel room window, looking at his car, waiting to shoot anyone reaching under the bumper. Not worth the risk. The Observer drove past Jonas' extended stay and pressed a button on a remote. The magnetic tracker dropped to the ground and rolled a short distance away from the Beemer. Twenty seconds later a seal was broken inside the device as a concentration of hydrochloric acid made short work of the components.

It was definitely time to take a trip to Toronto. Ontario is nice this time of year and the Canadian medical system is quite cost effective. The pink girl would wait. No more research tonight. It was time to close up shop.

The Observer headed home to begin the process of shutting down his life in Knoxville.

# Chapter Eleven

Anyone watching the Observer returning home would see a man walking calmly without a care in the world. No one would suspect he was about to commit the greatest murder of his renowned, if hidden, career. The man who resided in this simple house in the north Knoxville neighborhood would be found in the ruins of his home. *Pity. I liked this place. It has character.* None of his neighbors knew him well. He had made a point to be friendly enough so they would not think of him as a hermit, but not so friendly they would feel obliged to stop by for a beer.

Sitting at his bank of computer monitors, he looked out the window to see the darkened window of his next door neighbor. Ruth was the one exception to the rule. His blue-haired flirtation would be the one who would call the police and the fire department in an hour. The sound of the gas line explosion would be a sure fire way to get her to look out the window. Her grief over the loss would make some reporter very happy in the sadistic way reporters enjoy the pain and suffering of others. The Observer hit a series of keys as his computer began the process of copying everything to flash drives, wiping the hard drives, and shutting down. Making this look like an accident was crucial so he could not use a magnetic pulse to totally destroy them. This would be sufficient wiping so no one would be able to recover anything of substance.

The killer strolled to his kitchen where a special place in the wall housed the second to last piece of his puzzle. A simple pull on the section revealed a hidden alcove with a freezer door. Removing the contents of the freezer, the Observer carried them across the living room and into his bedroom where he placed the body in his seldom used bed. He even took the time to tuck in his body double. The electric blanket would help defrost the body, but the explosion would leave little to be found. Sometimes having a bedroom directly over the main gas line was very convenient.

The Observer went to his basement to begin the final act of his Knoxville life. The pipes of this century old home would not be a cause for concern for a fire investigator and they were an integral part of his plan. There was a section of the old gas line which would have long ago given way if not for the addition of a new piece of PVC pipe that acted as a patch. Donning a mask, the patch was removed and a slow gas leak began to fill the basement.

Glancing one last time around, he knew there would little left to identify the body who was a close match to the Observer. The explosion would take care of the details. Setting the timer on a propane heater, he slipped quietly out the back. He didn't even glance at his home. Jacob Raines would be found dead shortly. The Observer had liked Jacob. It's why he had kept him the past eight years in the freezer. Time to find a new home in a new city.


Abby and Jonas arrived at the FBI office in Abby's car. After Jonas had done a thorough check and found no trackers, he decided her car would be safe. As they passed through the checkpoint showing their credentials, the security guard waved them through with a smile.

"I knew I should've made you take a cab," pouted Abby. "This is going to be a long day." She maneuvered her car to the spot which had been hers since arriving in Tennessee.

"Oh dear, sweet Abigail," began the jesting Jonas, "they will all be jealous of us having such a night of passion and pleasure."

Abby tried to backhand the Interpol agent, but he caught her hand before it even got close. Resisting the urge to smile at his reflexes, the profiler stated, "You really need to teach me some of those moves you're using. What is that? Krav Maga?"

Nodding, Jonas smiled and said cryptically, "Among other things. Sometimes you need to have a few moves in your back pocket to keep the bad guys guessing. Klaus is one I would very much like to try some of my moves on. I don't like being the prey."

Concerned, Abby asked, "How dangerous is he? Do you think he'll know we found his camera?" They had touched nothing and left everything as it was.

"I doubt it, but there is no way to be sure. He is a smart son of a bitch. I'll give him that." Jonas had considered going back for his car but decided to ask Mathis tow it in. There was no telling what else was on it.

Walking through the rain, the two agents made their way through security and to the elevators. From behind them came a familiar New England accent. "Good morning, kids. You both look exhausted. Long night?" asked Tina, with a salacious tone in her voice.

"I didn't get a wink of sleep," said Jonas, playing along with the lustful banter. "How about you, Abby? Were you able to get any rest with me using my toys in such fun ways?" Tina's mouth dropped open. She leered at her friend as the doors closed on the lobby with only the three in the confined space.

Abby was not up for the playfulness. "Will you two grow up? He is talking about a helicopter, Tina."

The doors opened with Tina's confusion and curiosity battling one another. "Okay. That's something I haven't tried. Jonas, could you make me some diagrams?" Before anyone else could add to the tension building in Abby, two other voices could be heard in hallway outside Abby's office.

"She said we needed to be here at seven. It's all I know, sir," said Marcus.

Jeremy was more agitated than usual. "What the hell is going on? I'm pissed at this sudden change."

Abby chose the more important battle. Ignoring Jonas and Tina, she addressed Mathis. "Jeremy, we have a serious problem. Someone is spying on Jonas and me. Can we please talk in the conference room? The Deputy Director is waiting for our call."

This caught the attention the special agent in charge. "What do you mean you're being spied on? What is going on? Lange, is she serious?"

"I'm afraid so, Mathis. There is something going on here which you all need to know. But I'd prefer to tell the story one time, and Mike Billingsly is waiting for us." Without waiting for confirmation, Jonas strode past Jeremy, heading straight for the conference room.

Abby, sensing the confusion in her colleagues, tried to explain as they walked. "He's serious. We have a major problem with this unsub. He found us first." That did nothing to quell the questions coming to the minds of these naturally inquisitive individuals. "Please, wait until Lange can brief you. It's complicated."

Once they were in the conference room and the security system activated, the screen on the far wall came to life with the face of the Deputy Directory looking concerned. "What's happened?" he asked without preamble.

As everyone took a seat, Jonas took charge. Gone was the jokester and flirt to be replaced by the serious agent. With his low, deadly tone, Jonas began, "After dinner at Abby's with Marcus and Tina, as I drove back to my hotel, something felt wrong to me." He proceeded to tell the entire story of finding the bug on his car and the camera pointed at Abby's apartment. "Mike, I stayed there and kept her safe. I had no idea he would move this fast. It may have spooked him when I let him find out I was here."

The Whale asked, "Are you sure it's Klaus? If this really is him, we need to move before he disappears. Will it work?"

Jonas looked around the room at the expectant faces. Even Abby did not know the full extent of this plan. "I think so. Or he will run. I think we need to bring everyone up to speed, Mike. With your permission?" There was an unspoken communication between the two men over the video call.

After a pause, the Deputy Director replied, "Do it, Jonas. Call me when you're done. I want to talk to all of you after the briefing." The screen went blank as all eyes moved to Agent Jonas Lange of Interpol.

"You are all going to hate me before this over," said the still serious Lange. Sitting at one of the monitors, he nodded to Marcus who mirrored Jonas' screen to all other screens in the room. Logging onto the internet, Jonas quickly went to the Interpol secure download site and downloaded a file named "The Observer".


The Knoxville fire department arrived within a scant twelve minutes of the explosion. The police arrived a few minutes later with the paramedics not far behind. The flames were consuming the once beautiful home in the historic neighborhood as people filled the streets gawking at the inferno. Ruth was standing on the opposite side of the street, weeping openly at the loss of someone she only thought she knew.

Watching it all from several blocks away was the Observer. Three years ago he had begun visiting an elderly man who was suffering from dementia. He had no known family until the Observer had hacked into the database and added one of his aliases as a nephew. He had gone faithfully every week at different times due to his "odd work schedule". The staff was accustomed to seeing him, his entrance was met by joyful greetings even at the strangest times.

While sitting with his "uncle" on the top floor of the high rise senior citizen apartments, the Observer witnessed the explosion and the ruckus that ensued. He had even called in others to watch the burning building through the telescope he had brought his uncle who used to like star gazing. His escape plan was in place as he watched his old life burn away.


The screen showed passport photos of five different men. Each one had a very distinctive look. Two of them had black hair. One had red hair. The other two were somewhere between brown and blonde. Three wore glasses. Each one had different colored eyes. Beside each passport photo was a surveillance photo from a customs counter. Jonas dropped the bomb. "This is the man we're looking for. I know him as Klaus. He has gone by at least eight names we have been able to discover."

Marcus raised his hand like he was back in third grade. Getting a raised eyebrow from Jonas, he asked, "How do you know these are the same man? They all looked pretty different to me."

Opening another window within the Interpol database, he typed: {Shon, Marcus Kim, Knoxville, Tennessee, United States}. A series of pictures of Marcus appeared on the screen ranging from formal suit wearing professional to Panama hat wearing party animal. The jovial Jonas returned. "I believe the last one was from Spring Break in Cozumel."

"Dude, you are so wrong. It was Cancun." Marcus was trying to hide his shock behind humor.

With an evil smile, Jonas retorted, "No that was Cozumel. This was Cancun." Another picture popped up and showed a bleary eyed Marcus holding a small bucket. "You really grossed out the customs agent."

The serious Jonas snapped back into place so fast Abby thought she was going to get psychological whiplash trying to keep up with this enigmatic man. "These are the same man. Facial recognition is being used by Interpol to track terrorists has been watching for him for three years now. If you will look," said Jonas as an analysis of the pictures overlaid the photos. Showing ear definition, eye width, nose height and lip fullness, it was apparent these all matched perfectly.

"I call him Klaus Kempler," said Jonas as one of the brown-haired men filled the screen, "We have no idea what his real name is. The only people who meet him seem to disappear or have an accident. We wouldn't even know about him if it weren't for Kristin McAdams of MI5." Abby was watching the Interpol agent as he made the presentation looking for details he kept hidden. For the first time, she saw a chink in his armor. There was a barely discernible trace of sadness in his voice as the name of the MI5 agent passed his lips.

"Who was McAdams?" asked Abby, intentionally using the past tense to see if his armor had any more vulnerabilities. "What was special about her that she discovered something that no one else found?"

Jonas maintained his poker face but looked at Abby with a coldness in his glowing green eyes which was disconcerting to the psychologist. "Kristin McAdams was working with the *Serious Organized Crime Agency* in Scotland where they were tracking a series of three murders. While setting up a listening device, she happened upon a conversation between two men. One was a local and the other was an American. The way the American was trying to avoid the Scotsman made her wonder about him. She took the time to make some subtle inquiries about him."

Mathis broke in. "Not wanting to talk to someone is hardly a reason to become suspicious. If that were the case, Chilton would be on the Most Wanted List." Abby shot him her "You're an asshole" look.

Jonas was unperturbed by the interruption. "True. Unless you are an American in Scotland. Most of you seem to want to talk to other people when you are traveling." Switching to his joking voice, he threw in, "It is part of what makes you just so darned lovable by the international community." Jonas' sarcasm was not lost on anyone, but Tina was the only one who chuckled. "But you have to realize that people on the other side of the Atlantic have a stereotype of Americans and he didn't seem to measure up."

"So she did racial profiling on him?" asked Abby.

"In a way. But if that would have been it, she probably wouldn't have noticed anything. The next day, the Scotsman died in an auto accident on a lonely road. The coroner wanted to rule it an accidental death, but Kristin pursued it. She convinced him to do a full autopsy and they discovered he had been Tasered and stabbed. The accident was nothing more than covering up the murder. When she tried to find the American, he was gone leaving nothing behind but a false name and a fake London address."

Mathis was trying to reassert control as he asked, "This is a sad story and I'm sorry for them, but can you get to the point, please?"

"Jeremy, there is a reason I'm telling you all this. Be patient." The two men stared at each other until Mathis nodded for Jonas to continue. "Kristin began to make some inquiries into local businesses and found an American matching the mystery man's description had been in the area doing some computer security for them. That's when Kristin called me. She knew she might need me to work some magic over here. She knew I had some pull with the FBI."

Abby took advantage of a pause in his story to ask a question she knew he would not like. "So why did she call you? Why not call the local Interpol liaison? Was there something between you two? Inquiring minds want to know." She was trying to push him to get a reaction. What she got was not what she expected.

"Mike was right. You're good," said the German with a trace of admiration. Jonas became ice cold as he answered. "She was my ex-wife."

# Chapter Twelve

The Observer bid farewell to his pseudo-uncle who continued to stare off into oblivion, never knowing he was there. He told the woman at the desk he would be moving. He didn't know when he'd be able to see Uncle Conrad. As was his custom, he put some money in Conrad's account so various luxury items could be purchased. This time the accountants would find an extra ten thousand dollars in the account of Conrad Morgan. The Observer felt as though he and Conrad were now even. Conrad gave him a place to watch his alias die and he ensured Conrad would be comfortable for whatever time he had left. It was the little things which often made the biggest differences.

In his pocket were four 256GB USB drives that had everything he would need to continue his work and play in a new locale. It was a pleasant thought knowing he had a terabyte of data. Everything else he needed could be bought or was stored online.

Taking a cab to the airport, he was ready for his flight to Buffalo and the day's work. Life for him was good. Death for someone new was better. A peaceful smile crept across his face as he dozed on the ride.


"What the hell?" said both Mathis and Tina in unison. Had Jonas peeled off his face to reveal he was one of the gray skinned aliens from Roswell, he wouldn't have caused more of a reaction out of the FBI personnel. Abby gazed at him, trying to maintain her practiced face of passivity. On the inside, she echoed Jeremy and Tina's reactions. This explained a great deal to the profiler. Jonas revealed the reason he was driven to solve this case. It also showed how compromised he had become.

"Dude, I'm a computer geek and even I know you are tap dancing with landmines on this one," declared Marcus. Everyone watched Jonas, waiting for him to say something. He looked at them with a practiced look which betrayed nothing. Finally Marcus looked at Abby. "Tell him he's a few scoops short of a banana split, Abby."

So many thoughts and scenarios were racing through Abby's mind as she stared deep into the green eyes which had turned her direction. Was this man so cold that he could track the man who murdered a woman he had once loved without it making him into a serpentine creature lusting for vengeance? Could Jonas be the kind of man who would allow the animal who had killed Kristin to weave his way through the judicial system for years or even decades? Maybe he was using all of them to find this killer so he could rip him apart with his bare hands. Abby didn't know, but she was determined to find out.

"I want to hear what Agent Lange has to say." Abby's voice was the one of reason and each person looked to the Interpol agent for answers. "Jonas?"

The German took two long, slow breaths that were a calming balm to those around him, their body language eased slightly with the words from his mouth. "I know what you are thinking. I'm either trying to use you to find Klaus so I can kill him, or I'm a cold blooded sociopath who is doing this out of duty and nothing else matters to me. The truth is somewhere in the middle. Was there a point when I would have gladly torn his arms off and beaten him to death with his own fists? Absolutely. Do I want to see him dead? Yes. But not the way you think. I'm in America because you have the death penalty and you have been known to use it. Hell, I'd love to bust him in Texas. They have a gas chamber with a revolving door down there." His humor made Marcus chuckle nervously.

"Lange, you do see why we all might be concerned that you're a loose cannon, don't you?" asked Mathis. This was his office and there was no way he would let East Tennessee turn into the gunfight at the O.K. Corral.

The old Jonas was back. "Of course. I would be worried about your sanity if you didn't question mine. It's why I've been handcuffed to the beautiful Agent Chilton. Billingsly wouldn't even let me in the country without a list of conditions that made me very uncomfortable. I'm still wondering why he insisted on the strip search by those supermodels, but I'm not complaining. Did you know that models don't know THEY are supposed to strip YOU?" Abby began to wonder who he was behind all the masks. Her intuition had been working on it in the background all night and into this bizarre briefing. Humor was a defense mechanism, like so many others he used. But she also began to see it was something more.

"Jonas, what are you going to do when we find him?" asked Abby. "I understand the need and desire for revenge. It is part of the reason the Deputy Director shackled us together. But we need to know that we can trust you to take him in if we can. Something tells me you know how to pull a trigger if the chips are down, but do you know when not to?"

For a split second, Abby could have sworn he lowered his shields as she saw something inexplicable in his eyes. There was a level of sadness and pain, mixed with strength and courage and something else she could not quite read. Then it was all gone and the laughing green eyes were staring through to her soul making her wish for sunglasses.

"You know, Abby." His words made her want to believe him. There was something almost hypnotic about this man. She glanced at Tina who was staring at him with a dazed look. Neither Marcus nor Jeremy looked convinced.

"I will know before all this is over. I promise you that," she said, defiantly resisting his influence. "Did Billingsly know all this? I mean ALL of this?" The smile on Lange's face answered the question for her. Abby was pissed and didn't even try to hide it. "Of course he did. Machiavellian to the core. Get to it, Lange. What haven't you told us? There is something you're holding back and don't even try to play the 'Why, Abby, whatever are you talking about?' card. Not buying the bullshit. And I'm pretty damn sure you need my help to stay on this case or Billingsly will ship your ass back to Deutschland in a Berlin minute."

It was a rare occasion when anyone surprised Jonas. Quickly recovering, he joked, "Such hostility, Abby. It's not like I wanted to use you as bait to try and catch this psycho by making him think he could go after a second woman who was linked to me." He faked a thoughtful look. "No wait. This is what I had planned. Now the hostility makes sense." The silence in the room was deafening.

Suddenly everyone was speaking at once.

"Excuse me?" demanded Mathis. "You want to do what? Are you out of your mind?!"

"It's not going to happen!" declared Marcus.

"No, no, no, no!" insisted Tina.

The other three in the room seemed to fade away as the profiler and spy shared a silent moment. The missing piece of this puzzle had slipped into place. She now saw what Jonas was willing to do and what he was capable of doing. He would do anything it took to catch this killer, making any sacrifice to do it. Perhaps even her. There was a very fine line between light and dark for Lange. If he had to dance the tango with the devil to catch one of his minions, Jonas would insist on leading. He was controlled. Not being an opportunist, he created opportunities to get the job done.

Abby calmly got up, silenced everyone in the room with a look. She walked over to the controls for the video call and connected to the Deputy Director. The screen lit up with the face of Billingsly looking directly at Abby.

"Mike, you are a son of a bitch!" said the profiler. The look of shock and awe on the faces of her three colleagues would normally have been one she relished. She didn't even recall they were in the room.

Unperturbed by the insolence from his protégée, Billingsly replied with some amusement in his voice. "I know. But out of curiosity, is it for letting Jonas use you as bait, or that I found the one man who is as much of a single-minded, driven, pragmatic sociopath as you are?"

Abby stared daggers at the Deputy Director. "Both. You know this is really wrong, Mike."

"I know. But I also know you will do it without forcing me to make it an order." There was a confidence in the man Abby found infuriating.

"True, but I also know I own his ass. You will send him packing if I won't play." Abby looked right at Lange. "This is my sandbox now, he has to listen to me."

"Do I get to bury her up to her neck?" asked Jonas. "If we can come to some kind of arrangement..." His voice trailed off, letting the joke hang in the air.

Folding his arms, the Whale asked, "Are you both done?"

"Well, I had this whole routine about the cats burying shit in the sandbox, but I can save it for another time," said Jonas.

"And I was going to compare him to a useless toy in the sandbox," said Abby.

The Deputy Director settled the matter, "I will take that as, 'Yes, Director Billingsly. We're done.'" Hitting a couple of buttons on his keyboard, he said, "Abby Chilton, you are officially designated as Interpol Liaison for the duration of Operation Observer. You are now freelance with access to any resources you may need. Jeremy?"

The Special Agent in Charge of the Knoxville Field Office spoke up for the first time on this call. "Yes, sir?"

"Agents Chilton and Lange have carte blanche. Whatever they need, get it on my authorization. The e-mail which takes responsibility off your shoulders is waiting for you. But I need you to set aside any ego. There are lives at risk here. I want them to find this psychopath as soon as possible. Any questions?"

Jeremy had a thousand questions but knew better than to ask. "No, sir." He used the same tone Abby used when implying "asshole" with her "sirs". There was a glimmer in Mike's eyes but he chose to let it pass.

"You two are the best. Find this bastard." With those words the screen went dark.

"Looks like we have work to do," said Jonas with the air of a man preparing to do something as simple as taking out the trash.

Mathis rose and walked up to Abby. "Chilton..." he began and then softened. "Abby, are you sure about this? I can fight this for you. This is a huge risk for anyone and you never take this kind of chance." With those words, Jeremy showed an unknown caring side to Abby. But he also showed he really didn't know her at all. This was why Abby was an agent. She was willing to risk it all to get the job done.

"Thanks for the offer, Jeremy. But I have to do this. People are dying and I can help this fool," pointing to Jonas, "find the bastard who's doing this."

Shaking his head in acquiescence, Mathis replied, "Let me know what you need." With those words he pressed the button to release the privacy filters and walked out.

Looking at her two friends who had been drawn into this strange situation, Abby said, "Worry about your work. I'll talk to you later. I need some time with our favorite Germ."

"Call me as soon as you are done," ordered Tina, grabbing Marcus by the hand before he could make any useless threats to Jonas. Abby closed the door and activated the privacy measures.

She walked up to the smiling Jonas and slapped him hard across the face. Since he had easily disarmed her the previous day, she was pretty sure he let her do that. Abby didn't care. He deserved to be slapped and he knew it. The smile never left his lips.

"Feel better?" he asked as his cheek began to show a red outline of Abby's hand. He resisted rubbing away the sting, not wanting to give her the satisfaction.

"Actually I do." She grabbed his head and roughly pulled his mouth to hers as she locked her lips upon his. Her tongue invaded his mouth as his circled around hers. Their arms entwined around one another in a symmetry which matched the teasing and twisting of their tongues. The pent up passion exploded as the kiss deepened, a reaction below the waist on the man from Interpol was apparent. Then it was over as Abby pushed him away. "And that is a sample of what you could have had if you hadn't used me for bait."

Jonas gawked at her, still unsure of what had transpired. He tried several times to come up with some witty banter to recapture the moment of passion. The ringing of his phone saved him from having to say anything. "Lange," he spat into the receiver. "Sí." He listened. "Sí," Jonas said again with a raised tone which told Abby it was important. "¿Cuando lo ha encontrado?" Abby's Spanish was weak, but she was pretty sure he was asking about finding something. "Enviar la información a mi teléfono. Gracias. ¡Eres el mejor, Ronni!" The Interpol agent ended the call and looked expectantly at his phone. "A friend of mine in Chile was tracking Klaus. She says she found him and is sending the info to my phone." The tension in his voice was the first tension she had really heard in the man.

"And if this works out we may actually have a lead on where he is?" asked Abby. She was torn between being hopeful and discouraged. It couldn't be this easy after all the shit they had gone through. That would be a disappointment and she would be back to counseling by the end of the week. *Hell no! I'm ready to get back out there.*

"Abby, look at this without hitting or kissing me, please." Jonas held his phone so she could see what was coming across the screen. Pressing closer than necessary, she made sure he felt her breath on his neck. They had a name and an address. "Shall we take a casual drive? I want to see what kind of house Klaus lives in."

"You're not going to shoot first and ask questions later, are you?" asked Abby, genuinely concerned.

"Only if he resists arrest," replied the Interpol agent. "And we can talk about the kiss on the way."

"No we can't," retorted Abby. "Ever."

# Chapter Thirteen

The flight attendant announced it was safe to use portable electronic devices. The Observer pulled his tablet out of the seat pocket and booted it up. The plane had Wi-Fi for a price, of course. There was no need to go online. His work could be done without leaving an internet trail which would need to be hidden later. A flight attendant offered him the customary drink and snack. He accepted both. Coffee and pretzels were a modest celebration for a job well done.

Looking to the left at the empty seat, a smile crept across his face. It costs a great deal to buy two seats for a flight, but it is far most costly to have someone examining the very sensitive information displayed on his screen. He wouldn't want anyone to have access to Abby Chilton's personal data. That would be a breach of confidence and etiquette. Also, it would mean someone would have to die. His day was already so filled with activities, he simply didn't have time to kill.

The data on Abby was extensive. The bots – programs that searched the internet for information – were exceptionally good at what they did. The Observer had written the code himself and knew it would find more content than he would ever need. Now he began the laborious task of sifting through the false trails. That was the problem with detailed bots. They found so much that was not related to the person being investigated. He had adapted the filters over the years but still preferred to sift most of the data himself. The best part of the bots was the way they left trails leading to someone else. Internet searches of high profile people tended to be noticed. The Observer took great pains to avoid anyone noticing him.

Opening a separated word processing document he titled it: Profile - Chilton, Abigail Renee. Initial reaction: Abby Chilton is obviously intelligent and well educated with a PHD in psychology. She is attractive with a well-groomed appearance even after a long day. She is shorter than expected, but not so small that she would feel a need to compensate by being overly aggressive. She was able to resist the charms of Jonas Lange meaning she is either in a relationship, or is not one to let anyone in her bed too quickly. Check information for past lovers and/or marriages. Gut reaction: she is a woman to be considered a threat. Perhaps she is profiling me as I am profiling her.

The Observer closed that window and opened one with over one hundred and thirty pages of data on all the Abby Chiltons out there. Finishing his last sip of coffee and munching on a pretzel, he began to weed out the false leads to discover details on this new playmate.


As they entered the FBI SUV, Abby took the wheel. She took pleasure in his discomfort as Jonas quickly fastened his seat belt. "Don't like not being behind the wheel?" tormented the profiler.

"What can I say? I have control issues. Now, ask what you want to know," stated the uncharacteristically serious German.

Pulling into traffic, Abby smiled to herself. "Oh there are several question I would ask. So now I have permission? Let's see..." began Abby.

Jonas interrupted her pseudo-considering. "Kristin and I worked together on several cases and became involved thanks to an attraction and the stimulus of the action. We were married five years ago. It lasted two."

Entering into counselor mode, Abby asked, "What happened? Was it the strain of having domestic tranquility? That happens a lot."

"I don't think we ever had any domestic anything. You know how work can get." Jonas looked nostalgic. "But we both got busy with work and loneliness gets in the way and then temptations get the better of you."

"What was her name?" asked Abby as she tried to sympathize.

"His name was Phineas." There was a very loud silence in the Tahoe. After making certain that Abby was uncomfortable, Jonas continued. "Kristin met him on a mission in Wales. They went undercover as a married couple and took the cover a little too far. She left me for him. But at least I have the comfort of knowing he left her for the next woman he was under the covers with."

Abby had to ask. "But you still kept in touch and worked with her?"

Jonas' accent changed to something that most people would expect from a German speaking English. "Vell liebchen, I am German und ve have an image of being very pragmatic in matters of emotions und vhat vorks on zee job."

"Really?" asked Abby not buying the stereotype.

Smiling, Jonas' accent returned to normal. "Hell no! It took eighteen months of Interpol ordered therapy before I could say the bitch's name without wanting to kill her. And trust me, that's not an exaggeration. In time we found a way to work together. It did feel good when I told her to go to hell when she tried for booty calls." Abby laughed in spite of her training. Sometimes Jonas' could be too funny for his own good. She stopped herself but Jonas chuckled, "I can laugh about it, too. I don't think I'd laugh if I had paid for the therapy, though."

Abby and Jonas stopped over a block away from the address Jonas' contact had uncovered. Fire trucks and police cars were blocking the street making any further progress impossible. Turning on the flashing lights, Abby got out of the vehicle with Jonas in tow.

"I have a bad feeling about this," said Abby.

"Me too," agreed Jonas. "How do you feel about coincidences?"

The serious look on her face matched the tenor of her voice. "I'll let you know if I ever find one." Approaching the nearest uniform, she pulled out her I.D. "Special Agent Chilton, FBI. What's happening, Officer," she made a point of looking at his name plate, "Lawrence?"

He looked like he had been out of high school for a month and out of the police academy this morning. "Explosion, ma'am. Looks like a gas line. We done shut off the mains and are doin' a house by house search to make sure it ain't somethin' else."

"Who's in charge, Lawrence?" asked the agent in her best "I'm an FBI agent so get out of my way" tone.

"That's Lieutenant Drake. He's the one yellin' at everyone. Can't miss him." The officer moved off to stop others from entering the secure area. As they approached the makeshift command center, Drake stood out. Beside him was a face Abby knew well. Roger Walker was one of the best detectives in the KPD and was also the

FBI Liaison officer. His presence was about to make her life easier, she hoped.

This detective was one of the most successful on the Knoxville police force. Criminals tended to underestimate him and he liked it that way. He was five foot ten inches with brown hair, brown eyes that were framed by average looking glasses to match his average looks. Since he looked average, people tended to assume he had an average mind. Criminals regretted that assumption.

"Detective Walker," called Abby. The detective smiled at her approach. Abby and the cop had met on a few occasions when he had acted as liaison. Abby also interviewed him for his posting with the FBI. It turned out that he was intelligent, driven, not prone to hating Feds, and had a stable home life. Based on her recommendation Walker had gotten the job. He owed her a lifetime of favors.

Shaking Abby's hand before he had even stopped moving, he drawled, "Agent Chilton. What brings you out of the padded cells today?" He offered his hand to Jonas. "Roger Walker, KPD. Don't think I've had the pleasure."

"Jonas Lange. Interpol." He was using his best smile to try to charm the detective. Walker was not falling for it.

Looking back at Abby, the detective asked, "Interpol? What is going on, Chilton? Does this have anything to do with that wild goose chase from yesterday?"

"Yes and no. I'm sorry about that. That was an internal miscommunication," lied the profiler, shooting a look at Jonas. "We thought there was an issue, but it turned out to be a prank played by an immature asshole. You know the type. They get off on making people who are already busy trying to do good work go around in circles doing stupid shit that comes to nothing." To his credit, Lange remained impassive to her barbs.

"You would not believe some of the shit we have to deal with," agreed Walker. "But what's going on? Throw me a bone so I can pave the way with Drake. He's a hard-ass."

"Allow me to deal with him. Hard-asses are my specialty," jested Abby, tossing a challenging glance at Jonas. She boldly strode over to the Lieutenant.

Watching curiously as she walked away, Roger Walker asked Jonas, "What is she going to do? And will it make my life harder?"

Smiling at what was unfolding before him, the Interpol agent shook his head. "I have no idea, Roger. But I promise you, it will be fun to watch. And it is a roll of the dice as to how this will affect your life. Trust me on that one."

Holding out her I.D. as she approached, Abby began, "Lieutenant Drake? I'm Special Agent Abby Chilton with the FBI and I'm..."

"What the hell are you doing here?" demanded the irritated cop.

Jonas whispered to Walker, "Ever heard about getting enough rope to hang yourself?"

Fire burned in her eyes as Abby stared the bully down. "As the lead Forensic Psychologist of the Knoxville Field Office, I have been asked by Chief Clausen to perform field psychological tests on his commanders to determine if they are respecting their underlings and treating those with whom they have contact in a way befitting a leader of the Knoxville Police Department." Turning to walk away, she called back, "I won't waste any more of your obviously valuable time. The Chief will have my report on you by the end of the day." She began dialing her phone.

The detective whispered to Jonas, "Is that why she's really here?" He was trying hard not to smile at the situation.

"Nope. But I would be willing to pay for the study myself for no other reason than to make him squirm," replied Lange who didn't try to hide the smile. "She is something else. By the way, don't piss her off. Trust me. You don't want to be on her bad side."

The detective chuckled. "Looks, brains, and hell on wheels when pissed. She reminds me of my wife."

"Me too," replied the Interpol agent.

The scene being played out was nearly comical. Drake stood stock still, his face going pale and his mouth hanging open. He took a few halting steps to follow Abby, unsure how she would react. The FBI agent stopped in her tracks, made a show of canceling the call, and turned back to Drake. "On second thought, let's try this again. Hello Lieutenant Drake. I'm Special Agent Abby Chilton, CHIEF

FORENSIC PSYCHOLOGIST of the Knoxville Field Office. How are you today?"

Drake was not sure what was happening but became the most charming man that Abby had ever met. "Good morning Agent Chilton. It is a pleasure to meet you. How can I help you today?" His over solicitousness was more than Roger Walker could take as he burst out laughing. Drake eyed him concealing his anger.

"Well the uniform was telling me that you have something happening here. What's going on, Drake?" asked Abby. She was enjoying having this man as her pet for the moment. Not looking at him, she got out her phone and sent an email to the Chief of Police offering her services to do what she had suggested to the Lieutenant. Sometimes the best ideas come in the heat of the moment.

"Well Agent Chilton, we had an explosion. We have shut off the gas to this area but, as you can see, the house at 2318 is pretty much ruins. It's a miracle that no one else was hurt. We have..." He continued speaking but Abby didn't hear any of it. As soon as he had said the address she looked at Jonas who had been listening. Their eyes locked and they both had the same thought. *He's on the run.*

Jonas broke the train of thought of the man who was trying his best to impress Abby with his care. "Lieutenant Drake. I'm Jonas Lange with Interpol. Did you find a body in the house?"

Drake was thrown with the introduction and the question. He looked from Abby to Jonas and back again. "What is going on? Let me see your credentials before I answer any questions... please." The "please" sounded like an afterthought.

Jonas showed his I.D. and asked again. "I need to know if you found a body in the house that was destroyed. This is important, sir." Jonas tried his best to say "sir" like Abby, not quite getting the same inflection.

Abby maintained her poker face as the befuddled policeman answered. "Yes they did. It's being taken to the morgue. Cause of death seems obvious but we have to do an autopsy in cases like this where..." Jonas walked away.

"Detective Walker is my liaison officer," said Abby to the bully. "Roger, will you please accompany Agent Lange and myself? You don't mind if I borrow Detective Walker for a few hours do you, Lieutenant Drake?" Without waiting for a response, she walked away with Walker in tow. Drake stood there with a "what happened?" look on his face.

Jonas was sitting in the passenger's seat of the SUV waiting for them. He was obviously bothered. Abby was concerned, too. Roger Walker was totally in the dark, still smiling from the spectacle he had witnessed.

"That can't be him," Jonas said in his quiet, dangerous voice.

"It might be, Jonas. We will know shortly. Roger, who is the best coroner in the city?" asked the profiler.

"Well, I'd have to say Dr. Ariziz from the UT Med School. He teaches the stuff." Since he had helped, Walker felt that he had earned the right to ask, "Can you please tell me what's going on?"

"Well, the man I have been chasing for two years may have been blown up in a freak accident." Jonas was not in the mood to explain as he sent an email from his phone. After Abby got off the phone with Mathis, she told Roger all the details as she knew them with Jonas adding bits a pieces here and there.

"So we have a psycho in Knoxville? That kind of thing doesn't happen here." The detective was finding this hard to believe.

"We'll soon see. Mathis is arranging to have the body sent to the UT Med School. Let's go tell Dr. Ariziz he has a patient." Abby and Jonas glanced at each other. Neither one thought the body was the Observer. Neither one of them had that kind of luck.

# Chapter Fourteen

The final leg of his flight ended in Buffalo, New York. The Observer knew from long experience that traveling from the States to Canada was usually easier by land than by air. In a car, he could easily cross the border with little notice; whereas a flight would subject him to numerous unwanted cameras. Though the flight from Detroit to Buffalo was an uneventful ride, it was not as productive as he had hoped. He chose to rest instead of working on the Abby profile since he was not able to get the extra seat beside him. The well-dressed man next to him had given the customary "hello" and head bob and quickly became lost in a report of some kind. After making certain the man was not a gadfly, the Observer drifted off into a restful, dreamless sleep.

Crossing the Tennessee River to the University Of Tennessee Medical Center, the trio of investigators had ridden in silence long enough for Roger Walker. "So what is going on between the two of you anyway? Love affair gone wrong?"

Lange smiled for the first time since leaving the wreckage of the house in North Knoxville. "We are working associates. But she does have some unresolved sexual tension around me. I'm considering filing a sexual harassment charge." The men laughed.

Abby was not one to be outdone. "Want to know a secret, Roger? He keeps checking out my ass every time I walk away. Let him look. That's as close as he will ever get." Walker laughed at that, too.

"How long have you known each other?" the cop asked.

"About a day now," replied the profiler.

"Day after tomorrow," stated the detective without elaboration.

A sly smile danced across his lips as Lange asked, "What is happening the day after tomorrow?"

"Based on years of experience working with people in interrogation, I have learned a thing or two." Roger Walker knew he had their attention. "The day after tomorrow you will either have your hands around each other's necks or around each other's bodies. I'd recommend the bodies because I don't need a double homicide investigation right now."

"Walker, you are so full of shit," spat Abby with all humor and none of the venom she usually used. "We have some serious trust issues here. He's Interpol and I'm FBI. That makes for strange bedfellows."

Roger's voice showed mirth as he said, "Good. You both need some strange bedfellows. The sexual tension in here is so thick I want to go home and have a nooner with my wife. Can you two tone it down a little?"

"Well, Roger. I can't help it that I'm irresistible to Abby. But I promise not to nail her on the hood in the parking garage." Jonas showed his evil, playful side as he amended, "Well, not today at least."

"Or tomorrow," added Abby.

Roger feigned exasperation. "I know not today or tomorrow. I already told you it'll be the day after tomorrow."

The three laughed together as they found a parking place. Roger Walker led the way through the labyrinth that was UT Medical Center to the attached Medical School. Jonas was peculiarly quiet as they walked. He was reading something on his phone. Abby tried to sneak a glance but Jonas was not having any of that. He winked and turned his phone so she couldn't even pretend to glance at it.

Winding through the corridors leading to classrooms, they found their way through the maze to discover the small Department of Forensic Medicine. Appropriately, it was housed in the basement of one of the Medical School Buildings. Hovering over an old style microscope was one of the most unique men Abby had ever seen. The top of his head showed dark tanned skin that looked like it had been pulled too tightly over the skull beneath it. Wisps of gray hair formed wings that looked as if they wanted to carry the bald head away from its body. The same head looked entirely too big for the tiny torso that supported it. Abby estimated his height as somewhere around five feet three inches. He may have weighed one hundred and twenty-five pounds, soaking wet and wearing several layers of clothing.

Abby's profiler nature revealed that he was left handed based on the positioning of the pens and pads. Dr. Ariziz was also a tea drinker based on the steaming cup beside him and the eight mugs around the room with different levels of liquid remaining. He was either absent minded or got so involved in his work so that he forgot to finish his drinks before they got cold. Most likely both. There was no wedding ring or trace of a wedding ring. Easy assumption is that he was never married to anything other than his work, but could be long divorced or widowed. Age was difficult to determine, at least in his sixties.

Walker cleared his throat. The wizened doctor jumped at the sound. "Hell's bells, Roger. Don't scare an old man like that." His voice did not match his body. It was deeper than Abby had expected with a force behind it that made it entertaining to imagine him challenging students twice his size. The doctor moved around the lab table to greet the detective, giving a handshake-hug. "What brings you down into the bowels of the Med School? And why don't you bring pretty ladies every time?" Approaching Abby and kissing her hand, he continued, "Hello there. I'm Paolo Ariziz. Please tell me you are looking for a husband and have a thing for weird looking old men?"

"Special Agent Abby Chilton. Meet Doctor Paolo Ariziz," introduced Roger. "And this is Agent Jonas Lange."

"Nice to meet you Lange," said the good doctor without taking his eyes off Abby. "You didn't answer my question, fair maiden Abigail." Abby could tell that he loved playing the role of doddering, dirty old man, but there was much more to him. Looking into the dark brown eyes, she saw the massive intellect that was hidden behind the flirtation.

"Well, Paolo, I'm like you. Married to my work. But we can discuss a tryst." Abby watched the look in his eyes as they widened with joy. He was all about being playful on the outside since his specialty dealt with death and dissection. It all made sense since he had managed to flourish in this field for so long. Compartmentalization allowed each person in the room to do what they did.

"Excellent! I'm thinking margaritas and sopapillas." Looking for the first time at Jonas, he changed his demeanor to one of camaraderie. "Well, Agent Lange. Please forgive me for ignoring you. I'm sure you're cute, too, but she is more my type. How are you today?"

Jonas had been enjoying the show while still keeping one eye on his phone. Turning his full attention to Ariziz, he said, "Hello there, Paolo. Nice to meet you. What had you so absorbed over there?" He motioned to the microscope but Ariziz was still looking at him without moving. Lange stared back at the man he towered over by nearly a foot. There was a sizing up passing unspoken between the two.

"Germany or Belgium?" asked the forensic physician. Abby looked at the doctor with even more respect. He was very good if he could detect that from his voice.

"Germany. But I do have some Belgium roots, too." The Interpol agent was careful not to betray his shock, Abby was sure it was there behind the bravado. "I'm impressed. I thought my accent was almost perfect."

The joy in the doctor was obvious. "It is, dear boy. But you need to work on your American stance a little more. The shoulders are a bit off and the rest was written all over your facial and skeletal structure."

Detective Walker interrupted the lesson in anthropology. "Paolo, we need your help with an autopsy. Abby?"

Abby and Jonas filled the coroner in on all the details. At the conclusion, the old doctor was smiling a broad, too white, smile. "Now we may have an issue with security clearance, but I'll see if I can get Mathis to fast-track that."

"I don't think that will be an issue," said Ariziz with mischief in his voice. Abby again looked at the little old man before her, hoping for more information. He merely shrugged and said, "A guy has got to have his secrets."

Jonas jumped in. "I'm sure his top secret clearance from the CIA will make anything you need him to do a cake walk, Abby." The only person more surprised than Roger and Abby by that revelation was Ariziz. Jonas continued, "Doctor Paolo Ariziz was one of the lead forensic pathologists in Sarajevo in '93. His analysis was instrumental in the war crimes convictions of many of the criminals for the International Criminal Tribunal. Well done, Doctor." Holding up his phone, Jonas simply said, "I know people."

"Europol or Interpol?" asked the impressed Ariziz.

"Interpol," smiled Lange. "But I have friends all over the place."

Abby's phone beeped. She looked at her message and announced, "It seems that no further clearance is needed. There are parts of a body waiting to be told where to go, Paolo."

The Lilliputian physician headed toward the door. "If you will excuse me, I have a jig-saw puzzle to play with. Ta ta." He was gone without another word.

Jonas moved around the table to look at the microscope. "Jonas, what are you doing? That's his," insisted Walker. "Leave it be and let's get out of here."

"One second," replied the spy. Adjusting the focus, he looked in the microscope. He looked at his two partners, smiled and looked back down again. Shaking his head and laughing he walked out muttering, "I had no idea they made nude pics that small. Not very flattering if you think about it."


The Observer found his rental car without anyone really noticing him. Online rentals were a godsend to a man who liked keeping a low profile. Checking in over his phone, he had been able to walk straight to the car without any meaningful human contact. Once in the nondescript Ford, heading toward the Canadian border, the Observer reflected on his productive day. His life in Knoxville was over. He had his choice of eight new lives ready to be slipped on like a comfortable robe covering his bare psyche. He chose to be Richard "Rick" Draper from Rochester, New York. Week after next, he would head to that fine city to create a life. For now, this would work for his Toronto Trip.

The line to cross the border was longer than he had hoped. His Draper passport was perfect and ready to be waved at the customs officer. He doubted it would be needed at this low risk crossing, but you never know. As he approached one of the many booths, the Canadian customs officer asked the routine questions about produce and tobacco. The Observer stated his trip was one of business and explained his trip to Toronto as a cyber-security consultant. Unfortunately, that information intrigued the officer.

"What kind of cyber-security do you do?" Using his profiling ability, the Observer saw that this man was not a master spy seeking information about a serial killer. He was a bored man looking for a new career. The question was not out of customs curiosity, more of a personal perusal.

Laughing his engaging laugh, the Observer explained. "Companies hire me to break through their security. When I get in, I help them find ways to keep hackers out. Basically I use my superpowers for good instead of evil."

"How's the pay?" inquired the customs agent. "I bet it's better than this." he gestured to the booth behind him.

"Your government loves the taxes I pay when I work here, that's for sure." As he pulled away and onto the General Brock Parkway, the customs officer went on to the next car without a second thought as to the white hat hacker he had allowed into his country. Ninety seconds later, the video file of that hour's crossings was sent to a supercomputer in Lyon, France where Interpol facial recognition software began looking at all those who had crossed from America to Canada that day.


Abby and Jonas had dropped the detective off at his car with a promise to call if they had any information that would help with the house explosion. The laborious Lieutenant had already ruled it an accident, Walker was determined to make sure the truth was revealed. The plain-looking, plain-clothes detective ambled off, examining the wreckage of the Observer's house.

Heading down the road, Abby stated, "You love having info that you get to drop on people. That little CIA bombshell was a nice touch, but it pisses me off."

"I know. But I have to have some fun or this job will eat my soul. I don't know about you but I kind of like my soul intact." Changing topic, Lange asked, "So where are we off to now? Art museum? Model train store? Sex shop?"

Agent Chilton was still surprised by this man's mind. Did he ever reveal more than glimpses? Doubtful or he wouldn't be good at what he did. "Well I have to get back to the office and get to work on a preliminary profile of this Observer of yours. You are on your own for the rest of the day. Go hit the gym, practice your American stance on Market Square, eat some fried green tomatoes. You need to stay out of my hair while I sort through all the crap that you left in my email."

The grinning Interpol agent teased, "You know you love it. Besides, reading what I have on Klaus will help you figure me out. Even Walker could tell you wanted me. Too bad he didn't know you want my mind more than my chiseled body." Abby could see him winking at her in her peripheral vision.

"You think you are so irresistible, don't you?" laughed Abby as she continued to profile this man who was never what he appeared. "Or is it all a show to cover up some hidden insecurity?"

Jonas still gave away nothing. "It doesn't matter if I think I'm irresistible. It only matters if you do." There was a puckish pucker to his lips as he blew her a kiss. "I need to check out my SUV. Hopefully, Mathis had it towed by now. I want to know more about that little gizmo on the bumper. I'll let you know if any of my contacts find out where Klaus is going. Right now Ronni and Rikka – some associates of mine – are doing some questionable searching of a few databases." Abby shot him a sideways glance that silently communicated her question. "Don't ask. You really don't want to know."

"I'll get Tina to look into the finances of the house he blew up today. Maybe there's a money trail that will help us." Abby took her eyes off the road long enough to look at the enigmatic man next to her. "What if that really was him in the house?"

"It wasn't. It can't be that easy. My life doesn't work that way. Too much bad karma." Abby knew better than to ask, adding that to her profile of Jonas. *He has guilt over some of the things he has done.*

Arriving at the FBI building, they both went their separate ways. Abby tried to tell Jonas how to get to the garage but saw he was heading in the right direction. *How the hell does he know all this shit?* Recalling his words she began to debate whether she really wanted to know or not.

# Chapter Fifteen

Abby arrived in her office and collapsed in her chair. She couldn't believe how much her life had changed in the past twenty-four hours. She was suddenly thrust into a manhunt for a serial killer who could be one of the most prolific in history. There was a new man in her life who was jamming her profiler radar so much that it was a real turn on. To top it all off, she had been manipulated back into the field by Billingsly. *Damn him!* The profiler reached for her phone. Her hand stopped without touching the receiver.

Rising, Abby left her office and headed down the hall to find a cup of coffee and Tina. When she arrived in the break room, two agents were talking animatedly until they saw her. She had heard her name from the hallway and it did not take a great leap of logic to discern the topic of conversation. She was in no mood for water cooler gossip. One look from her and the two agents quickly left the room leaving her to mosey on over to the coffee pot. There was a thick brew already made and waiting for her. Looking around, Abby cautiously poured a cup and took a sip. It was good. Very good. Too good. Few people know how to make a decent cup of coffee, and this was one of the better ones.

The profiler had a bounce in her step as she headed down a corridor that led to the forensic accountants. She saw that Tina's door was open and could hear the New England accent that was clearly upset.

"I don't give a damn if he says there is a rational explanation. The numbers don't support the 'rational explanation' so trust me when I tell you the bastard is hiding assets in Tel Aviv." Abby could see she was on the phone as she peeked around the door frame. Tina motioned her to come in while rolling her eyes at the person on the other end of the line. "Listen to me. You asked me to see if he was hiding anything. It isn't my fault that he was or that you don't like what I found. My analysis is in your e-mail. Do with it what you want." She slammed the phone down and spat at the abused set, "I also blind carbon copied your supervisor and my supervisor so you can't cover up for your marine buddy, dipshit."

It didn't take a profiler to see the tension in her friend. "Rough day at the office, dear?" asked Abby, trying to get a smile out of the accountant.

"I am so sick of people asking me to dig into someone's finances and then they get pissed off at me when I do my job a little too well and find something they didn't want to be there. I am not the one funneling money to a Mossad front." Tina took a deep breath followed by two more. As her composure returned, she asked far too sweetly, "So, how has your day been?"

"Thanks for making the coffee," she said, toasting her friend. Tina gave Abby a winning smile at her pleasure. Sitting down, Abby tried not to profile this time and updated her on all the things that happened. She failed at not profiling by noticing the twitching of Tina's index finger on her left hand that was one of her tells. If the analyst had been playing poker, Abby would have known to fold. As it was, Tina was already beating her to the request.

"So what is the address on this house? There has to be some kind of paper trail we can use to track down this son of a bitch." Tina was starting to bounce in her seat. Abby always found it amusing how Tina loved profiling money as much as she loved profiling people. As soon as she had the address Tina quickly became lost in her computer while dialing the legal department to get the warrants for what she was already doing.

Jonas walked into the FBI garage, maneuvering his way through all the vehicles. Passing the remains of one vehicle, he paused for a moment to make sure it was not his BMW laying in pieces all around him. The color was right but there were not enough parts. He nodded to the techs working on the remains while moving around the parked FBI SUVs. He found his new X6 up on a lift. Mathis was standing nearby as Lange approached.

"Jeremy," nodded Jonas. "So have they found anything interesting?"

Mathis faced the Interpol agent. "You really sure there was something on there? They haven't found anything. What was it? Let me see that pic," demanded the Special Agent in Charge.

Jonas had a rare moment of confusion. Pulling up the pic from the previous night, he handed his phone to Mathis as he moved to the place where the tracker had been. With the X6 raised it was not difficult to examine the bumper in great detail. The German went straight to the spot where the device had been. "Hey. Look here." He pointed to a round spot where the road dust was not as thick. "That's where it was." Turning to the technicians around him, Lange asked, "Who brought my car in?"

A middle aged man in blue overalls stepped forward. "That would be me. I know what you're thinkin' and I can guarantee that we didn't lose a thang when we put it on the trailer. And we sealed it so nothin' got out." Jonas smiled at the man's accent and made mental notes to duplicate it sometime.

"Easy there, grease monkey. I wasn't going to ask that. Did you see anything under it that may have looked like this?" Lange retrieved his phone from Jeremy and showed it to the tech.

The mechanic looked from the picture to the bumper and back. "Nope. But ya know it has been rainin' and if it came off before we got there it may have got washed God knows where. Damn rain."

Mathis broke into the conversation. "Erickson, have you found anything else?"

"Nothin', sir." The man looked at the raised vehicle. "It is a nice ride though. Those BMW X6s are damn solid. Don't s'pose there's some money in your black ops budget for a few of these for the motor pool?"

Jeremy smiled. "Don't hold your breath on that one." Turning to Jonas he said, "I need to talk to you, Lange." He walked away with the expectation that the man from Interpol would follow. He looked back when he discovered that he was walking alone. Jonas was under his BMW talking with Erickson. Jonas held up a hand making the sign for "one minute". After three minutes, Jonas joined him and walked out of the garage.

Entering the first room they found, Mathis closed the door behind them. Looking Jonas in the eyes, he spoke in a low tone. "I am not sure exactly who the hell you are but I will find out. It doesn't matter to me who your friends are or how powerful they are positioned. If anything happens to Chilton or any of my people, you will pay. Understood?"

There was a long silence in the room as the two men locked wills – neither one willing to back down. It was Jonas who smiled and spoke first. "Jeremy Mathis. You sneaky bastard! You've got some balls. I didn't think you had it in you. You have my word that I will do everything I can to keep your people safe." Offering his hand and holding it out until Mathis took it, he added, "And if anything happens to any of your people or even to you, he will not live long enough to pay. Deal?"

"I do believe we're on the same page," replied Mathis, trying hard not to smile. "I'm still not sure about you, but if the director trusts you I don't have a whole lot of options."

Opening the door for the FBI man, Lange laughed as he said, "You always have options, Jeremy. Right now, none of the ones around me are very good. Welcome to my world."

"I like mine better," said Mathis. Both men went opposite directions.


Queen Elizabeth Way was a beautiful highway along Lake Ontario leading to Toronto. The Observer was enjoying the drive when he saw a sign for Grimsby Beach. Since he was not due to meet his clients until tomorrow, he had plenty of time for some relaxation and took the exit. The beach was right on the lake with a view that most people found breathtaking. For the Observer it was a nice place to rest and work on his profile of Abby Chilton. Finding a bench, he ignored the view and examined the information on his tablet.

He had developed some new insights since he had looked at her information. She was a single-minded workaholic who was more married to her job than she would ever be to a significant other. One of the files that had been mined from her computer was a series of links about an FBI shootout with a pedophile almost two years ago. Following the links the Observer was delighted to learn why Abby had left field work. She and her partner had been shot. He died and she was in the hospital for two weeks and on restricted duty for four months. Fourth months was a long time to be off. *Post-traumatic stress? Maybe.* The Observer wasn't convinced. That did not fit with her psyche as he was seeing it. What had she lost?

The Observer continued his delving into her past and made notes to hack the database of the University Hospital in San Antonio. *What happened to you, Abby?*


*What happened to you?* Seven hundred miles away, Abby Chilton was wondering the same thing about the Observer. She was sitting at her computer reading through the pages of data that Jonas had accumulated on this strange killer. The pictures he had taken of his chats revealed the most about this killer. She knew it was impossible to take his statements at face value, but how he said things caught her attention. There was a playfulness about his online persona that allowed Abby to discern many traits.

He was a killer who was organized in the extreme. If what he claimed was true, he had killed over two hundred people and had never been suspected until Jonas' ex. Kristin had been the first law enforcement to even take note of him. That was only by bad luck on the part of the Observer. If the truth were told, most of the time it was luck that led to the capture of the most intelligent serial killers. This one was scary smart. Brilliant even.

As she read through all of the conversations, she realized this killer knew Jonas better than she did. This guy had actually gotten under Lange's skin a couple of times. There was one conversation where the Observer and Jonas chatted about Kristin.

Klaus: {So how long since you talked to Kristin?}

Jonas: {It had been a while.}

Klaus: {We can talk about something else if you want. I'm sure losing her was quite a shock.}

Jonas: {We weren't that close.}

Klaus: {Really? I thought we understood one another, mate.}

Jonas: {Why would you think that, dude?}

*Both men were trying to make a point. Klaus that he was British and Jonas that he knew he was American. Two alphas battling in a chat room. Nerds of the world unite!*

Klaus: {You know I know who she was to you, don't you?}

Klaus: {Jonas?}

Klaus: {Jonas? Did I lose you?}

*No time stamps so I can't tell how long Jonas was silent. Must have been a while.*

Jonas: {I'm here. Who do you think she was?}

Klaus: {You didn't read my e-mail did you? You really need to keep up with that.}

Jonas: {What email?}

Klaus: {Look for one with an attachment called "Kristin". Tea time. Must dash.}

Jonas: {Catch you later.}

After some digging Abby found the e-mail with the attachment entitled "Kristin". She downloaded the file and hit the button on her phone to speed dial Marcus. "Can you scan a file on my computer for me? I don't want any repeats of yesterday."

Marcus' sigh could be heard through the line. "Give me a sec. What's the name of the file?"

"Kristin. I saved it to my desktop," answered Abby.

After a few windows popped up and disappeared Marcus declared the file clean. Hanging up but not wanting to take any chances, Abby unplugged her computer from the network and double clicked the file. A video began to play.

A pretty woman with short, raven colored hair was sitting in a chair with hands and feet secured with some kind of rope. Her eyes were looking right at the screen as she spoke.

"You don't really believe you will get away with this do you? You cannot kidnap a government agent without a reprisal." Her voice had an English resonance without sounding snobbish.

"Maybe not. But even if they don't, there are others who will find you and make you pay," continued the woman. Half of the conversation was missing. Abby was only hearing the woman.

"Listen to me you, sick bastard. It doesn't matter where you go or where you hide, my contacts in Interpol will find you." The defiance in her voice showed bravery and confidence even though she knew she was going to die.

Whatever was said to her caused her face to change from courageous to frightened. "How did you know that? Who are you?" asked the woman with real fear in her voice.

"You don't know him. Even though we aren't together, he will still track you down." The woman's voice had a trace of pleading and hope.

"Of course I do. I never stopped." The person filming said something. "He knows," she said. After the videographer said something else she visibly deflated. "I'm sorry, Jonas. Know that you were my last thought."

After those words, the camera moved closer as gloved hands shoved a piece of clear plastic wrap over the face of the woman. She struggled but, with limbs bound, could not win against the man behind the camera. Her eyes stared into the lens as her attempts to breathe through the plastic became weaker and weaker until the light went out in her eyes.

From her doorway, Jonas voice broke the silence. "Yeah. That was Kristin."

# Chapter Sixteen

The internet cafe in the suburbs of Toronto was perfect. They served the stereotypical coffee with the right amount of cream and too much sugar. The tables were scattered around the room in a chaotic pattern that allowed some the illusion of privacy. Others could position themselves so that no one would be peering and leering at whatever was being seen on the screen. Then there was the kind of privacy that the Observer added to keep his location a secret.

After bouncing around the world on various proxy servers, he made his way to the University Hospital in San Antonio. They had a better than average security system. Their firewalls had firewalls. Their secure database was commendable and would keep out all but the most sophisticated hackers. Fortunately for the Observer, but unfortunately for the hospital, he was one of those sophisticated hackers. He had gleaned information about the doctor who had treated Chilton from the information he had mined from her computer. A little digging and the Observer discovered the basic information on Doctor Priyanka Chopra. With a few password tries, the name of her first son gave away all the secrets in the database.

*That is sad. I need to make a call on that hospital and sell them my services if their doctors make it this easy to crack in.* With a few keystrokes he had found what he was looking for. *Abby, Abby, Abby. Losing a baby and your reproductive ability all because of a wound in the line of duty. That must really mess with your head.* After downloading all of the data in the archives, the killer logged on to his special chat room through a website that sold classic shag carpeting to see if his playmates had sent any messages. Sadly, there was nothing waiting for him. They had not even logged on. *It would be tragic if they really believe that was me. I was looking forward to playing with Abby.*

Jonas walked all the way into the room, closed the door and sat down on the love seat across the room from Abby. His casual way of half sitting and half reclining made him look totally at ease. All

Abby could do was look at him and wonder how he could appear so calm after hearing what he had heard. *Does he re-experience it each time he hears it?*

Jonas waited until the silence in the room had moved from uncomfortable to painful before he said simply, "Ask what you want to know?" There was something akin to a smirk on his face, he knew what Abby was going to ask before she said it.

Rising from her computer and sitting in the chair next to him, Abby looked long and deep into his amazing green eyes. Feeling the pain that he tried to subjugate, a tear tried to escape her eye as she asked, "Were you still in love with her?"

"In love? No. Love her? Yes," he answered. He refused to break the gaze. Waiting again in uneasy quiet Jonas seemed to open up for a fraction of second to share what his words lacked. The pain and horror, the pleasure and passion, flooded through as his eyes spoke volumes without the need for words. Abby could see his joy that reached higher than the Himalayas and the torture his soul endured dragging him down deeper than the ocean trenches. And then it was gone, his shields back in place. "Have you ever really been in love, Abby? I mean soul stealing, power draining, betray your values, rip your heart out, in love?"

Abby had to break away from looking at this man who had known pleasure and pain beyond anyone she had ever met. Considering his question carefully, she answered, "I don't think so, Jonas. But I have been..."

"If you don't think so," interrupted the man from Interpol, "I can promise you that you haven't. It's something that will make you as strong as you will ever be and weaker than you ever feared possible. It's something that you can only feel. It can never be explained." There was a pause as an internal struggle played out behind his ever-present mask. "It's something that I will never feel again. I won't let myself have that kind of weakness... ever." There was almost a tone of regret in his voice.

Abby was in full blown counselor mode. She did what she always did when she had a client who was stuck in pain. She asked a question. "Why do you consider that weakness?" Her tone was one of beckoning that she had perfected over years of practice.

"Why do you ask questions when you know the answer?" retorted a smiling Jonas. The mask was back in place and the smartass was challenging the counselor.

Abby was determined to not break the silence knowing that silence was the friend to the therapist. Jonas was not going to break the silence because he wanted to hear how Abby would try to coax more information out of him. A knock at the door after ninety seconds of a battle of wills allowed both to say, "Come in."

Without preamble or even greeting, the computer expert burst into the room. "Ronni is amazing!" stated Marcus. "She has mad skills and her GUI is to die for. Is she single?" All his words ran together in his excitement.

The man from Interpol smiled. "She is seeing someone this week. Right now she is into girls, but a month ago she had a thing for short Korean men so you might have a chance when this romance fizzles." Rising from the couch, he winked at Abby as he consciously moved so there was a chair between them. Jonas avoided her gaze and looked at the computer expert. "So what has you all hot and bothered other than Ronni's picture?"

Marcus smiled salaciously, "I haven't even seen her. I did share some data and some screen shots." Jonas raised an eyebrow. "Of her screen, you pervert," laughed Marcus. A couple swipes of the screen on his phone and Marcus' phone beeped. Looking at the picture message, the Korean's eyes widened in shock and pleasure. A very exotic beauty was looking at him. "That's Ronni? Dude, once we catch this guy I want an introduction and plane tickets to Chile for a month vacation."

Abby, tiring of the male bonding and the testosterone in the air, asked, "Are you two done?" She didn't even try to hide her irritation at the interruption and he noticed it in her tone.

"Easy Abby. Whatever you two were doing in here can wait when you see what I found." He looked at Abby, who gave away nothing, and then to Lange who merely shrugged and smiled. "Since you are not asking, I will. 'Marcus, what did you find?' Well I'm glad you asked. There is something wrong with the computers from that house. While you two were out playing with professors I was examining hard drives. That bastard had several terabytes of storage!" Abby and Jonas both had blank looks that conveyed that meant nothing to them. The computer geek sighed and spoke with the condescension given to a child, "That is a lot of hard drive space. But that's not the real issue..."

Tina strolled into the office with a huge smile on her face that said she too had news. Interrupting, she declared, "I found something interesting." She looked at Marcus who was giving her an evil stare for breaking in on his dramatic reveal. "Oh, I'm sorry," she said with mock apology in her voice. "Please continue with the nerd news."

"Thank you, Teeny." Reclaiming the conversation he continued, "When a hard drive is damaged in an explosion or a fire there are gaps in the data or at least places where you can still find bits of bytes. These hard drives are pristine. Well except for the places where they looked like they were attacked by a ninja with a flaming hammer."

Jonas asked the question that Marcus was looking for. "So they were wiped? Can you get anything back? You computer gurus do that all the time, right?"

"Normally I would have already done that and be handing you a print out of what I was able to brilliantly recover." Marcus took a break as he lost a little of his bluster. "Not this time. These things were wiped and the spots were covered with gibberish. It is like recording over something. What was there has been replaced by computer white noise. There is nothing to recover. That's the thing. This was too good to be from the house being blown up. Someone didn't want me seeing what was on those hard drives. Ronni agrees."

It was Tina's turn to take over. "That makes perfect sense with what I discovered. Jacob Raines bought that house eight years ago and totally changed his life. He moved here from Boise after a rough divorce. He came out pretty good on the settlement and was able to pay cash for the house here. Instead of going to work in banking like he had done in Idaho, he suddenly became a computer expert and has been working as a freelance computer security specialist based out of Knoxville. Almost all his transactions have been online. Every bill, every pizza, every book, every movie was all purchased by computer. Hardly anyone really had any contact with Jacob."

Abby knew her friend well enough to tell when she was holding something back. "Hardly anyone?" The two women shared a knowing smile.

"Well there seems to be one or two people who knew him by sight. One was the person who sent a lot of work his way. His name is Ian Edos, the CEO of *Cryptos*. It's one of those internet security companies. They seem to have transferred 1.8 million dollars to his account in the past six years." Turning to Marcus, she smiled an evil smile and asked, "Has the FBI paid you that much?"

"Not as far as they know," said the hacker cryptically. "I know about Edos. He is one of the best at white hat hacking for profit. If he hired this guy he must have been damn good."

Jonas was done with all the chatting. "Sounds like we need to have a talk with Ian." He shared a look with Abby and said, "Well, I do. Abby still needs to work on her profile."

"No way, Jonas. I can work on this later. You need me to profile this Ian guy. Besides, I so enjoy your company." The sarcasm in the last sentence was not lost on any of them.

Stepping between Tina and Marcus, Jonas put his arms around their shoulders and said, "It is so hard to get away from her when she wants something, isn't it?" The innuendo was thick and his smile played the game as well.

Abby finally rose from her chair. Looking at the trio she countered, "When I want something, I get it. And," taking on a seductive simmer to her voice, "the thing that makes me roll my eyes back in blinding ecstasy is profiling a killer. I have the big O when I get to see the bastard behind bars. Hurts so good." And then she walked out with her three friends staring after her.

Not taking his hands down, Jonas asked, "Did she say what I think she said?" The FBI analysts on either side of him nodded without speaking. "Does she say that kind of thing often?" They shook their heads. "She is very complicated. I like complicated." Jonas broke away and followed the profiler down the hall.

"At least their children won't be bored," said Tina.

"In therapy, but not bored," agreed Marcus.

The Observer was back on the road and heading toward his hotel. There are some things in life that create simple, unadulterated joy. For some it could be the first laugh of their baby. Many others found the pleasure and passion of either the action of sex or, more intimately, the act of lovemaking. For the Observer, joy was a mystery. As close as he came was finding the linchpin moment in someone's life. That moment was the source and stem from which the flower of their psyche grows. Every person who seems to be a budding or blossoming rose has some kind of thorns that enable them to remain safe by keeping others away.

The Observer was proud to have played such a pivotal role in making Jonas into the damaged man he had now become. The death of Kristin had been incredible in the way her eyes had locked onto his and remained there defiantly until they saw nothing more. The tiny camera in his glasses had captured it all to be shared with Lange. To this day Jonas was still unaware that the Observer had watched him when he saw the video for the first time. The desolation of the man was truly extraordinary. That would be his defining moment and the Observer had orchestrated it. He had created the thorns.

It was with melancholy that the Observer discovered Abby already had her defining moment. Losing so much so traumatically would haunt her for the rest of her life. It would either be a source of great strength or catastrophic weakness. Either way, this was going to be a fun thing to play with. *I wonder if she could have an even greater loss to redefine her defining moment. I wonder if she is the one...*

As the beautiful Canadian landscapes of the suburbs gave way to the business and busyness of Toronto, the Observer smiled his evil smile. He wondered how long before they sent him a message letting him know they knew he was still alive. It is the simple things in life that mean the most.

# Chapter Seventeen

Abby made a call to the offices of *Cryptos*. According to Marcus, they were one of the leading internet security firms in the United States. Abby knew the name only as one of the companies based in the area. It was by no means one of the big employers or major sources of tax income by big business standards. That being said, they were a force to be reckoned with if push came to shove. The very courteous and evasive receptionist explained that Mr. Edos would be out of town until late tomorrow morning. While talking she checked in with the boss. After texting him she was suddenly extremely accommodating and scheduled an appointment for Agent Chilton at 1:00pm the next day.

Abby hated herself for enjoying doing that to people. She got over hating herself quickly as she hung up and looked into the green eyes of Jonas who had a smug look on his face. He had sensed her pleasure in putting the secretary in her place.

"What?" she asked defiantly.

"It is so nice to see you enjoying yourself." Jonas was typing something on his phone while still maintaining eye contact with Abby. It was annoying that he could do that. "Do you also like to burn ants with a magnifying glass?"

"Shut up. You love it, too. I've seen the look on your face when you make everyone else look stupid. Especially those of us who are smarter than you."

False confusion appeared on the German's face. "Why Agent Chilton, I have no idea what you're talking about." With a mischievous grin he changed the topic. "So no *Cryptos* until tomorrow. That gives you time to work on the preliminary profile and I can get some exercise. Do you have plans for dinner?"

The question caught her off guard. "Um. No. Not really. I was going to work late. What did you have in mind?" She was unsure where Lange was going with this.

His too green eyes appeared to have a darker verdant hue. "Well, fair maiden Abigail, would you do me the honor of joining me for a repast? I know this very nice spot. After all the trouble I have caused I think dinner is the least I can do."

"Only dinner, nothing else?" asked Abby. She wasn't sure if she was asking that trying to dissuade him or persuade him. He was such a difficult person to read. There was some serious damage there but also something that reminded her of a lost puppy. Or was it that he looked like a blonde Adonis that got her going?

Jonas read her internal battle. "Why don't we start with dinner and see where things go. Personally, I am looking forward to a relaxing evening without feeling like I'm being watched. But then again, for all I know, Klaus has binoculars on us right now."

"You have a gift for ruining a mood," pouted Abby. "Let's have some dinner and chat about something other than a sociopathic serial killer."

The impish smile remained on his face. "Serial kidnappers it is. I'm going to try out the gym here. I need some exercise. Catch you later." With a wink, he was gone.

Abby looked after the conundrum of a man who walked out her door. There was something about him that she was missing. What was it? *Abby, you need to focus on this killer. Leave Jonas alone for now. But think about a few questions to dig a little deeper over dinner.* She began digging a little deeper into the information that Jonas had gleaned from his conversations with the Observer.


The computer store was surprisingly well stocked with options for the Observer. He usually preferred to work on a desktop due to the expandability, but a laptop would do for now. His new life would allow him to build any kind of system he wanted. But he needed to work and the 3.4 GHz laptop would do what he needed with plenty of power to spare. Paying with cash, he got all the bells and whistles he wanted. He smiled as he enjoyed the lack of paper trail. *Let's see if Marcus and Tina can track this transaction.*

The Observer had found a place that suited his needs. It was an extended stay motel that catered to the business elite. It was expensive but it provided what he needed – privacy. The suit was billed to one of his clients who would never even know they had paid for it. He sat down and plugged in the first of his USB drives.

The computer booted from that external source and began wiping everything off the hard drive to install the Observer's operating system on the terabytes of empty space.

Within an hour and a half his new computer would be ready to be the beast he needed. The Observer sat back on his bed and continued working on the details about Abby Chilton. *So, what would it take to break you further?*


After two hours, Abby needed a break. She had climbed inside one of the sickest minds she had ever encountered. He was by far the most twisted person she had even read about. She had created two lines of thought on the Observer. The first was the facts. The second was the unreliable information that he had told Lange. The reliable data was scant. The speculation was incredible in a horrendous kind of way. If there was even a smattering of truth to his claims, he was one of the worst serial killers in history. It was too much to stay inside his mind for longer than a couple hours at a time without becoming lost in the abyss. *Time to lighten up.*

Rising from her desk, she walked out her office with the intention of getting some coffee. Strangely she found herself walking to the elevator without her cup. Abby went down to the second floor and began heading to the gym. She didn't delude herself into thinking she was going there for a workout. The profiler wanted to see if Jonas was still there.

Entering the large gym, she saw a group of people around the sparring mat. Abby didn't remember a class being held at this time of the afternoon. As she got closer she saw why there were so many people around the perimeter. Jonas was testing his skills against Andy Oswald – the field office's hand to hand combat expert. Both shirtless men were drenched in sweat. Andy was the more muscle bound of the two, but there was more definition to Jonas' physique. How had she gotten the idea that he had only been in decent shape? *Damn that man! Always trying to throw me off.* He had slouched to create that illusion.

Looking around the room, Abby noticed that well over half of those watching were women and every one of them was watching Jonas carefully. It looked like he was getting the better of Andy. No one ever got the better of Andy. The FBI agent moved toward Lange with a combination of Taekwondo and Muay Thai boxing that was notorious in the field office for leaving men and women on the mat wondering what happened to them. With a move so fast that Abby couldn't keep track of it, Jonas stepped inside the arms of Andy and gave him an open handed hit under the jaw. With a closed fist, that hit would have left the FBI agent on the mat out cold. Jonas moved behind him, ready for another pass.

Andy, although unaccustomed to looking like a child beside a master, was not one to allow his ego to trump his judgment. He gave Jonas a head bob and a small clap of his hands acknowledging the superior move. The German smiled and took a half-bow, graciously accepting the compliment, and then sprang at the other man as Andy readied another strike. The move Jonas used looked something like a form of jujutsu where he flipped himself and the other man so both ended up on the ground with Andy in a headlock as the German used his legs to deprive the American of air. With a pat on the mat, the match was over, the Interpol agent being the clear winner. Abby looked around at the women who were sweating even though they had not exerted themselves and felt a twang of jealousy.

Both men flipped themselves up, bowed and shook hands. It was Andy who asked, "What the hell was that last move? German ju-jitsu?"

"Very good. Most people don't recognize that. I teach it when I get the time." Jonas did not sound arrogant or cocky. He said it in a simple way as though it were a foregone conclusion. Looking around, he said, "That will be all for Fight Club today. Remember the first rule of Fight Club: don't underestimate the German." The disarming smile made the joke even funnier.

Several women approached Jonas with numerous questions about his technique and whether he would have time to teach a class. The Interpol agent was gracious, declining to teach while shaking the hands of all his admirers. Abby was certain that he had been palmed more than one phone number. With a little effort, he was able to disentangle himself from the gaggle of people and approached the profiler.

"Aren't you supposed to be working?" asked the gregarious German.

"I needed a break so I thought I'd see how you were doing. I see you are doing well. How many numbers did you get?" She tried to hide her green-eyed feelings about the green-eyed man with a smile intended to convey curiosity. Abby knew he saw through it but was not about to give him the satisfaction of seeing her jealous.

Reaching in his pocket, he pulled out five slips of paper. "Four of them are interesting, but this one from Howard is a little off my normal taste," laughed Lange. He walked over to the trash can and casually dropped in the slips of paper. "How's the profile coming?" he asked as he grabbed a towel and took swig from a bottle of water.

"He is one twisted bastard. How many of his claims do you think are true? If half that shit's true, he may be the most successful killer I've ever heard of." Abby was hoping her instincts were wrong on this.

Jonas wrapped the towel around his neck, took another pull and drained the water bottle before answering. "You already suspect what I know, don't you?"

"He's not lying, is he?"

"My instincts tell me he's not," agreed Lange. "I think he has wanted to share his – for lack of a better word – hobby with someone." There was a slight hesitation that went beyond his heavy breathing from the workout. "He started with Kristin and then moved on to me. He says he started over ten years ago killing every two weeks. Have you gotten to the count as of two weeks ago?"

"Two hundred and sixty-eight," stated Abby, her voice quieter than she had intended.

Jonas nodded grabbing a second towel, drying himself further as they walked through the gym. "I'm sure the number has risen to two hundred and sixty-nine after last weekend. But I have a feeling that he is losing interest in me. He has already done his damage and all I am is someone to talk to. I'm no profiler, but I think he liked making sure I saw Kristin die as much as he enjoyed killing her. He teased her for months and when he got bored he killed her.

"Now that he's bored with me, Klaus will try to kill me and make you watch. But that won't be as much fun. As much sexual tension as there is between us, it's not quite as intense as the relationship I had with Kristin. My dying would be a tragic loss, but not devastating for you." Abby kept walking forward without looking. Jonas stopped, pointed to the sign that said 'men's locker room' and smiled. "You have to wait here. As much fun as showering with you might be, I don't think this is the right place for it." As he disappeared around the corner, Abby heard greetings from others who were cheering the German's fighting skills.

She turned to go back to her office. *How can he be so casual about being the target for a serial killer?* As she continued to think about it, she realized what Jonas had not said. She was going to be the new play thing for the Observer. It all came to her in a rush. That is what Jonas had meant when he said she would be the bait. If something happened to him, Lange needed someone like her to continue the search to find this psycho. He was not the son of a bitch he claimed. Abby was the insurance policy.


The fourth USB drive was removed and placed in a special envelope. It would be mailed to a drop box he used to hold mail until called for. Better to not have that on him in case of problems. His new computer rebooted and showed his operating system. It was a form of Linux that he had customized to his own needs. It could now be booted in normal mode or – as he jokingly called it – abnormal mode. The normal mode would show his work and had his hacking tools for breaking into secure systems to help them see their flaws.

Abnormal mode was the fun mode. It required a fifteen stroke password during an invisible six second pause as the computer booted. This one allowed him to see any potential targets; profiles of Kristin, Jonas and Abby; and the only list he kept of past kills. It was the closest he ever came to a memento. The only real reason he kept that was in case Jonas caught or killed him. This was the reward for the one who beat him. He never even looked at the list. The only time he opened it was for the addition every other week.

He had worked on Abby's profile enough today. It was time to look for someone to track down and watch the light go out. The killer pulled up his list of potentials and looked at the two highlighted in green. These two were ready. A toonie, the nickname for the Canadian two-dollar coin, came out of his pocket and was flipped. Tails meant that it would be Andrea Gaston. Excellent. She had been on his list for over a year.

Checking his internet search bots, he found that much of his information on Andrea was still up to date. There were a few changes. She had gotten a promotion. *Good for her!* She had changed boyfriends again. *That is shocking – not.* This was the fourth boyfriend in the year she had been on his radar. She was now a red head instead of a blonde. *I will never understand why normal people change their hair color so much. It makes those of us who need to seem so shallow.* All this was good to know, but it was nothing that would cause him to change his plans. In ten days, Andrea would disappear forever.

# Chapter Eighteen

It wasn't until seven that Abby and Jonas were ready to leave the office. Abby had put finishing touches on her preliminary profile, but knew she needed to sleep on it before presenting it. Jonas was working on something in his temporary office and being very secretive about it. Soon they were sipping glasses of wine and enjoying the flurry of activity on Market Square. There were many opportunities for outdoor dining in this downtown area. Jonas had chosen one that had some of the best food in Knoxville.

"How did you know about this place? I love eating here," shared Abby, trying to open a dialog.

Jonas smiled a different smile than she had yet seen. To her trained mind, it was the first real smile she had seen on the man. "Well, there are some things that a guy shares and some secrets he must take to the grave." Jonas left it wide open for more to be said. Laughing, he confessed, "I looked it up online. It has a great rating." Raising his glass in a toast. "Here's to a night away from killers. Prost."

Touching his glass with hers, Abby amended, "Assuming we're not being stalked, cheers." There was a glint in Jonas' verdant eyes that made her ask. "What?"

"We're alone. He's not in Knoxville. I have a feeling. Tonight we need to unwind a bit. How's the wine?" Jonas had a confidence that was infectious. Abby was sure he knew more than he was saying, but she had learned by now that pestering him would not work.

"The wine's pretty good. I didn't think they served Chateau Ste Michelle Riesling here."

A new smile spread across his face as his voice took on a cultured British resonance. "They don't. However, the waiter found a twenty dollar bill in his hand and brought me a bottle that I had waiting."

She raised an eyebrow as she considered the creativity of the man. How did he know she loved a British accent? *All American women like an English accent. It's not that much of a leap, Abby.*

"Well, mate. Jolly good show," she replied in a terrible attempt at the same style of accent.

His accent didn't falter. "You may want to consider elocution studies, Abigail. That was less than pleasing to the ear," teased Jonas with a glint in his eyes. "I could keep this accent if it is something you prefer. It is all the same to me."

Laughing at his jest, Abby countered, "Speak any way you want. It's all the same to me, too." She was lying and he knew it. The profiler decided to try distraction. "May I ask you a semi-serious question?"

It was Jonas' turn to raise an eyebrow. His voice returned to a normal American accent as he replied, "Please do. This should be good."

Abby knew he was ready for any number of questions. She could have asked about his home or about family. She sensed he was ready for questions about his career in Interpol or about cases he had completed. The one she asked through him a curve. "What is your real accent?"

She couldn't tell if the look of mild confusion on his face was real or if it was merely part of this persona that he chose to portray to keep her guessing. After a pause that was the perfect length, he replied, "To be honest, if I'm not speaking German, I really don't have one. I learned how to speak English originally with the Received Pronunciation that we all tend to learn in Europe. I also picked up other accents in my multinational studies. I can do pretty good English accents and a passable Scottish accent. Irish is a breeze thanks to my buddy Sean who spent a month with me in a training seminar with Interpol. And then there are all the American accents. It takes a while to learn one to the point you don't sound like... well... like you sounded just now."

Abby wanted to stick her tongue out at him but felt that would be childish. She flipped him off instead.

"Maybe later," replied Jonas. "Or was that intended as an insult instead of an offer?"

Abby could feel the blood rushing to her cheeks. *Damn that man and damn this wine.* She rolled her eyes while shaking her head in an attempt to play it off as exasperation instead of embarrassment.

"So tell me what kind of accent do they have in Phoenix? I've never been there." What appeared to be an innocent question caused Abby some apprehension. She had not told him that was where she had been born and raised. Her mother still lived in the house she and her now deceased father had bought forty years ago. The FBI agent had a feeling Jonas knew all about her family and her life. That was not fair.

"I'll trade you an answer for an answer. Deal?" The disarming smile and nod of the head told her that the German agreed to her terms.

As she was about to answer, Lange spoke up. "As long as the questions are of the same level of intimacy." That damnable gleam in the storm-laden green irises told Abby he had chosen his word with precision, intention and deviousness. He was trying to keep her on the defensive.

It was her turn to smile. "Deal. So the Phoenix accent is nonexistent. There are too many transplants from all over the country since it's a choice retirement community."

"Ah. That explains why a pulmonologist would relocate there. Did your father have a practice focused on the aging population? It seems like there would be quite a few people there with lung issues as they age."

How the hell did he know all this? Abby made a mental note to discuss with her mentor the propriety of sharing her personal and personnel information with people from Interpol. "Pretty much. But I'm sure he was able to use some of the tech that your dad invented." Two could play this game. Abby hoped the German would be surprised by the knowledge she had been able to discern. As usual, he gave no sign. They would have to play poker sometime. *Strip poker?* Her libido was asking questions. *Shut up.* Abby's logical side made a half-hearted attempted to reassert control.

"I'm sure he did. What's your next question and if it is about my side of the bed, I don't have one." Abby was certain that Jonas had read Sun Tzu's *The Art of War* and was using some of those tactics on her right now. She turned that around on him.

"Do you apply Sun Tzu's methods to every part of your life?" asked the profiler as their dinner arrived.

Jonas thanked the waiter as a second bottle of wine appeared on the table. Pouring them both full glasses of the elixir, he answered her question. "Not every part of my life, but many of them. There are some things that require the art of peace." Both reached for the same glass of wine and their fingers brushed one another. The spark that was felt by both was as unmistakable as it was undeniable. Their fingers remained barely touching as their eyes locked. The attraction was palpable as electricity passed in the touch and the unwavering gaze the two shared.

With some effort, the sizzling air was calmed by breaking contact. Jonas raised his glass in another toast. "Here's to... what shall we drink to, Abby?" The playfulness in his eyes was far too seductive to be accidental.

"How about to the Sunsphere? It is now one of my favorite places to meet new people?"

"To the Sunsphere," toasted the German. He waited until she was taking a drink to add, "And to not getting shot while meeting new people there."

Abby sputtered as wine dribbled down her chin from laughter. Jonas was quick with a napkin, taking his time as he dabbed at the wine. Moving up her chin, the napkin lightly brushed across her mouth leaving a light golden stain on the linen and quivering lips on Abby. Before pulling away, Jonas finger brushed those lips, fanning the spark of attraction into a flame of passion.

Breaking the intensely erotic touch, they stared deeply into one another's eyes. Abby knew that her Chicken Marsala and asparagus with hollandaise sauce would not be good later. Jonas considered how his Chicken Parmesan would taste later and came to the conclusion that it would suffer a great loss of flavor. Abby and Jonas looked back into each other's eyes and simultaneously waved for their waiter to bring doggy-boxes.


The Observer had completed all the preparation for his ten o'clock meeting the next day. The law firm would be both shocked and pleased. Shocked that all their secrets were so easily stolen. Pleased that the Observer had some quick fixes that would make certain their secrets would be far more difficult to steal in the future.

He had also made sure to leave out a few details in his solution that would leave them vulnerable to his skills should he need to access their network again. Besides, in a couple years he may want to charge them for a follow up visit.

Changing his computer to its abnormal mode, he decided to check in on his targets. He would drive out to the suburbs later tonight and replace batteries in the camera that watched over Andrea. She had been left unobserved for far too long. He needed to begin checking on her and making his plans.

Now was the time to check in on Abby. The feed from her camera was still strong but when the screen came up there was something wrong. It looked like a branch had fallen across the field of view. That was an odd coincidence. The camera had been in place for such a short period of time and it was already blocked. Since he was dealing with Jonas Lange, the Observer did not believe it was random chance. Jonas was far too clever and dangerous to think he would not have been looking for this. If he knew about the camera and the tracker, this took the game to a whole new level. Jonas was a little too good and a little too close.

If Jonas found him again it would be time for the man from Interpol to join his ex-wife.


Abby entered her apartment with Jonas close behind. She dropped their overfull doggy bags on the end table and turned to face Lange. With two quick strides she closed the distance between them, wrapping her arms around him and pressed her lips to his. His mouth opened to share the sweet breath of wine and the spark of passion as their tongues met in the kiss. It was long and deep as they explored the pleasure of first passion.

Not breaking the kiss, Jonas spun them both around, pressing her against the hallway wall. His mouth was pressed harder on hers and the heat of his body warmed Abby's in ways she had not felt in over a year. Jonas' fingers were making the tiniest circles in her hair while his fingertips danced and tickled her scalp. Abby pulled him closer as her nails dug into his muscular back through the royal blue Paul Fredrick dress shirt.

Jonas pulled away from the kiss to look into Abby's eyes. No words were needed as the shared passion communicated more than words could express. Pressing Abby even harder into the wall, Jonas began kissing at the point where neck and shoulder met with a combination of kisses, nibbles and a tongue that glided over her skin. A moan escaped Abby as his kisses moved up her neck, teeth running along her bare throat, to reach her ears where he bit hard enough to bring pleasure without too much pain.

Abby pushed him away, reaching for the buttons of his shirt. The first button came undone without an effort but the second was stuck. Without thinking, Abby yanked the shirt and sent buttons flying in every direction. His chest had a light smattering of blonde hair that tickled her lips as she kissed his chest moving to bite his nipples. She barely even noticed that her blouse was being removed and sliding down to the ground alongside the discarded dress shirt.

Suddenly realizing that she was nearly topless, Abby's hands moved to cover the scars from her surgery and began pulling Jonas to the darkened bedroom. He stopped her in mid-stride, gently turned her to face him, and knelt in front of her. She wanted to resist as he began kissing her tight abs, but surrendered when he moved her hands away from the scars to cover them with his lips. The tiny marks where she had been shot and the thin lines of the surgeon's scalpel had left places that were constant reminders of what she had endured; of what she had lost. He kissed the blemishes of her battle as if he could take away the pain and what they had cost. His kisses and licks were a sensation on the skin; but the passion was felt all the way through the scars as, for the first time, she felt a hint of healing from the emotional damage that the physical scars represented.

As his lips kissed a place that Abby had never dreamed would be an erogenous zone, Jonas' hands moved to free her breasts and move gently against this well-known sensual spot. Her nipples rose to meet the circles his fingers were tracing. Abby sighed as he first gently and then more firmly pinched her firm, pink areolas. His mouth moved up and kissed the breasts that were beckoning to him as his hands found the clasp of her slacks.

Jonas half led and half carried Abby to her bedroom shedding their remaining clothing along the way. Looking deep into each other's eyes, Jonas moved on top of the beautiful woman who had entranced him from their first flirtatious meeting. Teasing her, he moved so slowly it caused the ache within her to blossom and she greedily pulled him into her. The pent up craving caused the desire to explode as their bodies moved in perfect synchronicity with Abby rising up to meet each of Jonas' deep thrusts. Drops of sweat glistened on their bodies as they moved together, over and over, creating a cacophony of sensations. The slick, sweet sweat stimulated all five senses as their bodies encompassed one another drawing more and more pleasure.

As Jonas paused, tempting and teasing her with eyes that glowed with passion and lust, Abby grabbed his shoulders and threw him on the bed. She moved over him and slowly lowered herself onto him, and quickly sank all the way to the hilt. She moaned as she moved up and down over and over again. Dropping down as deeply as she could, Abby reached the point where she imploded, shaking and quivering, unable to even make a sound as pleasure reached every cell of her body.

Jonas, not one to let a great moment escape, continued his movements in fast circles. While Abby continued to rock back and forth as he found spots of pleasure she had never known she had. The combination of movements created sensations that caused them to groan in pleasure. Their shared ecstasy was reaching a point when neither one was even aware of the world around them. Gone were all thoughts of the dangerous man they were tracking. Gone was all the pain and loss each one had suffered. All that existed were two people locked together finding pure joy in the desire of shared bodies and spirits. As their eyes were locked in the soft glow of the room, they could see what the other was without any of the games or masks. Two broken people who needed each other both body and soul.

As Abby cried out in another implosion, Jonas moaned as he exploded long and deep while their bodies hungrily shared in the feast of passion they had denied themselves for so long. Collapsing on top of Jonas, Abby could feel every muscle in her body turn to jelly. She was totally spent. Jonas moved his hands through her hair, twisting it in tiny circles.

"Next time I get to play with your g-spot," taunted Jonas, in a voice barely audible.

"Promises, promises," sighed Abby.

The two lovers needed no more words as they lay in the afterglow. Both drifted off to sleep, sated and drained, knowing that tomorrow would be a whole new kind of day for them.

# Chapter Nineteen

The Observer was lying in his hotel room staring at the ceiling. He needed a few hours of sleep, but his mind would not let him rest. He had already checked his camera at Andrea's and replaced the batteries. It would last long enough for him to make a detailed profile of the traffic in and around her small home. Outer suburbs were one of his favorite places to kill. They tended to roll up the sidewalks after dark giving a stalker plenty of shadows where he could play. He even added something new. After seeing the limb in the way of Abby's camera it became apparent that Jonas was closer than he should be. If anyone opened the birdhouse at Andrea's, there would be little left to identify with his homemade version of C-4. It would be tragic if a bird lover was checking it out. Sometimes others must suffer to keep someone more important safe.

By all rights, Jonas should have been the one on his mind right now. *That damned Interpol agent is closer than anyone had ever been.* The Observer had no one to blame but himself. He had been toying with the man. Now that he considered it he realized his own need for validation had prompted him to contact his nemesis all those times. But the German could be dealt with very efficiently. The Observer had the advantage of knowing how Jonas looked. If the investigator had any clue as to his appearance, it would be spotty at best.

What could not be explained was the person who was causing this rare moment of sleeplessness. Why was Abby Chilton on his mind? *Think this through. What is so special about her?* The Observer opened his tablet and looked over all the information he had discovered about the FBI agent. She was pretty, looks never mattered to the Observer. He was not attracted to people of either gender for companionship or even plain-old, tension-relieving sex. Abby was more intelligent than most people he had been in contact with. That was a plus in her favor. She would be more fun to manipulate than Jonas. What was really going on? As he moved down his list of traits he shook his head. Profiler? No. Sarcastic? No. Loyal? No. Confident? No.

When he got three quarters of the way through the list he came upon the word 'broken'. *Broken? Could it be that she is broken and I can't be the one to break her? How arrogant is that?* He continued down the list and briefly considered the word 'driven' before dismissing it as something he had already found in Jonas. His eyes kept looking back up at 'broken'. That made no sense to the Observer. *I'm better than this. I don't need to break her to win. I can use what has already been broken to my advantage.* As he tried to convince himself of that another part of his brain was beginning to work on details of a plan to break Abby even further to turn her into something else.

He opened up his laptop, logged in to a website that sold pink pumps and found himself in the chat room. He typed one phrase and logged off.


Abby woke to the sound of her alarm going off. 5:30am is an ungodly hour. If you are still up it sucks that you have to keep going into a new day with no sleep. If you are in a deep refreshing sleep as Abby had been, it was one of the worst times of day to wake up since the sun was not out. Abby was not a morning person. She smiled to herself as the events of the previous night came back to her. She reached to the other side of the bed hoping to find part of Jonas already awake. She kept reaching.

She opened her eyes and looked at the empty space beside her. *How am I going to deal with this at the office?* There was no scenario where this was going to be a good day. *What the hell was I thinking?* "Dammit," she muttered under her breath, burying her fist in the pillow he had used.

"What's wrong?" came a voice as her bedroom door opened. Jonas was standing there, silhouetted in faint light from down the hall. He was carrying a tray with sliced fruit, bagels, cream cheese and something that smelled suspiciously like coffee. Standing there in nothing but a pair of boxer briefs, he looked even better than the breakfast he was carrying. Approaching he asked, "Did you really think I was gone?" With the light behind him she couldn't see it, but she knew there was a smirk on his face.

"Shut up and give me the damn coffee," said Abby trying not to smile. She failed. Sitting up she let the sheet fall revealing what had been covered. She reflexively reached for the fallen sheet but found that it was suddenly out of her reach as a tray was placed in front of her. She took a careful sip of the java and was pleasantly surprised to find it was drinkable. "Not bad," she admitted. Giving him her best demure look, she asked, "Any regrets?"

Jonas appeared to be considering his answer making Abby hesitate as she lowered her coffee. "Well, there is one thing. I think the breakfast is premature." With that he moved the tray and began kissing her.

At 7:45 the two were pulling in to the FBI parking lot to park beside one another. They were unprepared for the ambush. As they rounded the corner, two people were waiting for them. Tina and Marcus were standing there, arms folded and doing their best to look like disapproving parents.

"Where were you last night young lady? What were you doing? Is this how you treat me? I was waiting up for you last night." teased Tina in a mock scolding tone.

Marcus tried to stare down Jonas. "Are your intentions toward our young Abby honorable?" Then he stage whispered, "If you say 'yes' she will be very disappointed."

"Marcus! We were supposed to drag this out. You broke after the first sentence." Tina had hoped for more tormenting. Looking at Abby she said, "Men. They don't know when to..." She looked carefully at Abby. "You got laid!" Tina gave her a bear hug that would have lifted the profiler off her feet if it weren't for Tina's tiny stature. She still tried her best. Abby blushed so brightly Jonas feared she was about to pop.

Jonas looked at Marcus when he offered a high five. Reluctantly he pressed his palm into the Korean's. "Dude, she really needed that. Good job. Now maybe she won't be so uptight for a while."

Jonas looked at the blushing Abby as they all walked to the entrance. "I will always love how open Americans are about things like this. I do appreciate it better when I'm watching and not receiving." The jovial tone of his voice told everyone that he was lying. Jonas liked feeling like one of them for the first time.

Abby finally spoke up. "You get used to it."

"How would you know? Did you have to use the Jaws of Life on her thighs?" teased Tina, causing a raised eyebrow from the agent at the security desk.

"Don't say a word, Mike, or your next psych eval will really suck," said the psychologist to the man at the desk. He merely smiled and raised his hands in surrender. Abby led the way to the elevator shaking her head. "Shit," she muttered under her breath as the doors closed.

As they stepped out of the lift the two analysts went one way and the agents went another. Walking down the hall, they were met by Barbara. "Hey, Abby. Hello, Jonas." She paused a little too long as she appraised them. Abby became paranoid until she noticed that Barbara had not even looked at her. She was trying to be subtle as she checked out the German. "Word has spread about you and your talents, Agent Lange. No one has been able to do what you did. Congratulations."

"Thank you. It comes from years of practice and a lot of dedication," said Jonas modestly. Abby was about to go into shock. She could not believe how casual Lange was being about all of this. This was no one's business.

"Have you considered teaching a class? There are many of us who want to see firsthand what you can do." asked Barbara. Abby was sure she was about to have a stroke.

"Barbara you have no idea how flattered I am that you would ask. Do you really think there is that much interest? I'm sure there are others who are nearly as good as I am." Abby has serious doubts as to the honesty of that statement.

Barbara was gushing. "Jonas Lange, everyone is talking about you now. Do you have any idea how many have tried and failed? Please consider showing us. Think of how much you could help the female agents." Abby began praying for a heart attack or something that would cause instant death.

Jonas glanced at Abby, realized what she was thinking, and smiled a devious smile. "I'm afraid I won't have time for that. But don't worry about it. Andy has things well in hand." Andy? Suddenly Abby realized this discussion was about the martial arts from the previous day. She moved past Barbara to go and hide in her office.

Barbara called after her. "Mathis wants to meet with you at nine." Abby gave a noncommittal wave. Turning back to Jonas, she asked, "What's wrong with her?"

"Something must have gotten into her. I'll make sure she's all right." replied Jonas, laughing to himself as he headed toward Abby's office.


At 8:15am, the Observer walked into the law offices of Lockwell, Crosby and Chase with too much on his mind. He needed to focus on the job at hand but he was still thinking about the FBI profiler. With more will than he was accustomed to needing, he prepared for the meeting. After presenting his card to the receptionist he was shown into a conference room to wait for the partners. Within thirty seconds he had placed folders around the table and set up his laptop and projector. He was going to show him how he had cracked into their system. It was the fun part of his job. Showing lawyers what he could do to them was even better. He really didn't like lawyers. They were always so pretentious. He had killed five lawyers in his day. They didn't even die well.

After being made to wait until 8:45, the three partners came in together chatting about something they had learned on a case of some importance. The Observer was not worth their notice until they sat down and to give him the illusion of attention. Looking at each of them, the Observer saw all there was to see.

James Lockwell was in his fifties. He was doing his best to hide the hangover he felt this morning, but the lines around the eyes and the faint trace of anti-nausea medication told the Observer more than the partners knew. The enlarged size of the lower part of his nose coupled with the almost immediate drumming of the puffy fingertips showed the Observer that this was a normal state for the man who depended on alcohol to deal with the stress.

Benito Crosby was trying to maintain his youth even though he was obviously in his late forties while trying to look in his early thirties. The Observer had researched them and knew that Crosby considered himself the playboy of the group, though his computer had more porn than all the others in the office combined. The practiced smile was returned by the computer specialist. Crosby would likely have told his partners about his liaison last night with some kind of hot babe. The way he was sitting and moving told another story entirely. After twenty minutes he had to excuse himself to go to the bathroom. When he returned he was substantially more flushed than before he had flushed. Having chlamydia was a painful experience for some.

Though Janice Chase was also in her fifties, her face had lost most of its ability to show expressions due to the amount of Botox that had been injected. It amused the Observer that this woman – married for thirty years with three children – was having an affair with the young woman who had brought in coffee and doughnuts. It always amazed the Observer how no one else could see what was screaming to his senses.

The lawyers gave him their best counselor looks to humor the computer nerd at first. When he showed them by the amount of damage that could be caused to their clients but – more importantly – to the law firm and their profits, he had their undivided attention. No one could ever duplicate what the Observer had done. After reassuring them that he could fix all their problems, they came to an understanding about payment. Once they realized that he had seen everything in their computers, all agreed the fee was more than fair. The Observer spent five minutes uploading and testing the software he had already prepared and then spent the next five hours pretending to fix and test the system.


As the Observer was entering the law firm in Toronto, a different kind of negotiation was happening in Knoxville. Sitting in her office and laughing at Abby's panic attack, Jonas refused to become more serious. "Abby, you can either be secretive about what happened last night or let people know. To be honest, the way you're glowing we may want to post it on the message system."

Abby was sitting behind her desk with her head in her hands. "Can we please get back to work and talk about this later?"

"And I thought it was the German who was supposed to be the one who tried to hide everything behind an air of indifference. Or is that the British? I get us confused." Lange was enjoying himself far more than Abby.

"We need to work now. I have the preliminary profile ready; but I want to read it through one more time before I present. Do you have something you can be doing until nine?" Abby was doing her best to be professional.

"You are so cute when you do that?" smiled Jonas.

"Do what?" asked the profiler with more than a little trepidation.

Walking to the doorway, Jonas grinned. "Trying to be FBI-like while you're thinking about me standing in your doorway in my undies." He left before she could reply. Abby was pretty sure she heard him laughing in the hall.

One minute later, the door burst open. Marcus was at her desk holding a laptop with Jonas a few steps behind. "It's him! It's him! It's him!" the computer tech was saying over and over. He sat the computer on her desk while trying to catch his breath.

Abby looked from Marcus to a shrugging Jonas. "No clue. He ran past me in the hall and told me to follow. I'm guessing it's something about 'him' whoever 'him' is." Realization hit them both as their eyes locked.

"I made a secure computer to chat with him." Marcus was still out of breath, but was so excited he had to share. "It checks that chat room every hour. Look what it found this morning."

Inside the chat window was one phrase. {Miss me yet, Abby?}

# Chapter Twenty

While considering the ramifications of those words, the profiler was also considering her Interpol partner. Jonas stared at the blank screen. Abby was learning how to read the man, but this time there was nothing showing through his stoic expression. The lack of reaction was more disturbing than an explosion of outrage and anger. After a prolonged silence, Lange looked up and said, "Please excuse me for a minute. I need to make a call." Without explanation, he left the room.

Excitement and enthusiasm had been transformed into confusion in the computer guru. "What the hell does that mean?" asked a perplexed Marcus.

Abby had already processed the meaning behind those words. For her it meant that she was now the focus of the Observer's attention and Jonas would be relegated to being a peripheral interest at best. It could also mean that Jonas now had a death mark. For him this would be playing out the role that Kristin had played. No wonder it rattled the man.

"I think I know. Meet me in Mathis' office at nine so we can bring him up to speed. I'll find Jonas," replied Abby. Leaving her office, she looked in his temporary space and was not surprised to discover and empty office. She followed her instincts and headed straight for the conference room. She passed agents and others beginning their work, totally oblivious to any greetings that came her way. The door to the conference room was not locked, but she knocked to make sure she was not interrupting some other meeting. The door opened and she was waved in by Jonas.

"Bist du verrückt?" he was demanding into the phone. It was the first time Abby had seen him angry. A stream of what Abby assumed was questions – sprinkled with colorful expressions – followed with her name interspersed among the German. Finally, Jonas said, "Hold on. She's right here." Hitting a button on his phone he continued, "You're on speaker."

"'Ello, Abbee," said a voice with a very thick French accent. "I am Frédérique Veilleux, but please call me Rikka." Abby already hated her for the cute accent. "Yonas and I work together at Interpol."

"Rikka is my liaison with the rest of Interpol when I'm in the field," explained Jonas. As his eyes examined her he could see the twinge of jealousy on her face. "One second Rikka." He hit the mute button. "In case you're wondering, this is Rikka." He turned his phone to show the face of a striking woman around sixty. He unmuted the phone. "We're back."

"Really, Yonas? Again? 'Ow many 'earts are you going to steal before you let one in, mon loup? You can't mourn forever. 'E showed you my picture so you would be not jealous, no? Abbee, I am like 'is mother. If you can get 'im out of 'is monastic life, we would all be grateful." The care in her voice was obvious.

"Nice to meet you, Rikka. I'll see what I can do," replied Abby.

There must have been something in her voice. Rikka inquired, "Yonas, is zere something you want to tell Mama?" She had the knowing sound of any good mother who had caught a kid with his hand in the cookie jar.

"Yeah. Tell your nephew to stop flirting with me. It's not going to happen." Laughter came from the phone. "Now tell Abby what you told me."

There was silence on the phone for longer than necessary. "Are you sure? Zis is classified."

Jonas tapped his phone several times and said, "Check your screen. She now has clearance. Please tell her."

"Mon dieu. Welcome to ze 'arem, Abbee." As the sound of a keyboard clicking came through the speakerphone, Abby looked at Jonas and mouthed the word "harem". He mouthed back the word "later". "I am ready. Oh, Abbee, ze group of women who help Yonas, we call ourselves ze 'arem. 'E never works with too many men for some reason." Jonas gazed up at the ceiling with a look that was as close to embarrassment as Abby had yet seen on the spy's face. "IFTAS found ze Observer crossing ze border into Canada from Buffalo, New York yesterday at 1:12pm Eastern Daylight time. 'E was also tracked at ze Detroit airport before zat based on a ninety-two percent probability assuming 'e did not change 'is appearance during zat time. 'E used an American passport with ze name Richard Lang Draper." Abby caught the joke and laughed. Jonas looked at her questioningly. Rikka's voice showed her confusion. "Is zere something I'm missing by being zo far away?"

Abby stopped laughing and explained. "His name is a joke and a slam at the same time. The slam is using Jonas' last name as his middle. The joke is that Richard Lang Draper means 'designer long dick'. The nickname for Richard is Dick. Lang is German for long. And a draper in the fashion world is someone who assists in the designing of the clothes. That fits with my profile of him."

"Wait. You have a profile? 'Ow did you do zat? We 'ave been trying to get zat done for some time." Rikka was obviously impressed. "I zee why you like 'er, Yonas."

Abby had questions. Most she saved for later but one she wanted to know about. "What is IFTAS? Some kind of facial tracking system?"

Jonas spoke up. "It's the International Facial Tracking and Analysis System. We use it to find the bad guys. You will have it in a few years. Right now it is still being tested but I have a bypass protocol for new technology. Rikka is heading it up when she is not being a mother hen."

"Zis mother hen found your Observer. Show some respect to your elders. Abbee, I sent my contact data to your mobile phone. I would like a copy of your profile for my database on ze Observer, please." Even though she said please, Abby noticed that she did not ask.

"As soon as it is ready, you will be one of the first. Did Jonas tell you why he called you?" The look Jonas shot Abby made her glad that looks couldn't kill. But Jonas was giving it a really good try.

"What 'as 'appened, Yonas?" demanded Rikka. "I will find out so tell me now." The concern in her voice showed the real motherly love she had for him.

"His focus has shifted to Abby," said Jonas, without any inflection in his voice.

"Merde! Are you certain?" The level of Rikka's voice was rising.

"Yes," said Abby. "He left me the message in the chat room. He asked if I missed him." All three of them knew the significance of that.

"Abbee, please watch over Yonas. 'E thinks 'e's never going to die. 'E is such a little boy sometimes." Rikka's tone took on one of tenderness. "Yonas, if you let 'im get to you 'e will 'ave to answer to me. I am not as kind as you."

"Understood, mother. Now get back to work and tell me where he is now." Jonas closed the line and finally sat down. "To answer your questions in order. No, there is nothing between us but a bond that is closer than yours to Billingsly. Yes, she did train me in much of what I know and she is still one of my closest friends on the planet. She also has fifty-eight kills on her record, most with a sniper rifle. The harem is what Rikka calls my network of contacts because I prefer to work with women instead of men since I can read them better. And last, but not least, I am not worried about me with the Observer. I am worried about you."

The last statement threw Abby off her game. She had prepared all kinds of snarky comments about his harem and his mentor. Being worried about her didn't make sense until she considered the man she was sitting with. Above all other things, he saw himself as a protector. Laying down his life for another was something that he could and would do. But placing her in harm's way was difficult for him in spite of the way he tried to make himself look like an asshole. He never thought she would really become a plaything of the Observer. And now she was.

At nine o'clock, Jeremy Mathis looked up to find four people in his office. "Please, feel free to invade. Have a seat." He gestured to his sitting area and joined Abby, Jonas, Tina and Marcus. "I take it things have taken some interesting turns." He looked at Abby and asked, "Are you doing something different with your hair, Chilton?"

"No, Jeremy. Let's focus on what matters here." She shot an 'I'll murder you in your sleep with a dull gravy ladle if you say anything to him' look to the other three seated around her. Strangely, they all understood exactly what she meant. "The Observer has become... what is the right word here?" she asked to no one in particular.

"Enamored?" offered Jonas.

"Fascinated with?" threw out Marcus.

"In lust with?" suggested Tina.

Before Mathis' head twisted off from looking from one person to the next, Abby continued, "The Observer has taken an interest in me like he has with Jonas in the past."

"Enamored was better," pouted Jonas.

"How so?" asked Jeremy, ignoring the commentary.

Abby proceeded to explain the events of the previous day and the activities of the morning. "It seems I have a fan."

"I would say so. So what is your next move and how are you going to stay safe from this psychopath?" inquired the Special Agent in Charge. He had been shooting looks in Jonas' direction all during the update. The question about Abby's safety was directed at him.

Abby was ready for that question. "I need Marcus and Tina assigned to me for a few days while we track him down. We're pretty sure he is out of the country right now. I really need them to be focused on this case."

Mathis handed her a folder that had the case name 'Observer' on the tab. When she opened it, there was an order that had been signed yesterday releasing the two analysts to her task force. There was also a third order that would allow her to take Rupert Michaelson off any current cases should he be needed. *I hate it when he shows off.* Abby was secretly grateful for his foresight.

"Michaelson? Really, Jeremy?" queried the profiler. She knew what he was planning.

Mathis was ready for her resistance. "He is obnoxious and green as hell, but he also has the most potential. Besides, he pisses you off and that makes him less afraid of you than others around here."

"And the pissing her off factor makes him more fun to use in this case. Mathis, you have a twisted side I never appreciated until now," said Marcus, with more bravery than he usually showed around the boss.

"It's the little things that matter. And don't get cocky." Having put Marcus back in his place, he turned to Lange. "You had better be damn careful with my people. They may be pains in the ass but they are my pains in the ass. Understood?"

"Jeremy, we're working from the same playbook." Smiling his impish grin, Jonas asked Mathis, "Plus, does that make me hemorrhoid cream for taking care of the pains in your ass for the moment?"

The Special Agent in Charge shook his head and turned to Abby. "Next steps?"

"We will be meeting with the president of *Cryptos* after lunch. It looks like the Observer did some freelance work for them under his Jacob Rains identity. We will see what we can get. Hopefully the coroner will have some information for us as well. At four I'll deliver my profile."

"Meeting room at four then. Do we need Billingsly for that?" asked Jeremy.

"Wouldn't be a bad idea. My report of everything will be in your email before we leave for *Cryptos*.

Heading to Abby's office, the four talked amicably. When they passed Michaelson's desk Abby spoke up. "Rupert, can you spare a few minutes, please?"

"I'd love to but I'm right in the middle of..." began the agent. Abby handed him the order that would override his current case. He looked up with a grin. "I meant, sure Abby. Let's go."

When they arrived in her office, the rookie agent was brought up to speed. He remained silent, taking in all the information and asking no questions. When he had received all the data, he asked, "So what do you need with me? You have the wiz kids and Captain Interpol here."

"You're our backup with the FBI. If I call, it means I need you to come running. You are the proverbial cavalry to come to our rescue." Abby was buttering him up but he didn't even notice. The flattery worked like she knew it would.

"Consider me there," beamed Rupert.

"I'll keep you in the loop but don't need you right now. Keep your phone handy though. You are officially on call." The rookie practically bounced out of the room.

"Does she ever do that to either of you?" asked Jonas.

"Play us like a Stradivarius at the London Philharmonic? God, I hope not," said Marcus.

Abby looked at the clock and declared, "If we leave now, we can have a bite to eat before our meeting at *Cryptos*." Heading for the door, she looked over her shoulder at Jonas and asked with a twinkle in her eye, "You going to sit there all day checking out my ass, or are you going to follow me to meet our new friend?"

As Jonas rose, he kicked at Marcus who was mimicking playing a violin.


The Observer was having a wonderful day. He made fifty thousand dollars off the attorneys. There was a new person in his life to play with. He had managed to use the Wi-Fi where he had been working to hide his research on his newest victim. Even though it had been less than a week since his last kill, he was feeling the urge already. Andrea was so tempting, but he knew that another kill so soon could lead him into an escalation in his behaviors. It was better to control his desire and make sure everything was safe. No need to get caught now. *But if I'm careful...*

*No. No. No.* That was not how he worked. What was wrong with him? He had marshaled these kinds of desires years ago. Every two weeks was plenty. The desire to watch the life leave the eyes could be a potent narcotic. The release was akin to the orgasm of lesser individuals or the high achieved by the gutter scum addicted to the drug of the day. He was better than all of that. He was in control of his desires. They would not control him. *But if I could safely kill Andrea now...*

What was going on? This was wrong. Was Abby already inside his head? This would not work. Since focus was becoming difficult he would need to kill again this Friday and get back to normal so he could concentrate on the task at hand. *I wonder if Abby is online.* No. No. No! This was going to lead to trouble. Forgetting Abby would be the best move to make. *She doesn't matter in the long run.*

# Chapter Twenty-One

First Tennessee Plaza was the tallest building in the Knoxville skyline. Abby was pleased to see the offices of *Cryptos* were not on the top floor. It was a standard rule of thumb that the higher up the office was in the building, the higher the people thought of themselves. That usually resulted in either sucking up or intimidating the people who worked there to get what was needed. She hated sucking up. Since *Cryptos* was only on the seventeenth of the twenty-seven floors there was a decent chance that Ian Edos would be a decent guy. But, she had thought Jonas was an east Tennessee native. Her confidence in her deductive powers was not at its best.

While riding the elevator, Abby's phone went off. She glanced at the caller I.D. and was surprised to see Roger Walker's name. "Detective Walker, how are you today? I'm surprised to be hearing from you so soon." The warmth was somewhat forced, she knew Roger would not be calling with good news.

"Good morning, Agent Chilton. Like so many other men in your life, I can't seem to stay away," joked the Knoxville police detective. His tone changed. "Abby, I did a little bit of digging for you. Did you know that Jacob Raines worked freelance for a local company called *Cryptos*?"

Abby put him on speaker so Jonas could hear. "You're on speaker. Yeah, Roger. We're actually on our way up to see the CEO now. Someone named Ian Edos. We don't have a whole lot on him. Do you know something we don't?"

There was a pause on the other end. "Watch yourself, Abby. Is Jonas with you?" The door to their floor opened but neither stepped out. Lange hit the button for the lobby. His instincts were sending him signals he did not like at all. Even though Jonas had not known the cop long, he knew the type of man he was. This must be important if he was rattled.

"Right here," chimed in the Interpol agent. "Roger, what's wrong?"

There was no pause this time. "Edos is a ghost. I have friends in high and low places and no one seems to know much about him.

He seems to have deleted much of his history off the net. Plus, when I try to dig into law enforcement databases I get blocked. There is something hinky about this."

For the first time Abby thought the German was struggling with a word. She was about to explain it when Lange spoke up. "Have you tried Interpol's database? We have anti-hinky software." He either knew it or figured out the word in record time. "Hold on a second." The elevator door opened a few floors short of the lobby. Abby's FBI badge held in the face of those trying to enter was enough to convince them to wait for the next one. "Go ahead."

The detective did not sound assured. "That's the thing that really bugs me, Lange. It appears that your databases have next to nothing on him either. How is that possible? I thought you were the masters of all information about everyone. Hell, I thought you knew what I had for breakfast."

If Jonas was surprised he was too professional to let it show. "You had waffles." Pulling the phone out of its home in his breast coat pocket, he began to text. "Let me have someone look into Edos. Thanks, Roger. You're the man!" Abby could sense a slight tension in Jonas voice not usually present. As he tried to jest and reassure Walker, he was trying to reassure himself.

"I'm earning my keep," said a slightly more upbeat Roger. The praise from Jonas had helped. "You two watch your backs. I have a bad feeling about this for some reason. Don't trust him."

"No problem, Roger. I'll watch her back and front," joked the man from Interpol as he stepped out into the lobby.

There was a pause on the other end of the phone. Finally Roger said, "Hmm, I think I underestimated you, Jonas. A day earlier than I guessed. Not bad." The words were followed by the click of the call ending. Abby stared at the phone for a moment and then looked into the smirking face of Jonas.

"Shut up!" she snapped and glanced at the elevator, trying to decide whether to go up or not.

Jonas looked at his phone. "Rikka and Marcus are checking into Edos. I'd like to have something before we walk in."

"True but..." began Abby, stopping as the elevator door opened.

Standing in the lift was a man who looked completely average. Average height. Average build. Average looks. He was neither handsome nor ugly. He had medium brown hair with no gray and only a scant few lines on his face, making him somewhere between late twenties and late forties. His only distinguishing feature were the two hazel eyes that shone with a glow that implied a hidden knowledge. "Agents Chilton and Lange? I am Ian Edos. I believe you missed my floor."

The Observer was sitting at his computer pretending to be spending time fixing the holes in the security system he'd repaired an hour ago. Positioning himself so that no one could see his screen, he was looking at his newest prey. She was quite lovely in a girl next door kind of way. Not that being a beauty or as ugly as Quasimodo meant anything to the Observer. They were all nothing more than prey to him. *Well, maybe Abby is something more than prey.*

He looked up from his screen when that thought crossed his mind. What was wrong with him? He was supposed to be profiling this woman who would help him satisfy his desire to see the life drain from the eyes of another living being. Why was he was thinking about an FBI agent who could be more dangerous than anyone he had encountered?

*Focus!* He would not allow Abby to become his downfall. He would be her downfall! But for now it was time to look into Miss Andrea and find the most satisfying way to end her life. Sorting through his files he saw the perfect way to take her out and it would both sate his thirst for death and be a fun challenge. *Now what kind of car does she drive these days?*

Abby went into her normal profiler mode as she spoke. "Mr. Edos," said Abby offering her hand as the agents stepped into the elevator. Edos shook it with a firm handshake that betrayed a strength that was well hidden behind a button up shirt that was best described as an elegant casual with a green and blue pattern that complemented his disquieting eyes. "Thank you for coming down but that was unnecessary. I had to take a call."

Jonas offered his hand as well. As the two men clasped hands, Abby could almost see the battle of wills happening right in front of her. Though the men only allowed their hands to raise and lower three times, no one in the confined space was fooled into thinking it was merely a greeting. The palpable tension in the eyes of both men filled the small area as two predators sized up one another.

"It is a pleasure to meet you both," said Edos, breaking the tension. "I have read so much about you. I am pleased to see you back in the field, Agent Chilton. It was a waste of your talents being behind a desk.

"I never thought I'd get to meet you in Knoxville, Agent Lange. I really have to say that your work in Milan with the stolen Pissarro was brilliant. May I ask how you found Tremalo? What I have been able to find did not give the details other than you were the one who helped Polizia di Stato make the arrest."

Both agents were in a quandary. This was a man who clearly knew more about them than they knew about him. Abby was able to discern much using her gifts. He was highly intelligent and had no qualms about showing it. He was accustomed to being in control of situations. That was apparent when he took the initiative to come down and meet them in the lobby. The demonstration of his knowledge of them was simply a way of showing off. Edos did not allow her to address the issue of how he knew that she had been out of the field, he liked to keep people on the defensive. Asking Jonas about a specific case he had worked, was an attempt to keep the Interpol agent off his game. *This guy is good, in an evil kind of way.*

Abby had noticed the cameras and wondered how many were hidden in and around the tower. Edos would likely have access to all the security feeds in the building, allowing him to see them coming up and returning back down. *He probably gets a deal on the rent for providing the snooping system.*

A powerful personality was key to his control of a security firm in such a competitive field. He did not have the same subtle sexuality of Jonas; but there was something that would appeal to a woman. There was a confidence in Ian Edos that made him more attractive than physical beauty. Or was there something else? Abby looked at him more carefully and saw that he had a practiced way of holding his face that was slightly awkward. *Was he holding some kind of disguise in place?* She had long ago learned how to look in drastic detail, seeing things in an instant that made long looks unnecessary. He was wearing some makeup that was hiding some of his features. Abby was convinced that there was much more to this man than he wanted others to see.

While Abby was analyzing the computer security consultant, Jonas was prying in his own way. "That was a fun case. I found him through hard work, doggedly pursuing the mysterious clues, and bribing an informant with more cash than he deserved. May I ask you a question now?"

As the elevator doors opened, Edos smiled a too white smile. "Of course, Agent Lange. I presumed that was why you came to see me. We have a mutual friend in Signore Fumagalli who spoke very highly of your talents in that case. My firm did a little work for his company following the theft of that painting back in 2006." Ian had answered the question before it was asked. Leading the way down the hall and into the office suite of *Cryptos* he held the door for Abby and said, "One of my associates was in Corpus Christi when you were shot. I hope your wounds have all healed." The man was frighteningly well informed.

Abby was a little annoyed that he knew as much as he did but would cut off her own arm before she allowed him the satisfaction of knowing that. "I have. Thank you." She walked into the conference room and took a seat at the head of the table. "Now if you don't mind I need to know about one of your employees."

The white, knowing smile creased Edos' face once more. "Of course." Raising his voice, he called, "Rachel." A middle aged, mocha-skinned woman entered the room carrying a tray with three drinks and three folders. She sat a diet Dr Pepper in front of Edos, a Red Thunder by Jonas and a cup of something that smell like a special brew of coffee by Abby. Three folders were placed by each of the drink recipients.

Abby smiled to herself as she added to the profile of Ian Edos. He made sure he knew what they liked to drink and didn't even ask if they wanted something. That was an attempt to ingratiate himself to them with the refreshments, even though he knew they were unlikely to drink anything. Abby took a long drink from her coffee. It was perfect. Ian Edos nodded to her. Jonas glowered from the drink to the man across the table. The host smiled again as he took a sip of his soda. Abby could almost feel Jonas' dislike of the man even though he showed no overt signs. She suspected that Edos knew it, too, and liked it.

"I took the liberty of making a dossier of Jacob Rains." He looked at Jonas and asked, "Unless it is someone else you wanted to ask about." Two alpha males in a confined space trying to show dominance was always interesting to the profiler. The testosterone was so thick in the room that Abby was wondering if it would make her boobs shrink.

Jonas smiled the smile of a predator. "No. Jacob Rains would be fine. Unless you have yours handy."

Ian laughed first. "Sorry. I don't have my CV available. But I'm sure Rikka and Marcus are digging up all kinds of interesting dead ends about me right now." He looked at Abby, making her both ill at ease and slightly aroused. Ian asked, "Do you mind if I ask why you're interested in Jacob? Does this have anything to do with his resignation?" His face had changed slightly. He was not quite as average looking now. Somehow he was relaxing his facial muscles and creating a fuller look to his cheekbones. The touch of his foot under the table told her that Jonas noticed the change in appearance as well.

"He resigned?" asked Abby, opening the folder. "When did that happen?" There was a picture of the man that they knew to be the one they were hunting. It was obviously taken from some kind of hidden camera in that very room. It showed him smiling with his mouth open in a laugh.

"He gave a two week notice about five days ago. It's a shame. He was really quite talented at breaking into computer systems. He was about our third best wracker." There was a little bit of pride in his voice which told Abby he considered himself one of the two who was better than Rains. "He proved to several of our clients that they needed our services."

The FBI agent knew that Jonas was wondering the same thing she was but would never ask. She came to the rescue. "Mr. Edos, may I call you Ian?" Without waiting for a confirmation, Abby continued. "Ian, you have to forgive me. What is a wracker?"

Ian chuckled. "Sorry, Abby." He used her first name without asking. "It is what we call our technicians here. It is short for 'white hat cracker'. We do the same thing as those to crack into computer systems, but do it to help them instead of causing harm." His eyes sparkled in a way that made Abby wonder if that was totally true. She was certain there was a dark side to the man across from her.

Jonas broke into the conversation. "So, Ian, what can you tell us about Jacob Rains?" The German smiled at the slight twitch in Edos' eyebrow when his first name was used.

"Well, for starters, that is not his real name." Ian was looking to them for surprise and showed his first sign of disappointment when they did not react. Abby saw that he realized they already had those details. Edos continued without losing his confidence, "Jacob Rains has no real computer skills. The man who used his name was hiding his real identity behind a man who disappeared seven years ago. The man who claimed to be Rains looked close enough to the real man to fool people who didn't look carefully."

Jonas put aside his dislike of the computer guru and asked, "How did you know that he wasn't Rains?"

Edos smiled his biggest smile yet. "Information is my business, Jonas." He made the name "Jonas" sound like an insult. "Did you think I would let someone work for me without knowing every detail about him? He slept on the left side of his bed. Favorite food was canned ravioli. He did not date anyone of either sex. He helped his next door neighbor with her trash cans. His cholesterol was a little high at his last physical." The man paused as if trying to remember some detail he had forgotten. It didn't fool either agent. Edos snapped his fingers, rose to his feet and said, "Oh yes. And his real name is Darren Dalton Smythe."

# Chapter Twenty-Two

"What do you mean you know his name? Are you sure? How the hell do you find that? Are you really sure?" Tina's questions were coming faster than Abby or Jonas could answer.

Jonas held up a hand. "Breathe, Tina. If our good buddy at *Cryptos* is right, then yes we have his name. I don't trust him. He's a bit of a self-important, over-confident prick."

Marcus smiled. "Takes one to know one, I suppose."

Jonas gave him a dirty look but a smile quickly snuck onto his face. "Touché. Anyway, let's find out what we can about Darrell Dalton Smythe."

Abby laughed out loud as she noticed something. "No wonder he's a serial killer. With initials like DDS he would be into inflicting pain."

Hitting a few buttons on his ever-present tablet, Marcus stated, "I've started a search for this shit-head. Shall we see if our favorite psycho's online? I want to see you play this bastard, Abby." Booting up the computer, Marcus had the chat room open in no time.

Abby took over the computer and typed one phrase in response to the previous question from the Observer.


While his mind debated the pros and cons of profiling Abby, the Observer's hands seemed to have a plan of their own as they explored the internet and discovered that he had a message.

{How sweet of you to ask but I really didn't know you were gone, Darrell} were the words waiting from Abby. He was not surprised. He knew that if she were truly worthy she would eventually find that name. Now let the games begin for real!

Two computer screens separated by national borders showed the same information. Two profilers stared at screens as if they could look through the internet and see one another. Both had the same thought at the same time. *I wonder if we could Skype.* The Observer immediately dismissed the thought.

Humming the tune to "Go Insane" by Lindsey Buckingham, the Observer typed, {I guess I'm not as memorable as I had hoped.}

Abby's pulse raced as the words appeared on her screen. Her phone rang as she prepared to chat with her nemesis. It was Paolo Ariziz. She put him on speaker. "Paolo, good to hear from you. How is the exam going?"

The rich, deep voice of the pathologist sounded good even on the speakerphone. "Hello Abby. The margaritas will be on you when you hear what I have discovered."

Tina and Marcus stared at Abby. Tiny mouthed, *"How many men have you been hiding?"* Abby rolled her eyes at them.

"Let me hazard a guess. The man who you have on your slab is Jacob Rains but he's been dead for at least eight years." Abby looked at Jonas who had a smile on his face that was a mixture of satisfaction and amusement. Abby totally understood why Lange enjoyed doing things like that.

The momentary silence from the other end of the line was followed by the voice of Ariziz saying, "I guess I'm buying after all. But you have to drink doubles. How did you know? I got the tests back that confirmed the presence of crystallization of the necrotic tissues that indicate this body has been frozen for quite some time. Possibly as long as ten years, but eight seems feasible."

"Well there are several factors. The most obvious is that I'm online chatting with the man we thought was in the house." Abby said it in such a casual way that Paolo was again, silent.

"You have a very strange life, Abby. I'll e-mail you my report this afternoon. I want to run a few more tests." Then, pausing to think, the pathologist asked, "What should be done with the remains when I'm finished?"

Abby considered that. "I'll get someone to track down his family and see what they want." She nodded to Marcus who pulled out his tablet and began a search. "Thanks so much for helping. Send the bill to my attention."

"Bill? What happened to the margaritas and sopapillas? You know you find me irresistible in a grumpy old man kind of way," jested the physician.

Abby flirted back. "Okay but I'm not a cheap date. I expect top shelf tequila and high end honey."

"Deal!" declared the doc and clicked off.

"Honey?" asked Tina with a raised eyebrow that questioned the use of honey and the salacious opportunities.

Abby sighed. "Haven't you ever had sopapillas?"

Tina was not letting it go. "No, but I'll look for them when I'm at my favorite toy store." Abby shook her head.

{Are you still there?} asked the Observer.

Abby typed, {Sorry. I had a phone call. I am so sorry about your house, Darrell.}

On the other side of the screen the Observer smiled and typed, {I will miss it but it was time. When did you realize it wasn't me in there?}

Abby decided to play along. {It never crossed our minds that it was you. Life is never that easy.} She intentionally used the word "our" to see if it would get a reaction. It did.

{Well I thought it might fool Jonas. I never really thought it would get past you though.}

Abby looked up at Jonas who was standing like a parent over her shoulder. He smiled the kind of smile that made her wonder what he would do if he ever caught up with this psychopath. She was pretty sure she didn't want to know.

{None of us thought it was you.} Abby wanted him to think there was a whole team assembled to try and rattle him. Based on her profile she didn't believe that he would rattle easily but wanted to test her theory.

The Observer decided to test a theory of his own. {None of you? Not even Tina? I didn't think she was that much of a creative thinker being a glorified accountant. At least Marcus thought I was dead, didn't he?}

A pin could have dropped in the room and sounded like a crash of thunder. Abby reached up and covered the built in webcam suspecting he was watching them through it. Looking at each of the others in the room, she was actually afraid for them.

Marcus' voice returned to him first. His tech side took charge of his tongue. "He can't see us. I disconnected the cam to be extra safe from this whack-job." He reached over and moved Abby's hand and waved his in front of the cam. "Not physically connected." He looked at Abby and Jonas and said the one word that conveyed what all wanted to know. "How?"

In a voice that was barely a whisper, Tina stammered, "He knows m-m-my n-name."

Abby's fingers danced across the keyboard. {Who are you talking about?}

Jonas looked around him. "I did not see this coming. I'm sorry." He began putting together the scenario where the Observer would be able to get this information. The proverbial light bulb went off over his head. The tracker! It wouldn't have been hard to put them on all the vehicles at Abby's dinner party. "He is scary smart."

The Observer smiled at her pathetic attempt. {Now Abigail, if we are going to have a conversation we must really try to be honest with one another. Insulting my intelligence is far beneath you. Let me guess. They are all right there with you as you type. Hi there boys and girl.} His cockiness was annoying to all present. Tina's face was three shades lighter than usual. Marcus had a visible tremor in his hand. Jonas looked as if he were made of stone; but Abby was certain that it would not take much to cause the dormant volcano of his rage to explode in a rain of destruction. She didn't want to be there when that happened.

Trying to reassure her friends she said, "Watch this." She typed, {My apologies. I know you are as intelligent as you are narcissistic. I should not have tried to lie to you. So what shall we discuss?}

{Let me guess. It was Edos who figured out my name. Tell Marcus not to worry about the search. He won't find anything.} There was a cockiness in his typing that bothered Abby.

{Would you like to know your profile?} Abby typed. She wanted inside his head in the worst way.

{Or are you worried that I know you better than the parent who continually beat you down?} she continued.

{Was it physical or emotional or both?} she asked.

Abby sent the lines in rapid fire succession trying to put him on the defensive. She was trying get under his skin as much as he had gotten under theirs. It worked.

The Observer stared at the words Abby had thrown at him. It was astonishing that she already knew him better than anyone else.

*So she guessed about Dad. Good job.* A multitude of possibilities crossed his manipulative mind, he decided to find out more. How good was she? {Interesting theory. What else have you profiled, Abby. Tell me about myself.}

In her office, Abby began to type but was stopped by the tender touch of Jonas' hand over hers. Looking deep into her eyes he said, "Be careful what you give him. He can learn about you as fast as you can learn about him. Trust me." The last words sounded like a prayer to her, the walls behind his eyes coming down as he showed her the pain he kept hidden.

"Trust me. I can own a corner of his mind. It will be my summer home," smiled Abby.

Jonas looked sad. "You don't want to live there." With those words he lifted his hand and silently acquiesced to what she wanted.

Abby thought about her next interaction and typed, {And what do I get out of the deal? You did not confirm or deny anything with that reply.}

The Observer had been prepared for this ploy to get more information. {I'll tell you what I have surmised about you. You have experienced loss unlike two of your colleagues. The death of your partner, the loss of your unborn child, and the loss of any chance to ever be a mother were enough to push most over the edge. You bounced back from that. You have some impressive willpower, Abby.}

Too late, Abby slammed the cover of the laptop closed. Jonas, Tina and Marcus had seen the words on the screen. Abby rose from her desk and walked unsteadily out of her office alone.


The Observer laughed as he typed, {Abby? Did I say something wrong?}

He had won the first round. The hits that she had landed were impressive but he may have scored a knockout. He hoped not. It was finally starting to get fun playing someone who was nearly his equal. She was really good. *I wonder what else she knows about me.*

He left the law offices feeling sated. After a very good day at work, it was time to have some fun. He walked two blocks to the nearest subway station. Paying cash for his ticket, he boarded the first train that arrived. From his pocket he pulled a ten-sided die and cast it to see where he would be exiting. As luck would have it, he found himself getting off at the King Subway Station right in the middle of the PATH – the famous Toronto underground shopping area. It was the perfect place to watch for new targets.

The Observer began wandering through the maze of shops and restaurants looking for a place to sit and watch the life around him. Which one of those lives would he pick to end? He was really starting to like this town. The die was cast and he chose the third bench he came to. Positioning himself at an angle that allowed for the best view, he rolled the ten-sided die four times. The numbers added up to twenty-two. The twenty-second person he saw would be added to his list of future victims.

Casually looking at all the people passing by, he counted each person he saw. It wasn't until the thirteenth person that he lost focus. It was impossible that fate could play this kind of game, yet it was happening before his very eyes. All his doubts about an early stalk of Andrea were whisked away as she walked past him, begging to be killed. An unbidden smile crossed his face as he rose up and began to follow the woman who was soon to die.

Without knowing, as he walked through the Toronto underground the Observer was caught on a total of eighteen cameras that were being monitored by Interpol's IFTAS. Across the ocean, Rikka received a ping from her computer. Smiling a vicious grin, she reached for her phone.


Jonas had tried to follow Abby out of her office but had been stopped by the hand of the tiny Tina. "I think she needs some time, Jonas." He considered ignoring her unwanted and unsolicited advice. The look in her eyes was pleading yet defiant. Lange knew she would fight him on this. After briefly considering picking her up and setting her aside, he decided against it. He relaxed and she lowered her arm.

The three who had been left behind sat down in silence. The Interpol agent asked, "Did either of you know about that?"

Tina was the first to respond. "No. To be honest, we don't know much about Abby before she got here. She is pretty tight lipped about her past. How did that prick find out? How did he know any of the shit he knows?"

The German answered, "He's as good at finding information and using it to manipulate and destroy people. He and Abby are opposite sides of the same coin. His computer skills are probably as good as Marcus'."

Marcus shrugged. "In some ways he's better. Well, 'better' might not be the right word. Evil? Yeah, evil works. Definitely not a white hat."

"Are we safe?" asked Tina timidly.

Jonas looked from one to the other and opted for honesty, "No, we aren't."

Abby had hoped that no one would follow her. That revelation had caught her totally off guard. *How the hell had that son of a bitch found out?* Being angry, stunned and hurt, she had no clue if anyone else was in the hallway. A nearby balcony was used by the smokers who would sneak out there for an illegal smoke on federal property was the first place she found. It was an unwritten rule that no one looked out there when the flowerpot was blocking the door. If you didn't see it, you didn't have to report it. The flowerpot was absent.

Abby stumbled through the door and looked around, relieved no one was out there. With the flower pot blocking the door, she sat down and took a deep breath. She could smell the aroma of the thick air of the Tennessee Valley mixed with the pungent smell of cigarette ash left by the many smokers who used the nicotine sanctuary. She didn't even care.

The violation she felt was indescribable. It was as if he had broken into her home, gone through her most secret possessions, and left them in the lobby of the FBI offices for all to see. Jonas would know the reasons behind the scars he had so tenderly kissed. Would it change how he felt? Marcus and Tina would know why she had left field work and would worry even more when she was back out there. Worst of all, Abby had not been the one to tell them. They had to find out from a narcissistic sociopath who was targeting her.

Abby sat there silently staring at the city. She wasn't sure how long she had been there when the words escaped her mouth. "Damn you, Jonas. What have you gotten us into?"

"I may have found a way out of this," came the German's voice from the doorway. He held up his phone, saying, "Rikka found him in Toronto."

# Chapter Twenty-Three

The Observer was living up to his name as he calmly stalked his prey. Andrea had no idea there was anyone watching her among the many milling around the underground world of Toronto. She had a spring in her step, lost in her own thoughts. The Observer abandoned his plan involving her car. He was looking for something new. A challenge to his ordered world would be nice. Always planning everything out in detail ad nauseam was getting tedious. If only there was a way to get the rush of seeing the life leave her eyes right here in front of everyone in the underground without anyone else knowing what he had done.

Four thousand miles away in Lyon, Rikka's hands were flying across her keyboard trying to gain access to the multitude of cameras in the Toronto underground. A map of the PATH was moved to a larger screen that took up most of the wall, red and green dots showing inactive and active cameras. With a few more keystrokes V-shaped fields of vision patterns came from each of those cameras. As each one was assessed, a window appeared next to it with a live feed.

On her smaller screen, a secure video chat window opened with the exotic Ronni looking back. "Ronni, I have found the Observer. He is in Toronto. Sharing screens. I need your help tracking him." The thick French accent she normally used was replaced by a perfect British English accent.

The face of the Chilean lit up with excitement. "Let's see if we can find him." As the sounds of keyboards being beaten into submission filled the ether between the two women, Ronni teased, "You know you really need to work on your Spanish. Sometimes I can't understand your accent in English. It sounds so French," joked Ronni.

Without missing a keystroke, Rikka taunted back, "Or you could learn French. Ze men love ze accent." Looking closer at her screen, Rikka shouted, "Look! Is that him?" There was a man who was the right height and build walking along looking too casual.

Ronni took over control of the cameras as Rikka moved to the large touch screen. She expanded the picture of the man. "That's him," said Ronni. "Beginning tracking."


"He's where?" demanded Abby.

Jonas smiled his most ingratiating and annoying smile. "Toronto. IFTAS was focused there because of where Rikka found him crossing the border. We got lucky thanks to the pic I sent her from Edos. The extra detail was all IFTAS needed to narrow the scan. Plus Rikka is damn good at weeding out the false trails. She's sending a live feed to the conference room if you'd care to join me." He offered his arm as an escort.

Abby flew past him speed-walking down the hall. Jonas was by her side within a few strides of his longer legs. Grabbing his beeping phone he looked at the screen to see Rikka looking back at him. "Still have him?" asked the German.

"Oui. 'E is walking through ze underground shopping mall. Is Abbee with you?" asked the Interpol officer, her accent back in place.

Abby turned the phone in Jonas' hand but did not let go when the camera was on her. "Right here, Rikka. What do you need to get on our screens?" Her hand tightened slightly on Jonas' with the thrill of what was happening.

"Ronni 'as already been in touch with Marcus. It is ready when you walk in. I wanted to make certain you were with 'im when 'e sees zis man." Rikka was being a good mother for her protégé.

Abby and Jonas blew into the conference room at a jog, startling both Marcus and Tina. The three screens were filled and active. One had a split screen with Ronni and Rikka staring intently at them. One had a map of the PATH in Toronto with the various cameras mapped out while a purple dot moved from one field of vision to the next. The third screen showed a changing live feed of the camera closest to their target. Seeing him live was a rush to all of them.

There were heads peeking in the door to see what had caused both Abby and Jonas to run past the cubicles. To no one in particular Abby barked, "Get Mathis!" Sherry, the secretary who had been enamored with Jonas that first day, shot toward the office of the Special Agent In Charge. "Do you need something?" asked the profiler to others peeking in the door, causing them to rapidly disperse.

Michaelson appeared in the doorway. "Is something happening?" asked the young agent with obvious enthusiasm.

Jonas looked up from the screen. "Yes. Sit down and shut up." Turning to the screen with his Interpol associates, he continued, "Have you contacted the local police?"

"Of course, Yonas," said Rikka, a trace of irritation in her voice. "Zey are trying to get someone to 'im now. I am relaying 'is position to zem, but I do not think zey are going to get zere before 'e is gone." The Observer looked right into one of the cameras and suddenly made a change of course right into a small boutique.

"Did he spot the camera?" asked Abby.

Ronni spoke for the first time. "He may have. That one was moving into position to follow him."


The Observer entered the tiny store that had a heavy scent of potpourri. He smiled at the bored clerk behind the counter and asked, "I'm so sorry to bother you. Do you have a toilet I could use? I drank too many cups of coffee at lunch." He was trying to look both harmless and helpless. That camera may have been turning to look at him. He had a feeling that he was being watched. If he could find another way out of this underground without going back out the door, he wanted to play it safe. *Surely they can't be tracking me. Or can they?*

The young woman glanced up at him and in a very rude, unCanadian way said, "We don't have a public restroom." Then she went back to a very important text.

The Observer approached her with two American twenty dollar bills in his hand. "Are you sure there are no exceptions? I don't like going where so many other people go. It is a germ thing."

The eyes of the clerk locked on to the bills in his hand. Suddenly she became very friendly and accommodating. "Of course, sir. It is right through that door. I can show you if you want."

The Observer considered that for a second. He could easily overpower her and leave her lifeless body in the restroom, but that would leave a trail. There was no guarantee anyone was watching him. Passing his hand over the counter, leaving the twenties he said, "Don't trouble yourself, dear. I can find it." Dropping a third bill he said, "That one is to help you to forget I was here."

"Who was here?" asked the girl, snatching the cash off the counter and returning to her text.

Going in the back and leaving through the service door, the Observer found himself behind the stores. With a quick look around, he was pleased by the absence of cameras. He strolled calmly down to the end of the corridor to the two doors marked with an exit signs. One had a peephole that allowed him to see it led back amongst the people shopping and the cameras snooping. Cracking the other door open, he discovered stairs heading up and out of the underground PATH. Stepping onto the first step he reached into his pocket and dropped a small device that looked like a piece of trash. This device would find a Wi-Fi signal and send a message to his phone telling him when the next people used these stairs and how many there were. It was always best to make sure instead of being paranoid.

Smiling to himself, he took the stairs two at a time and began making his plans to meet up with Andrea later that night. He was not sure if that camera had been looking for him but it was always better to be safe than sorry.


Screens flashed with different images but there was no sign of their target. Rikka's voice broke the silence. "Expand ze search to above ze ground."

Mathis entered the room. "What's happened?" demanded the SAC.

Abby tore her eyes from the screen to Jeremy. "We found him. He's in Toronto. Interpol was tracking him using CCTV in the underground. He may have spotted the cameras because he ducked into that store." Abby pointed to the one window that stayed steady as others all around it constantly changed.

"Where are the locals?" ask the ever-thinking Jeremy.

Jonas took that question. "We were hoping they could get there before he disappeared. I decided to keep the mall cops out of the loop. I don't think a Segway would be too intimidating and could get the guy killed." Looking at the screen he said, "They are entering the store now. Rikka, do you have their radios?"

"Sending zem to your screens now." replied the efficient Frenchwoman. Through the connection they heard her ask, "What is your status, officer?"

The speakers crackled as a signal was sent from Toronto to Lyon to Knoxville. "There was a man who was supposedly using the washroom who did not come out. We're continuing through the axillary corridor."

"Damn," whispered Abby.

The speaker crackled again, "Looks like he took the backstairs up and out. Sorry, but if he's on the street there is little chance of finding him unless there is a kerfuffle." There was silence in the room.

"Keep IFTAS scanning every cam in Toronto," ordered Jonas. "Give the city a level five. Raise all transport hubs to a six and keep all nearby border crossings back into the U.S. at a five until we spot him somewhere else. Rikka, I need the plane at McGee-Tyson in an hour." A nod from his mentor told Jonas all he needed as the screens went black.

"What does this mean?" asked Tina. "Is he going to be coming back here or is he gone for good?" She was still shaken up that he knew about her.

All eyes turned to Jonas for an answer. "I'd say he's gone, unless we draw him back for some reason. He's a survivor who tried to live in the shadows. But I'm not the profiler."

As if linked, heads turned to Abby. "Do you really want to do this now?" asked the FBI agent. Seeing that no one was looking away, she walked over to a monitor and pulled up a file from her computer. "The Observer. We believe his real name is Darrell Dalton Smythe. He is a sociopath so he does know the difference between right and wrong, he simply doesn't care. He kills people for pleasure and a need to fulfill some part within him that is dead. Since he did not react to my taunt about his father, I'd say there is a high probability that he was abused by that father from infancy to the point that the part of him that knows right from wrong was subjugated as a means of survival. It would not surprise me to discover that his father is one of his victims. The maternal figure in his life was either absent or did nothing to protect him.

"I do believe that he has killed over two hundred times. No one knew he existed until he got bored and began toying with Kristin McAdams of MI5. As careful as he is, there are signs that he is beginning to slowly devolve in spite of years of careful work. He is highly organized, making him very skilled at avoiding detection. For some reason, he has begun taking more chances recently.

"He is intelligent and skilled with both computers and psychology. His work for *Cryptos* shows his computer skills are on a level beyond even some of the most skilled hackers in the world. He uses those skills to find information about his targets so that he can kill them without taking too many chances. In his own way, he's a brilliant profiler who uses what he discovers on the computer to manipulate and mentally subdue an opponent as he did to Kristin and tried to do to Jonas. He will now be focused on trying to break me since he believes he has already created a breaking point for Jonas. As most of you now know, I have already had a defining moment – don't ask, Rupert – so he is in unknown territory with me."

It was Mathis who asked the question of the hour. "How much danger are you in?"

"I honestly don't know, Jeremy." Abby had a look that was too intense to stare at but was also impossible not to watch. "But I think Agent Lange is the one who is in the most danger. Smythe is tired of playing with Jonas so he may be ready to kill him. If it also plays into hurting me, he will definitely kill anyone to break me down." Looking at the German, she said, "I'm sorry, Jonas, but I have no doubt he's going to try to kill you."

# Chapter Twenty-Four

The Observer found a small bistro on Queen Street where he hoped he would be safe from the prying cameras all around Toronto. He was taking a sip of a cup of coffee when his phone beeped. The device he had left on the stairs had discovered that two people had entered the stairwell; but had not left by the same door he had. It was hard to say for certain; but it appeared that they had gone up, looked out the door, and gone back the way they had come. That was enough to convince him that he had been noticed.

*Damn, they are getting better. Ian must have given them a good picture of me. Time to go with a new look.* As he watched through the window of the cafe, he pretended to be reading a book on his tablet. After an hour, four cups of coffee, a croissant sandwich and a trip to the bathroom, the Observer decided it was safe to leave.

Once on the street, he found a small, hole-in-the-wall clothing store that was trying to be trendy. Entering, he smiled at the cashier and went straight to the section he wanted. He purchased several new brightly colored shirts, two new pairs of slacks that would look acceptable with the shirts, and a new light tan fedora. Being courteous but not so friendly as to be memorable, the Observer paid cash. He put on the fedora and took the rest of his purchases to head back onto Queen Street. Flagging down a cab, he climbed in while keeping his head down to avoid any attention and headed back to his hotel.

It took Abby and Jonas longer to extricate themselves from the FBI field office than it took to drive to the airport. Somehow, Jonas had talked Mathis into loaning Rupert to him to drive his BMW to Toronto so they would have it with all its gizmos in case they needed any of them. Rupert had looked like a kid who had been told he could have anything he wanted from the candy store when Jonas had handed him the keys and a credit card for gas and food.

"It has diplomatic plates so feel free to take advantage of that. I need it in Toronto as fast as you can." Thinking for a moment of all the spy movies the young agent had seen, Lange added, "And don't push any of the secret buttons. I don't want to hear my car died because you ejected yourself out the sunroof." The young man looked at the departing backs of the agents, wondering if the German was serious.

Both Tina and Marcus wanted to take them to the airport but Mathis had put his foot down, insisting the computer tech stay and work with the Chilean computer guru on tracking the movements of Smythe. Abby always had her go-bag ready and Jonas was always prepared to move at moment's notice.

When she dropped them at the hanger, Tina looked worried. "Are you two going to be all right? I'm worried that this sicko is still ahead of us and has a trap for you two. You sure you don't need an accountant to watch your backs?" Abby knew the offer was sincere, but also knew that Tina did not want to be in the same country as the Observer.

"If Jonas and the Mounties can't keep me safe, I'll call you. Bring a heavy calculator so you can brain him with it." The joke eased the tension enough for the two to embrace without shedding any tears.

Tina looked at Jonas who was carrying Abby's one bag and his two bags. "Keep her safe Lange or I'll slash your credit rating," she laughed. "Why do you have two bags and she only has one? I thought women were the pack rats on trips."

Jonas finally spoke. "It takes a lot of work to look this good. And I like my toys."

Tina raised an eyebrow. "Really?" Turning to Abby, she said, "I expect details." Without waiting for another word, she got in the FBI sedan and drove away. As the two agents walked up to the Gulfstream G450, Lange greeted the pilot.

"We ready Willis?" asked the man from Interpol.

The response was not what Abby had expected. "We are, Lange. Aren't ye gonna introduce me?" The Scottish accent was distinctive even to her untrained American ear. Her profiler instincts kicked in as she gave the pilot the once over. The man appeared to be in his forties or fifties. It was hard to tell since the smile lines made him look older than he was. He had the typical pilot's cockiness and swagger, plus something else. It was the broad smile as he looked at Abby. He had the physique of a fighter pilot but a casual air that contrasted the swagger. There was something in his eyes that spoke volumes more than the blue of his irises could say. This man had been through hell and had not lost his soul. He was more than he appeared. Much more.

The body language of both men told her that Willis was more than merely an acquaintance. The handshake was two fisted and lasted longer than most. They shared an unspoken communication with nothing more than their eyes. These men were friends. Jonas had a genuine smile when he turned to introduce her.

"Abby Chilton, meet Andy Willis. Andy, meet Abby." Willis took Abby's hand and pressed his lips to it in a gentlemanly kiss. "Andy is the best pilot I know. He helps me out from time to time. Don't let the gentleman act fool you. He's a player."

There was a look that could have been shock if it weren't for the fact that he couldn't maintain it and began laughing. "Better a player than a dick like Jonas."

*Yes. Definitely friends. Associates do not insult each other like that.*

"We're ready to go as soon as you get your arses in the plane," jested the pilot, walking around the Gulfstream for one final check.

Jonas and Abby took their seats in the comfort of a small corporate jet waiting for clearance to take off from Knoxville air traffic control. Abby was accustomed to flying, usually on commercial airlines. She had been in private jets before for agency business, but this was a little different. Jonas had managed to have a private jet at the airport, fueled and ready to go within an hour of his phone call to Rikka. She hated to admit it but she was a little bit awed. That pissed her off a little. *How could this one man have this kind of effect on me?*

As if he were reading her mind, Jonas smiled his most self-satisfied, knowing smile and asked, "So how much does the jet impress you?" Being a skilled interrogator, Abby could lie with the best of them. She was about to make some comment about it being an extension of his masculinity when Willis' voice came over the intercom.

"We're cleared for departure. Priority flight plan to Toronto. Flying time should be an hour and twenty minutes." The click told them he had released the talk button on the intercom only to hear it click back on. "She is impressed, Lange. I believe I've seen that look before...about a hundred times," laughed the Scotsman and the intercom clicked off again.

Abby punched the intercom. "I was starting to like you until now, Willis." Even without the intercom, they heard raucous laughter from the cockpit. "I'm not that impressed, Jonas. But this is a handy toy. What makes you so special?"

Jonas shrugged. "I was in the right place at the right time with the right credentials, I suppose." He was trying to make light of the situation which naturally made her more suspicious. Abby was not going to let him off the hook so easy. She was about to challenge him when he abruptly leaned over and kissed her hard on her mouth, his tongue tickling and exploring sending her mind spinning.

When he pulled away Abby caught her breath, looked him dead in the eyes and said, "If you think that will distract me, you're right." She grabbed his head and kissed him even more passionately as they felt the pull of the plane speeding down the runway. They didn't discuss anything for the rest of the all too short flight.


While Abby and Jonas were flying high and joining the mile high club, the Observer was preparing for a flight of his own. After entering the hotel through a service entrance, he made it up to his room with no one noticing him. Once there, he opened his bag and began his metamorphosis. The medium length brown hair disappeared as he stood naked in the closed shower with a cordless trimmer. The number three guard ensured he would have very little hair left when he was done. Once the hair was scattered around his feet, he gathered up most of it and placed it in a sealed plastic bag. The remaining hair was washed away as he took a shower to remove the traces.

What remained on his head was barely more than stubble but it was a brown similar to the color that the rest of his hair had been. With a few sprays of a bottle from his bag and the blowing of the hair dryer, it lightened several shades within thirty minutes. A few more items from his bag gave him fuller cheeks, blue eyes, and a pair of trendy glasses that made him look intelligent. The difference an hour made would have impressed the most fastidious makeup artist in Hollywood. Adding in the new flamboyant shirts, he would draw attention to himself in any of the CCTV cameras around Toronto. Hiding in plain sight was the plan for the day.

Calling down to the office, he explained that he needed peace to work so he would like to hold off on the room being cleaned for three days. He would be staying until the end of the week. After that, the bed was turned down and made to look as if someone had slept there. Leaving everything but his new purchases and his electronics, he walked out of the hotel through the front door and into the light of a Toronto afternoon.


"That was the best flight I've ever had," said Abby, as the wheels touched the tarmac at Toronto Pearson International Airport. They were both refreshed from the recreational activities a private jet offers. "Do you think Willis knows what was happening back here?" asked the slightly embarrassed profiler.

Jonas grinned. "I doubt it. But, he may have been watching us through the peephole." He enjoyed watching the profiler's face turn red. "I guess it's time to get back to work. My liaison with the RCMP should be here to meet us."

As the plane taxied to a hanger with the emblem of the Royal Canadian Mounted Police emblazoned on the side, Abby saw a white SUV of the Mounties standing there with a suited man scowling at the plane. "There he is," said Lange over her shoulder. "He looks like he's in a better mood than usual when he sees me."

"That's a good mood? What does a bad mood look like?" asked the FBI agent, halfway serious.

With a wink Jonas replied, "His pistol would be pointed at me. Again."

As Willis lowered the stairs, Abby led the way. "You really have a way with people. I totally understand why he would want to shoot you."

Walking up to the Mountie, Lange greeted him. "Hello, Rob. How are things in the great white north?" The hand that Jonas offered was ignored.

"Lange," nodded the Canadian. Walking past the Interpol agent, he greeted Abby. "Ma'am, I'm Inspector Robert Gibson. Royal Canadian Mounted Police. You must be Agent Abigail Chilton of the FBI. A pleasure." He shook her hand in a way that made her think he was being more than chivalrous. He was establishing a male dominance in the presence of Jonas.

Abby was both charmed and alarmed by this man. She turned her skilled gaze on the Mountie. He was a little below average height. Around five foot, eight inches. Neither homely nor handsome, he had dark brown intelligent eyes. The most unexpected aspect of Gibson was that he was black. The Mounties were notorious for not having many minorities in their ranks. Even though there was public progress in this area, that Gibson was an inspector spoke volumes to both his competence and his persistence. The ring on his finger told her he was married. The Mountie held himself with a pride that could be arrogance. There was something indefinable about Gibson that made Abby feel uncomfortable. Perhaps it was his manners. It was more likely that he had a distain for the politics of the situation and had ignored Lange in favor of charming the American FBI agent. Perhaps, it was that he just hated Jonas.

"Inspector, it is a pleasure to meet you as well," bantered Abby. "Thank you for extending the courtesy to me while I'm here."

The Mountie smiled. "If there were more FBI agents who looked like you, I think we would invite more of you to help."

Jonas joined the conversation. "You never know when you'll need a profiler, eh Rob? There are all those grizzlies out there with bad attitudes."

Gibson countered, "Well, we also need help with that doughnut smuggling ring." His eyes never left Abby as he sparred with the German. "But I think we need to get somewhere more official to discuss what is happening with your suspect." Finally looking at Jonas, he said, "After you." He gestured to the waiting SUV as he followed behind Abby and Jonas.

Once in the official vehicle, the inspector was all business. "Lange, we have no evidence this man is still in Toronto. I spoke to your woman in Lyon and she explained as much as she could. I also read a summary of who you think he is from the FBI. Can you give me anything that is not on paper so I can help you find him as quickly as possible?"

Abby was confused by his helpfulness until Jonas spoke. "I think he is the one who may be responsible for some of your missing person's reports that you were tracking last year. If what he says is true, he has a body count to rival Robert Pickton."

Abby knew the name. The Canadian pig farmer killer was well known in the United States. The Observer made Pickton look like an amateur. The last thing the Canadians wanted was a serial killer from America causing jurisdictional issues.

After a painfully long silence, Jonas added, "He is the one who killed Kristin and has his sights set on me and Abby." There was a palpable tension in the vehicle telling Abby that there was a significance to that statement that she did not understand.

Robert momentarily took his eyes off the road to glance at Lange in the back. "Jonas, we will get this bastard. For Kristin." Looking back at the road he added under his breath, "You weren't the only one who loved her."

# Chapter Twenty-Five

The Observer walked along the road without a care in the world. His changed appearance was all he needed to feel hidden among all the pedestrians along the road. The rich aromas that drifted his way from the multitude of coffee bars and cafés would have been intoxicating to anyone else. He played the role of the man who was captured by the allure while his thoughts were focused on the one who would help him with the desires driving him.

As the sun moved closer to the horizon, the Observer moved toward his goal. Sitting quietly on a bench, he pulled out his tablet and looked over all his information on Andrea. The voice that had guided him for years was telling him this was a mistake. There was no reason to kill her right now. It would be best to wait until the video feed could be studied for a few days. What difference would a few days make? *Another kill so soon could lead to an escalation and you have focused so hard over the years to prevent that.*

There was a new voice that contradicted the other. This one said, *It's time to live a little and let go. One kill would not lead to another and another.* It was a chance to blow off some much needed steam. The whole thing with Abby and Jonas trailing him had stressed him out. Watching the life drain from Andrea's eyes would help him calmly move on to Rochester. His new life was waiting there. *One quick kill and you will feel better.*

Thinking of Rochester and all the possibilities made him giddy. It was only a five hour drive to New York City where killing would be easy. A six hour drive to Boston or the DC area would give him other venues for prey. *I wonder how hard it would be to make a politician into a plaything.*

Getting up and heading to the bus stop, the Observer smiled to himself. *Time to kill.*

The conversation on the ride was a confusing combination of familiar and formal. There was a link between the two men that had something to do with Kristin. It was possible that they had been rivals for her affection and Jonas had won over Gibson. With the divorce it was not impossible that the Mountie had been involved with her, too. Her instincts told Abby that was unlikely.

As Abby's mind began to race, Lange interrupted her thoughts. "Before you hurt something, let me tell you. Rob is married to Kristin's sister, Kerri. They were identical twins. That is the connection. Nothing scandalous unless you count that I know what Rob's wife looks like naked since they were absolutely identical."

"Or that I know the same thing," added Gibson. "But I still don't like you, Lange."

Abby was confused. "What is the issue? Divorces happen." Abby wondered what she was missing here. It was Kristin who cheated on Jonas. Why would he blame Jonas?

"Let it go, Agent Chilton. It's none of your business." The chill in the vehicle dropped even further as the icy stare of the Canadian cop was leveled at her. It didn't work. All it accomplished was giving Abby another piece of the puzzle that was Robert Gibson. Like most cops, he was not above using intimidation. He was either confident enough – or dumb enough – to try it on an FBI agent. Not a smart move.

"Oh shit," said Jonas, knowing what was coming. "Bad move, Rob."

Abby took control of the conversation. "Inspector Gibson," she began, using his title since he had used hers, "You are working with Jonas and me to find a man who could be one of the most prolific serial killers of our time. If there is a tension between the two of you that could have any effect on this working relationship, I will make it my business. We may be putting our lives in each other's hands and I need to know that I can trust the two of you testosterone-filled, alpha dogs to have all of our backs so that I don't have to carry your asses." Her voice never rose in tone or timbre.

She took a deep breath and continued. "I am a trained forensic psychologist and I am the reason you know as much as you do about that fucker. But I'd rather face him alone than with two people who may choose to shoot each other instead of this killer. So I will ask you again," Abby changed her tone to one of false calm and sweetness. "What the hell is the problem?"

Jonas was sitting back smirking which did nothing to calm the rage within Abby. She had to admit to being impressed by Gibson's lack of intimidation at her outburst. He pulled over and stared at her for a good thirty seconds that felt like thirty hours to everyone in the SUV.

Jonas broke the silence. "If you don't tell her, I will." The smirk was still on his face but the steeliness in his green eyes would have made the most hardened criminal flinch. The look worked on Mounties, too, because Gibson flinched as well.

"Lange wouldn't give Kristin a second chance," he said plainly, as if that explained everything. Abby waited for elaboration that was not forthcoming. The burning Chilton stare appeared to have no effect on the asbestos infused side of Robert's head.

Since the battle of wills would have taken longer than the trip to the office, Jonas broke the stalemate. "About six months after we separated, two weeks before the divorce would be final, Kristin wanted to reconcile. I refused to even talk to her about it. We signed the papers. Robbie blames me for Kristin burying herself in her work. It was that work that got her killed."

The weight of that sunk in to Abby as she looked hard into the eyes of her lover. Did he blame himself, too? The German had his shields up so she couldn't tell what was going on behind the beautiful green eyes. *Damn his eyes.* They were too distracting. She pulled herself away from Jonas and looked again at the Mountie. "So you blame Jonas for Kristin's death? There has to be more to it than that."

"I hate psychologists," bitched Gibson. After a pregnant pause, he explained. "I know Jonas was hurt by Kristen; but when she tried to make amends, he treated her like garbage. I'm surprised he's even trying to catch this son of a bitch."

The silence in the SUV was painful. Abby was confused. Jonas had told her that he and Kristin had formed a kind of friendship. Robert was saying something totally different. Both sides couldn't be true, but she hadn't detected deception from either man. Something was missing.

"Let it go. Abby," came the voice from behind her. Jonas did not want to pursue this topic. She opened her mouth to ask him why when he spoke again. "Please," was all he said. Looking back at him, the sadness and fear in his eyes was all she needed to see to let it slide. Jonas mouthed the words, "He doesn't know she cheated."

When they arrived at the offices of the RCMP, one of Gibson's subordinates led them to a well-furnished conference room. The rich oak table and the maroon upholstery of the chairs created the atmosphere of a boardroom instead of a room for Mounties to chat. As soon as they were alone, Abby closed the door.

"How can he not know? Why do they think you two got divorced?" demanded Abby. She was confused and shocked by this revelation.

Jonas took a seat and motioned for Abby to do the same. She reluctantly sat across from the man she thought she knew, realizing there much more she didn't even suspect. Jonas looked deeply into her eyes and explained. "I never told them and neither did she. We got divorced, but I left the infidelity out of the paperwork. She knew and I knew. That was enough. Why drag her name through the mud? We told everyone that she let work get in the way. That was true enough."

Abby was stunned. She had seen the hurt in the eyes of the German and wouldn't have blamed him for taking out billboards telling everyone what she had done. But he had done something that very few others would have considered. Even after her death, he let her family hate him for not reconciling when it would be easier to tell the whole truth. *What kind of spy has that kind of soul? Who is Jonas really?*

"It's nice to see you at a loss for words once in a while," said a smiling Jonas. "Don't think I wasn't tempted. But in the end, who would it have hurt more? Kristin or her family? I can let them hate me so they don't have to remember her like that." Jonas anticipated many of her questions. "Abby, her father was a serial philanderer. All three of her siblings hated him for his constant cheating. Knowing that Kristin had done something like her father would be devastating. So, you see, I'm trying to protect them by being the bastard who wouldn't forgive their sister." There was a sad, noble smile on Jonas' face.

"You are amazing," sighed Abby, moving her chair back to stand.

Grinning an impish grin, Lange asked, "Are you still thinking about the flight?"

Before Abby could get up to kiss him, Inspector Gibson entered the room, killing the moment. Without a word, he went to the wall, turned on the large screen, and grabbed a wireless keyboard. He sat down and soon had the screen up with files that showed everything that had been sent about the Observer.

"So, how sure are you that his name really is Smythe?" asked Robert. He was all business once again.

"Two of our people are checking into that," said Abby. Texting Marcus, she said to Robert, "If you don't mind, we can link in with them and video chat." Nodding, Robert slid the keyboard over to Abby. With a few keystrokes she logged into the FBI secure server and found Marcus' smiling face in the chat window. "Hey, Marcus. You are live with Jonas and Inspector Robert Gibson of the Mounties. Behave," she warned.

"I always behave. But not always how you want me to," joked the computer guru. Out of the corner of her eye Abby could see a slight curling of the Inspector's lips. He didn't want to smile, Marcus made that difficult. "While you two have been doing whatever you field types do on long flights, I have been working." The hint of a smile faded on Gibson's face as he looked over at Abby with suspicion in his eyes.

Ignoring the look, Abby asked, "What have you found out for us?"

A new window opened up beside the image of Marcus. "This is the birth certificate for Darrell Dalton Smythe. It makes him a month shy of forty. The only problem is that this," another image popped up, "is the death certificate for Darrell Dalton Smythe from meningitis at the age of five."

"Damn," swore Jonas. "Will we ever find out who this guy really is?"

Robert chimed in. "So much for the infamous computer skills of the FBI."

Marcus had a look on his face Abby knew all too well. He had set them up and was waiting to drop his bombshell. She would let him reply to his critics. It was his show this time.

"Well, gentlemen and lady," began the analyst, "before you disparage the skills of one who can discover your account numbers at the CIBC, Inspector Gibson, you may want to wait to hear the whole story." He paused for effect. "The death certificate is a fake. Knowing how conniving this asshole is I had an agent from the St. Louis field office go and look at the physical records. While speaking to the clerk in Rolla, Missouri, Agent Caldwell discovered that little Darrell recovered and grew up. The clerk, who knew him from Sunday school, couldn't understand why there was a death certificate."

The pride in Marcus voice was obvious. Abby shot a glance at Gibson who was looking impressed in spite of himself. Finally, the Mountie spoke, "So, how sure are we that this is our man?"

"All of that means that it could be him," said Jonas, as he looked at the screen. "Or does my second favorite computer wizard have another trick up his sleeve?"

Abby spoke. "He does. Look how smug he is."

"Smug? I never look smug," defended Marcus. Abby tried for her best pseudo-withering look. "You are confusing smug with showing pride in one's achievements," replied Marcus, giving Abby a dictionary definition of smug. "Anyway, I did some searching online and found a copy of the Rolla High School Year Book and discovered there was no picture of Smythe. But Agent Caldwell did a little digging of her own and found an actual physical copy of the annual. Now, if you will look on your screen at the scanned picture of the Rolla High School annual." A page of an old high school yearbook filled the window next to Marcus' image. He zoomed in to the senior photo of Smythe. "He looks older now but I think we can be confident that our Observer is Darrell Dalton Smythe."

# Chapter Twenty-Six

The Observer made himself comfortable. Breaking into Andrea's home was child's play for his skills. Even though it was early evening, the sun had set an hour ago. Down deep, a small voice inside the killer was telling him to get out of the house. *Something feels wrong.* The louder voice was telling him to be patient. *Follow the new plan.* He went through the house and discovered little had changed since he first profiled Miss Gaston. No new items in the bathroom indicating no new men in her life. The bathroom trash revealed tampon wrappers and applicators which told him that she would not be bringing anyone home tonight for a one night stand.

Wearing a black body suit under his new dark clothing, he was prepared to leave no traces that he had ever been there. Normally, he would wear something to cover his head as well, but this time he wanted to see her reaction to his face. It wasn't like she would be telling anyone anything.

His gloved hands had found what he wanted in the kitchen. Andrea had the bare basics in her kitchen. A butcher knife would be perfect for the fun of the evening. It wasn't up to his normal creative standards, but it would do the job. The thought of her watching his face as her life slipped away was already giving him a high that would only climb when he drove the knife through her heart.

Excitement nearly overcame him when the car pulled into the driveway. The keys made a jingling sound like a melody of malice to the ears of the Observer. He really needed to make a recording of that sound for the times when he couldn't hear it. It was one of the most engaging sounds he ever heard. The deadbolt made a snapping sound and the door opened revealing the silhouetted form of Andrea. Leaving the door open, she walked to the kitchen carrying several bags of food. *That's why she was late.*

"Damn," muttered Andrea as she tried the light switch only to have nothing happen. She set her bags on the table and moved to the far wall of the kitchen to the fuse box. As her hand reached out to check the box, the killer's hand caught hers and – in one swift move – had her on the floor.

The Observer was straddling the struggling woman. Holding the knife to her throat, he calmly said, "Scream and I'll slice your throat." The scream that echoed through the house did not come from Andrea. Startled by the sound, the Observer turned to see another figure in the doorway with the light from the car leaving her face in shadow. Taking advantage of his distraction, Andrea twisted and was able to dislodge the Observer from his position of power on top of her.

"Run!" screamed Andrea to the woman at the door. That was the last thing she ever said as the knife that had been at her throat was driven into her chest by the recovered Observer. He was on his feet and sprinting out the door after the only person who had ever witnessed him at work. He heard the car door slam as the witness rocketed out of the driveway and onto the street. The taillights were disappearing around a corner by the time the Observer got to the road.


Ronni had joined Marcus on a split screen in the Mounties' office. The exotic Chilean was adding her insights into the details of the case. Ten minutes later the screen had another window with Rikka joining them. All three were taking turns sharing information with the fourth window showing the data.

After an hour long briefing, Gibson asked, "So, what you're telling me is that we have a complete psychopath loose in my city doing God-knows-what to God-knows-who. Right?" It wasn't as much a question as a statement of the situation.

"He's a sociopath, but that's about the situation in a nutshell," admitted Abby. She had read the expression on the Mountie's face and knew what he was about to say. She beat him to it. "I'm sorry we can't seem to keep our serial killers in the States. But, like Jonas said, he may have been here before. Rikka, have you found his work trail?"

The data screen changed. "As best we can tell, 'e 'as worked in Toronto, Montreal, Ottawa, and Halifax. Zat only counts 'is Jacob Raines identity. Zere could be countless others zat we have not discovered, yet."

"Halifax? That seems to be small for what he does," pondered Gibson.

Jonas broke into the conversation. "So is Knoxville if you consider population. But he also knows that those smaller cities have fewer resources to investigate missing persons or murders. It's actually clever in a sick, sadistic way."

Rikka chimed in. "'E may 'ave changed 'is appearance. I 'ave not been able to find 'im on ze CCTV around Toronto since ze underground. Zere are too many people for us to sort through. And 'e is very good at changing 'is appearance. Ze computers are working overtime on zis; but if 'e knows we are watching 'e may be avoiding places with too many cameras."

Abby was frustrated. "I want to meet the woman who let him get out the door in the underground. I doubt she knows anything, but it won't hurt for me to run a quick profile on her to double check."

Jonas shared her frustration. "While you're doing that, I want to go to that store and see if I can find anything the locals missed. You never know. One of us might catch a break."

Marcus spoke for those on the screen. "We will keep working from our end and keep you in the loop." The windows on the screen winked out as Abby closed the connections to the FBI and Interpol.

Jonas turned to Robert. "Okay, Robbie, are you going with me or staying with Abby?" He was trying to taunt the Canadian with his unique brand of humor. The look from the Mountie said more than words. "All right. Can you have someone else take me to the PATH?" Jonas' humor was a little different to Abby. He was not as comfortable with Gibson as he wanted everyone to think, but was trying to keep the mood light.

A few minutes later, Lange was gone and Abby and Robert were walking down a long hallway to an interrogation room. "I'm surprised you didn't meet us in interrogation the way you and Jonas get along," said Abby, trying to get more out of Gibson.

A smile creased his face. "I considered it, but since you were with him I thought I'd remind you that Canadians are polite even when dealing with Interpol bureaucrats. On top of that, this is serious and I need to be professional no matter what I think of my ex-brother-in-law."

Abby had a question on her mind that was like an itch that needed to be scratched. She thought for a few paces and asked, "Why did they get divorced? Jonas can be evasive about personal questions."

There was a slight break in his step, but Robert recovered. "He definitely can be. The official reason is that Kristin's work got in the way, but I don't buy that. They both knew what they were getting into. Something else happened that neither one would talk about. I think that something or someone came between them. And not only their jobs. What I don't understand is why Jonas is keeping the secret now. Kris is gone and it won't matter what he did anymore."

"Or what she did," added Abby, immediately regretting her words.

The Mountie didn't merely stumble this time. He stopped in his tracks. The profiler turned back to look at him as she read a sea of emotions on the man's face. He was showing confusion, anger, recognition, back to anger, but soon had a look that could best be described with a question mark.

Guiding her into an open doorway, he closed the door to the empty office. "What do you know?" asked the Canadian. It was more than a question. It was a demand. There was a fire in his eyes that was neither anger nor fear. It was a need to know. Abby discerned these thoughts were new to him. The idea that Kristin may have done something was not a possibility he had ever seriously entertained. Now, he was looking at the picture from a different point-of-view.

"You said it yourself. It's none of my business," replied the psychologist, knowing that would lead him down the road he needed to travel. "Why are you asking me when you should ask Jonas?"

"Goddammit, Chilton! Answer the fucking question! I don't need psycho-babble. Was it Kristin? Did she have an affair?" Abby keep her best neutral counselor look on her face and let the silence build. The ebony face of Gibson was tinged with red as his anger burned. "Why wouldn't he tell me?"

"That is a good question. If Jonas knows something, why would he keep it a secret? It's not like his personal life affects anyone else." Abby was playing the role of guide. She knew this question would make the Inspector answer his own question. "What is it that is part and parcel of Jonas Lange's personality that would make him keep a secret that is non-work related?" She could almost see the light bulb going off over the head of Robert. Maintaining her impassive look, Abby raised an eyebrow to ask an unspoken question.

"That son of a bitch," whispered Gibson. The tough guy image was crumbling as he turned away from Abby. "Dammit," she heard him mutter under his breathe. Abby placed a comforting hand on his shoulder. He reached up and placed his hand on top of hers for a few moments and then removed both hands as he turned to face her. "We have a witness to talk to." Heading toward the door, he opened it for Abby and muttered, "Try not to make her cry, too."


The Observer was on the run – literally. This is how killers got caught. He knew better. The small voice in his head that had been warning him was now screaming insults. *How the hell could you be so stupid? I told you not to do that.* A voice berating him was not what he needed right now so he told it to shut the hell up while he got himself out of this mess. It was time to move on quickly and quietly. He went back into the house and grabbed the bag with everything he needed. This was something that he knew might happen one day so he had prepared for it.

Ten debit cards that had $9,000 each plus the $10,000 in cash he always kept would give him all the resources he needed until he could get to his other bank accounts. He had not planned for escape from Toronto because he had not planned on this misadventure. Steadying himself, he quickly went through his list of possible escape routes and dismissed several. Stealing a car would be easy; but it would easy for the Mounties to track, too. The airport had far too many cameras and someone at Interpol would likely spot him. Trains offered the same problem; plus they could easily be stopped and boarded by all kinds of people that the Observer didn't want to see. There was really only one option for him. He smiled at the simplicity as he found his way to the bus stop, searching for the route that would take him to the harbor.

---

Abby entered the stark interrogation room with Gibson close behind. The young woman was nervously typing on her phone trying to get a signal. She slammed it down in irritation. Being disconnected from her e-world was making her surly.

"Good evening, Melanie. Looks like you have had an eventful day," began the Mountie. "Sorry about the phone. We seem to have issues with phones getting signal this deep in the building." As Melanie looked at her phone again in hope of finding one bar, Robert winked at Abby silently confirming what the profiler suspected. There was a jammer in the room to prevent anyone from making unauthorized calls or communications.

"Whatever. Can I go now? I've been sitting here forever. I didn't do nothing wrong. That guy said he needed to take a shit. I didn't think it was gonna hit the fan."

Abby could see past her bravado into the little girl who was scared to death. She was all kinds of worried that she was in serious trouble. That was something that the profiler would be able to use. This girl was no rocket scientist. She smiled inside. This girl was a few sprinkles short of a doughnut. Based on the file before her, Abby knew she was nineteen, unattached, and adrift as to a future. Looking in her eyes, there was no kind of serious deception; but it did look like she was craving something. Possibly a drink, but more likely a hit of her drug of choice. Pot probably.

"Melanie, I'm Agent Abby Chilton from the FBI. You have helped a wanted serial killer evade capture. It is my job to discover whether you are an accomplice, or if you did something stupid for a cute guy. Or maybe for some cash." When Abby mentioned the money, there was an involuntary twitch in the girl's facial muscles telling her that she was on target.

"Now, I think he paid you a couple bills," the girl's eyes widened as if she suspected Abby were reading her mind, "and you looked the other way." The girl was clearly thrown off by Abby's knowledge of the situation. "The only problem is my associate with the Royal Canadian Mounted Police doesn't buy that story. He thinks you are involved with this man and that you have more information than you have told us." Robert leaned back, folding his arms, looking the part of the disbelieving prick.

A deer in headlights doesn't look any more stunned than Melanie. She began stammering, "H-h-he gave me two American twenties to use the toilet. A-a-and then he gave me one more to forget I seen him. I swear to God. That's all I did." She produced the three twenties and placed them on the table. "Am I gonna get fired?"

Jonas hated not being in control of situations. Riding in any vehicle was never something he relished. He was one of the many who preferred to be behind the wheel no matter where he was. A new city was always best to be experienced as you learned your way around. Toronto was not a second home, but it was a familiar city thanks to his many visits with Kristin. Riding with a young Mountie who didn't look old enough to shave made it even worse.

The light conversation was amusing as the Canadian tried to be a tour guide to a man who knew the city better than he. After Jonas corrected him on the actual height of the Gibraltar Point Lighthouse, Officer Clark stopped trying to impress the agent. The remainder of the trip was passed as Jonas explained things about the city that the young Nova Scotian had never known.

When he arrived at the PATH, Jonas was pleased to see little had changed since his last visit. Some stores had new names and there was fresh paint in strategic spots; but the essential feel of the place still had the vivacity he remembered well. With some fondness, he glanced at several shops that still had the same name that he had visited years back with his ex. Pushing those thoughts aside, he strode confidently into the store where the Observer had managed to disappear.

The presence of a uniformed Mountie made any introductions unnecessary. The man tending the store was the owner who was all too happy to help in any way. Even without Abby to tell him, Lange could tell the man wanted to put this behind him so that it would not leave a lasting stigma on his little shop.

"The police have already looked around. I don't know what you're hoping to find but you are welcome to take a look." He was practically pushing them into the back room where the Observer had disappeared.

"Don't you love it when they are so helpful?" asked Jonas, with more than a little mirth in his voice. The joke was lost on the young Mountie. The Interpol agent held an arm up like a parent protecting a child from running into the street as Clark tried to move into the storage area. "Let me look around first."

There was nothing of note to be seen. The bathroom was clean enough without being immaculate. His instincts told him the Observer had not spent any time in here. Jonas looked in some of the more obscure places where most would not expect to find hidden objects. After satisfying himself it was all clear, he led the way to the corridor behind the stores. The barren hallway left nothing for him to consider as he walked slowly toward the two doors at the end. His ever alert eyes scanned the floor and walls for any traces that others may have missed.

Looking through the peephole at the end of the hallway, Jonas saw the same view the Observer had seen a few hours earlier. Opening the door and looking around, he satisfied himself that his nemesis would not have gone back into the open with all the cameras. Turning to the other door, he opened it and looked up the stairs. Jonas' gift was in seeing details that other's dismissed at unimportant. An American phrase that Jonas found appealing centered on things being as obvious as "a turd in a punch bowl." To Jonas, there were turds in punch bowls everywhere he looked. It was amazing to him no one else could see them. The first turd he saw was a piece of trash where no trash should be.

"What do you make of that, Clark?" asked the German. He wondered if the kid had any instincts.

"Well, it looks like the janitor hasn't been through here, but I'm guessing you see something else," replied the Mountie.

Jonas was disappointed that Clark missed the obvious, but pleased that he knew enough to look harder. Putting on a pair of gloves from his pocket, Lange picked up the piece of paper and revealed a small cylinder with motion sensors on either end.

"You Canadians throw away things I like to keep," mused the German.

# Chapter Twenty-Seven

"So you think that gizmo is from Smythe? How can you be sure?" Abby asked. Jonas had called her with an update on what he had found. She paced back and forth in the conference room, her level of tension rising with each breath. She could feel they were close.

"I'm not totally certain but as soon as Michaelson gets here with my equipment, I can tell you more." Jonas continued, "It looks like a wireless motion sensor, but that is not the kind of thing you throw away. And it's still charged. Someone could be trying to hide a motion sensor for some other reason, but it seems like…"

Abby interrupted. "Too much of a coincidence. I get it. How soon will you be back?"

Jonas voice was muffled as he checked with Clark. "About fifteen minutes and you will be trying not to stare at my eyes, again." Abby could hear the smile in his voice.

"See you then, asshole," teased Abby, trying not to let him detect her smiling as well. That man saw way too much for her own good.

Inspector Gibson came flying into the room. "There has been a killing in Milton. It could be your guy." He was breathing hard from the sprint to the room, but there was an excitement in his eyes. Abby felt like her stomach had dropped to her toes.

"A killing? Already? That doesn't fit his pattern." Abby was genuinely confused. "What makes you think it's our guy? Don't you have polite killers here, too?"

"Sure. Between fifty and sixty a year. But this is a strange coincidence, don't you think?" Gibson was moving toward the door. "Want to come see if your profiler vision can see anything? If nothing else, I could use your help and the Halton Police Service needs mine."

Abby grabbed her jacket and took a few quick steps to catch up to the speed walking Inspector. "I'll call Jonas and tell him where we're going," she said, as she caught up.

"I already told Clark to take him there," said a smiling Robert. "I had a hunch you'd want to see this for yourself." Abby hated it when someone got a half-step ahead of her.


Jonas and Clark diverted to the crime scene and arrived twenty minutes after receiving the call. The victim was a young woman. Jonas couldn't really tell if she was Smythe's type because he didn't seem to have one. The scene was unlike the other crime scene he had seen of this killer. The biggest difference was the presence of a body and the bloody mess. The dark, red cardiac blood was pooled around the victim on the kitchen floor. This didn't seem like the Observer's modus operandi. The Interpol agent was about to walk out when he overheard a conversation between the two officers who were standing at the door.

"Yeah, I don't know how she did either. But at least we don't have two bodies. She said he came out of the house after her."

"How good of a look did she get?" asked the second officer. Jonas walked up to join the conversation while Clark went outside to vomit.

The first officer started to answer. "I heard she saw…" Noticing Lange, he asked, "Can I help you, sir?"

"There was a witness? Please continue. I want to hear all about it." There was the beginning of a smile on the German's face that struck the officers as a little ghoulish considering what had happened.

Officer Tremblay continued cautiously. "Well," he looked at his partner for support, "There was another woman who came over for dinner. The victim was attacked but the witness was still in the doorway. She got away and called us. This is how we found everything. The detective is outside talking to neighbors."

Using his best Interpol agent voice, Jonas asked, "Where is the witness? I need to interview her. Now!" In a conspiratorial whisper, he added, "She may be the only witness to an international spy ring." The two officers ate it up like potheads munching on cheese fries.

"She's at the station," said the second officer, too quickly. Whispering, he asked, "Is it terrorism? Should we be on heightened alert?"

On the inside Jonas was laughing. On the outside he was as serious as a heart attack. "Gentlemen, please keep doing what you're doing. We will take care of this crisis. Keep everyone calm." Sometimes it was fun to mess with idiots. He understood why Abby did it.

Seeing that Clark was still heaving, he called Abby. "Hey there. This may be a wild Canadian goose chase but there is a witness. She's at the station, wherever that is."

"Really? We'll head there. How does it look? Any of those notorious insights of yours?" asked the profiler.

"Not yet. This is different. If this is his handiwork, he didn't leave the place spotless. An interruption would explain why there is actual evidence of a crime this time."

Abby followed his train of thought. "Well, with so few homicides in these parts there may be a connection." Hitting the speaker button, she continued, "You're on speaker. How did she die?"

"Stabbed through the heart. It is one of his methods. It still may not be him; but at this point, who knows? Maybe the witness got a good enough look to tell us something," replied the German.

Abby asked her driver, "Robert, do you have many deaths like this around here?"

The Inspector replied without having to think about it, "No. More gunshots than stabbings. And not through the heart either. That is unusual."

The voice of Lange came through the speaker. "I'll give this place the once over three or four times and meet you at the station. I don't really expect to find anything."

As he slid it into his shirt pocket, his phone rang again. It was Rupert. "Agent Michaelson. Tell me you're making good time." He really wanted his toys right about now.

"Not bad. This thing moves! I should be in your area in about an hour. Where do you want me to bring your badass Beemer?" Rupert was obviously enjoying himself.

After giving the agent the address, he added, "We may have another victim and a witness. I need my equipment to help me check this area. It's too dark to find much without infrared goggles."

Michaelson was animated. "A witness? No shit?! That could be amazing! I'll be there as soon as I can." Jonas wondered if Michaelson's training covered high speed pursuits without anyone to pursue.

The Observer got off the bus at the Toronto Musical Garden on the Toronto Bay. He had walked around there several times during previous visits to see the sights and look for people to add to his list. He first spotted Andrea near the garden. The hotels and parks were a perfect hunting ground for a predator like him. Tonight was another story. He needed to get moving and do it quickly and quietly. The bag he was carrying with the essentials was getting burdensome the longer he had it on his shoulders. Even though he had been sitting for some time on the bus, it had not been restful. He needed a place to take a break and get a little bit of rest until it was late enough to find a boat to steal.

Along the bay were luxury hotels and touristy destinations. What he needed was a place that took cash and didn't ask too many questions. Wearing his garish clothing, he strolled the short distance from the bay to discover the kind of place he needed. It was cheap, dirty, sleazy and private. Overpaying for a night plus a security deposit that he would never get back, the killer slipped quietly into his room after placing a small camera outside the door.

Abby and Gibson entered the police station with the confidence of professionals doing a thorough job. They both agreed that this was a longshot. Even if it wasn't Smythe, they could help with a homicide. After brief introductions, the Inspector and profiler were led to a waiting area where a frazzled woman was sitting. Abby had seen meth addicts going through withdrawal who didn't look as shaky as this poor girl.

In full counselor mode, Abby sat down beside her. "Miss Casey? I know it has been a trying time, but can I talk to you?"

The haunted eyes met Abby's for the first time. In them Abby could see confusion, terror, and a host of other emotions competing to get to the surface. "'Trying time?' I saw my friend stabbed and you think it is a trying time? What fucking planet are you from?"

Abby took a different, more aggressive tack. "I know what happened. I'm here to find the bastard. Do you want to help me?" Beverly Casey was startled by the abrupt honesty. Her eyes softened. She nodded, trying to hold back the tears but finally allowed them to flow. She collapsed in Abby's arms as the sounds she made became a jumble of inaudible wails and guttural cries. Abby sat there with the woman who was finally letting everything flow out in a tsunami of emotions until she was nothing but a sobbing mess.

After twenty minutes of groaning and crying, Beverly finally ran out of steam. Looking up, her makeup a disaster, she took a steadying breath and asked, "How can I help?"

Abby had waited for her to get herself back together. She had taken the time the woman was crying to consider all the possible ways she could approach this. Looking at her with sympathy, Abby asked, "Did you see the man who did this?" The direct approach was the simplest choice.

The fear was back all over the woman's face. She nodded slowly and said, "I will never forget the look in his eyes. He looked…" She looked around the small room as if making sure he wasn't sneaking up on her. In barely a whisper, she said, "He looked like he was enjoying himself."

Abby took out her phone and pulled up the picture of Smythe that Edos had given them. "Is this the man?" There was a brief flicker in her eyes as Beverley looked at the killer. She stared at it and finally looked away.

"I-I-I don't know. It may have been him if he changed his hair. That guy has dark hair and the man who killed…" She couldn't say her friend's name. "He had lighter hair and it was really short." She looked at the picture again and back into Abby's eyes. "Who is that? Do you think it's him?"

Abby had heard enough. "It's probably nothing, Beverly. This gentleman is going to take you to see someone you can talk to. Don't worry. We will do everything we can to find the man who did this."

After the woman had left the room, Abby turned to Gibson and said, "Jackpot! That is him."

The Mountie was confused. "I thought she couldn't tell for sure."

"Robert, all she needed to say was she saw any vague similarities and I would be convinced. But I saw it in her eyes. She is terrified. It's him!" Abby jumped up and dialed Jonas.

While Abby was interviewing Beverly Casey, Jonas had been going over the house and yard. In the house, he was able to place himself in the mind of a stalker. Clark and the two police watched him with a morbid fascination as he found where the killer had been lying in wait for his victim. After the coroner had taken the body, Jonas could be seen on floor, looking at the death scene from every possible angle. He even climbed on the table to get a bird's eye view of the situation.

When he stopped, Lange noticed that the two cops were staring at him. He was accustomed to that and he really didn't give a rat's ass what anyone thought of his technique. It was his results that shut them up.

When he was ready, he spoke. "All right. Here's what happened. The killer entered through the back door." Opening the door, he pointed to some barely visible marks on the lock. "These scratches are fresh where he picked the lock. It was a good job. Then he went through the house to make certain that no one else was here." He pointed to a disturbed area on the hallway carpet that looked like nothing special to the other three men. "If it were me, I'd even check in the bathroom."

Looking around the kitchen, Jonas moved to the corner by the backdoor and turned off the lights in the room. "If the lights were off in the house, there would be no way anyone would see him in this spot. It gave him clear access to the victim who would assume that the lights were out due to a thrown circuit breaker." He went over and opened the breaker box and returned to the spot. "When she reached up to check the box, he could spring at her and subdue her without any problem." Jonas demonstrated the technique he would use to do the same thing that the killer had done. Kneeling on the ground next to the pool of blood, Jonas demonstrated how Andrea had been held down.

"When the other woman screamed, it would have only been a moment of distraction. The killer would have to end the life of the first woman quickly," he mimed thrusting a knife into the chest of the victim, "and then leapt to his feet to pursue the witness." Jonas jumped up and ran to the door with the other three men following him, keeping an uneasy distance.

Looking back at them, he said, "Yeah. I know. It's creepy, but it is how I recreate the scene." He was gazing around the yard when another vehicle pulled into the drive. The smiling face of Agent Michaelson came bounding up to Lange. Looking at his watch, Jonas whistled. "I don't want to know how you got here so fast."

"It was easy," began Rupert. "I didn't…"

"I don't want to know," interrupted Jonas, with a smile. "But your timing is perfect. Let's see what we can find." Both men headed to the SUV with the three other men in tow. Jonas held out his hand and Michaelson reluctantly handed over the keys. The auto-lift on the back gate revealed several closed containers. Opening one, Jonas took out a device that looked like something that would be used to play disc golf. After tapping a keypad on the top, he tossed it toward the trees along the property. The other four men stared after it, trying to figure out what Jonas was doing.

Jonas walked along behind the slowly moving disc until it began hovering. A laser was pointing to a spot within the trees that had a birdhouse. Grabbing the disc out of the air and turning it off, Jonas went over to the tree and took the box down. With the disc in one hand and the birdhouse in the other, he went back to his SUV with four men stumbling over themselves trying to see what was happening.

Holding up the disc, he said, "High tech metal detector." He placed the disc back in its case. "Infrared googles didn't see any heat so I had to go with plan-B. I thought there might be something like this over there." He opened the birdhouse to reveal a camera and an array of batteries. What he hadn't expected was the flashing light on a package on the camera. Instincts kicked in as Lange hurled the birdhouse back toward the trees, yelling, "Down!" He tackled two of them.

The explosion was not as spectacular as the destruction of the Observers house in Tennessee, but it was big enough to knock down two trees. One came crashing down on the police cruiser and the other was lying in Andrea's dining room.

Looking up at what was left of the car, Jonas muttered, "Being right can be depressing sometimes."

# Chapter Twenty-Eight

As Jonas took the phone out of his shirt pocket, it rang. Wanting to share his news first, he answered Abby with, "Guess what I found?"

There was a slight delay before she replied, "Is it something like I have that tells us this probably was Smythe?" The smile could be heard through the phone lines.

Jonas was not expecting that reaction but recovered with a lightning fast verbal repost, "Sorry. Nothing here that says 'probably.'" He waited until he heard the psychologist take a breath. "But I do have absolutely, solid, conclusive proof, if that helps any." Lange heard that same breath rush out as if deflated. "I found a birdhouse camera like he had on your place but this one blew up when I opened it. I may owe the locals a new car. So, what did you find?" He was trying hard not chuckle.

"Do you ever do things the easy way?" Taking a deep, patience-giving breath, Abby shared her discovery. "The witness says it could be him but I am sure she recognized his face. She's afraid. But the camera makes this our case. Putting you on speaker."

"Robert, it's your jurisdiction. Your call. How do you want us to proceed?" asked the Interpol agent.

Lange could almost hear the wheels turning in the Mountie's head. "Okay, I'm increasing our presence at all departure areas. Also, border crossings will have a picture and composite so that we can try and catch him if he's crossing by car. I will need to call further up the chain of command and get back to you."

Abby's voice came back on. "Speaker's off. This bastard has gone so far off profile that I'm not sure what he'll do. Something has changed. This is out of character for him. It's time to rethink my whole profile. This doesn't make any sense based on what we know of him. What are you thinking, Jonas?"

"I'm thinking he is too smart to be caught by any of Rob's checks," began the German. "You're right. This doesn't fit. But, if he is getting sloppy, we may be able to catch him. Rupert and I will pick you up as soon as we can get there."

"Wait, how the hell did he drive up here that fast?" asked a bewildered Abby.

Shutting the back door of the SUV and motioning for Michaelson to follow, Lange replied. "I didn't ask and don't want to know."


The Observer tried to rest but sleep was out of the question. His phone had the feed from the camera perched outside his doorway and beeped every time it detected motion. He considered muting the warning, but he had made too many mistakes today to allow another. Getting out his tablet, he searched the internet for details on the marinas in the area. The nearest one was not an option. They had live streaming video of the boats available online. There was no telling how many other cameras were snooping that were not available for public view. *Damn, those cameras!*

Even without the resources of Interpol, the Observer had ways of detecting surveillance dangers. Orwell had truly been a visionary; but even he could not have fathomed the width and depth of the constant surveillance that everyone accepted as the norm. The killer made a mental note to write a virus to disable CCTV in the future. Right now, there was no time for something so elaborate.

Cracking into the systems of three different marinas, he discovered that two of them would be problems. They were too low tech. He found bills and receipts for hard wired, old school cameras and digital recording that was not online. That meant that Interpol wouldn't be able to control them; but he wasn't sure that was the case with local law enforcement. They could have someone watching in security offices for anyone out of place.

The third was another story. It was totally state-of-the-art. Multiple wireless cameras were linked into a system that had terabytes of storage. The website billed it as "a marina for the techno-savvy boating enthusiast." The owners could log on and check on their boat twenty-four/seven. It was perfect for his needs. After checking several of the slips, he found the boat that would get him where he needed to be. It would make the trip across the waters of the Great Lake and allow him to make his escape to New York.

The computer genius quickly delved into the server only to discover that each video had a date and time stamp at the bottom. With enough time he could fix each frame to allow him to create a false video feed that no one would detect until it was too late. Time was not something he had in abundance. The killer determined the path he would need to travel and loaded video from a year ago. No one would noticed the wrong year on the video feed. If someone was that observant, it would be chalked up to a computer glitch.

The two hour feed was ready to begin at 2:00am giving him two hours to get to the boat, steal it, and make a getaway across Lake Ontario. Now the Observer could rest until 1:00am. The plan was in place. The Observer relaxed a little bit. He still had a sinking feeling that he hoped had nothing to do with the boat.


Abby and Jonas sat in the front while Rupert was relegated to the back seat. Jonas drove his BMW back into the heart of Toronto. Inspector Gibson was following his own logical course of action, trying to create a net around the area. He knew it was unlikely to catch one as devious as Smythe; but it was still the most logical plan. Abby and Jonas had a different plan that left logic lying in the pool of blood at Andrea's house. The profiler was thinking like the killer.

"Since you are inside his head, where would you go?" asked Jonas. He wanted to know Abby's thoughts.

Abby was prepared. "Smythe knows the area. He's been here plenty of times. I don't see him going further into the countryside. He seems more urban than rural based on his past." Jonas nodded in agreement. "He's too smart to try for the main airport, but might try a smaller one. As far as I know, he doesn't know how to fly. Or does he?"

"Not as far as I know either," admitted Jonas. "If he needed a pilot then I think we can rule out the smaller airfields, too. Besides, I'm sure Rob has those covered." He spoke into his phone. "Text Ronni. Check and see if there are any places that have web-accessible, high-tech security that Smythe can hack and use as a getaway." The speech-to-text sent the message to the Chilean who would check for possibilities. "What else is going on in that pretty little head of yours?"

Ignoring the chuckle from the backseat, Abby continued, "Well, if he is in a car, we're screwed. He could be anywhere and the Mounties are the only ones who can find him."

"And if he's not?" came the voice of Michaelson from the peanut gallery.

"If he's not in a car, we have to consider where he will go and how he will get away. My money's on a car, though." Jonas reconsidered after he spoke. "Then again…" He left the thought dangling in the air.

"What?" asked the confused junior agent in the backseat.

Abby finished the thought. "Then again, when has he done what's expected." She looked over at Lange who had a mischievous smile on his face. "How wide is Lake Ontario right here?"

"It's a little over 20 miles to cross the lake and get to New York. About half that to get into American waters." The Interpol agent smiled even bigger. "Why, Agent Chilton, you're not thinking that Smythe would do something as illegal as stealing a boat and smuggling himself across Lake Ontario, are you? That would be disgraceful of him."

"Perish the thought," replied Abby.

"Both of you are too damn spooky," said Michaelson, adding what little he could to the conversation.


Ronni received the text from Jonas linked up with Rikka and Marcus. Having all three of them working on the problem, they would have a list for Jonas and Abby within minutes. Each had been updated on the confirmation that Smythe was the killer and that he was on the run. This could be their chance to catch him and end this bloodbath.

"I have found eight possible places where Smythe could use the technology to his advantage," said the image of the Chilean hacker. The data was immediately shared across cyberspace.

Rikka looked at the list. "Oui, mon ami. But I don't zee 'im using zee trains at Union Station. Too risqué."

Marcus loved the accent. "Risky. True. And I think we can say the same thing for the airport on Toronto Island."

Rikka dismissed two more places from the list. "And zere are too many cameras to be sure you 'ave got zem all at both zee car rentals."

"That leaves four marinas. Two of them are farther out than others; but that could be what he wants. He has had time to get there. There is one right on the bay, but he would have to come all the way back into Toronto to get to that one." Ronni was into gathering the data. She didn't like analyzing it. "Let's give these to Jonas and see what he thinks."


Jonas' phone rang. He sent it directly into the sound system of the BMW so all could hear and speak. "You are live with everyone in Toronto, Ronni. What do you have for us?"

"You have all three of us on this end. We have narrowed it down to four marinas. Sending the data to your phone." Jonas tapped a link button on the touch screen of the Beemer's middle console and the information was visible for Abby and Rupert as well.

Michaelson spoke up first. "Okay. That one," he pointed to one that was on the far east of Toronto along the lake, "would be a long way to travel if he is trying to lay low."

Abby glanced back at the agent. "Good point," she said, mildly impressed. "And this one," she pointed to the one at the opposite end of the screen, "is way too close to the border. He'd want to avoid as much attention as possible."

Jonas agreed. "It seems that these two are the best bets. I think we need to divide and conquer." Abby looked at Jonas. Something was wrong. "Abby and Rupert can take one and I'll take the other."

Abby could see something going on behind his eyes. *What is he thinking?* "Why don't we call Robert for backup? I'm sure he can spare a few Mounties to help. Or at least get a few locals involved." There was grunt of agreement from the backseat.

After a quick phone call to the Inspector, Abby was summarily dismissed by Gibson, who saw it as a fool's errand. He said he'd ask for a few uniforms from the Toronto PD to be there when they could; but the profiler knew when she was being placated. He didn't have the resources to help and had his hands full with the manhunt he was coordinating.

Punching the end button on the call, Abby looked over at Jonas. "You saw that coming, didn't you?" *God, I hate it when he's right.*

"Rob is a good guy and a dedicated cop, but he doesn't have much imagination. What we're doing probably sounds stupid to him, but he will let us do whatever we want. He can say he helped us and we helped with the manhunt. He's a skilled politician." Jonas spat the last word so that is sounded like an insult.

"That's too bad. I was really starting to like him," said Abby, more serious than jesting.


The Observer left his rented room at 1:30am. Thinking of the several cameras along his route, he decided to find a cab. He greeted the cabbie warmly and asked to be taken to the marina.

"Little late for a cruise," commented the driver.

The Observer had already thought of that. "Actually, it's a little early for fishing; but I couldn't wait anymore. You ever gone out deep lake fishing?" The driver promptly lost interest in the conversation. Dropping him off a little after 2:00am, the Observer tipped the driver modestly and walked toward the gate. Pretending to scan a card, he opened the gate that he had set to remain unlocked until 2:30am. Walking casually down the gently sloping dock, he looked around for anyone watching.

# Chapter Twenty-Nine

Someone was watching the casual ambling of the Observer. Abby spoke softly from her spot in the shadows. "Rupert, can you focus in on the guy coming down the gangway? I can't see him well enough from here."

From the security office, Michaelson replied, "I don't see anyone, Abby. Where is he, again?"

"He right on the main dock heading toward the split." The tenor of Abby's voice rose. She had a bad feeling about this. "He's right there," she whispered.

The voice of Jonas came through her earbud. "He may have hacked the video feed. Ronni is checking." Abby would have been more comfortable if Jonas were there, but she knew how to handle herself. The man turned away from her, walking toward the slips.

Rupert broke into her thoughts. "The date is wrong. The feed says it is last year. Jonas, he's here!"

"On my way," said the tense sounding German. "Don't take any chances." Abby was not sure who Jonas was warning.

"I'm going to take a stroll and make sure this guy is supposed to be here," said the profiler, leaving the shadows. She walked calmly after the disappearing back of the stranger. After, turning a corner, she was surprised to see no one on the long, covered dock. He could be anywhere on any of the boats. Something was wrong. She held her Glock in the ready position as she stalked slowly down the dock, making as little noise as possible.

A noise behind her caused her to turn, with her pistol raised to fire. Quickly, pointing her weapon up, she whispered, "Michaelson, you almost got your head blown off!" The young agent raise his hands in surrender, holding his gun above his head. Turning back toward the boats, Abby stalked on.

The gun above Michaelson's head disappeared as the Observer took it from his perch above him. Before a warning could come out of his mouth, the gun was turned and the face of young agent disappeared in a spray of blood as a bullet from his own gun ended a promising life.

Abby spun and prepared to fire but found herself aiming at the falling form of Michaelson. The sound of gunfire exploded in the air again as Abby found herself spinning to the right, pain enveloping her mind. Her gun clattered across the deck, making a splash as it vanished beneath the murky waters of the marina. The voice of Jonas was screaming in her ear but she couldn't focus on his words. She was trying to make sense of the wraith sliding from the rafters above. It was like a specter descending from the dark shadows.

The Observer had seen Abby halfway down the gangplank to the marina, far too late to turn back. The sound of her whisper had carried so he knew she was speaking even though he couldn't tell what was being said. After letting her pass beneath him, he had waited, hoping to catch Jonas following behind her. He settled for the FBI peon who was dumb enough to practically hand him the gun. Some people were too stupid to live.

"Hello Abby," began the Observer, stooping by the still body of Michaelson. "It is nice to finally have a chance to talk." He was searching the dead agent looking for the means of communication. He wanted to talk to Jonas, who was undoubtedly on his way. He found a walkie-talkie. Looking at Abby, he said, "This looks too low tech for Jonas." Pressing the button, he said, "All clear. False alarm."

"Did you shoot one of the boats?" demanded the voice of the security guard.

"Your precious boats are safe. I'm going to help Chilton out here. Let me know if you see anyone on the monitors," replied the Observer.

"Okay. But you better not be shitting me about the boats or it'll be your asses, not mine," replied the night watchman in the security office.

"Charming fellow, isn't he?" he said to the pained profiler. Sifting through what remained of Rupert's head, he found the ear bud in an ear. Placing it in his own ear, he heard the voice of Lange. "Goddammit! Someone talk to me!" screamed Jonas.

The subtle voice of the Observer answered. "Of course, Jonas. I'm sorry but Abby is indisposed. And her friend seems to have lost the ability to speak. But I'll be glad to chat."

There was a moment of silence as the words sank in. Lange, rage barely controlled, spat back, "If you hurt them, I will fucking kill you so slowly you will beg to die." The sound of squealing tires could be heard through the link.

"Oops. I really wish you would have told me that sooner. What was the agent's name with our dear Abby? Well, it really doesn't matter. It will be a closed coffin." The Observer was actually having fun. "Now, as to Abby. I'll let you control that. You come here by yourself so we can chat and I won't do anything else to her. You may want to hurry. I really don't like bandaging bullet wounds"

"You son of bitch!" grunted Jonas.

Laughter filled the ears of the com. "We will be on the second dock on the left. Slip twenty-seven. Excuse me while I drag her down to my new boat."

The cry from Abby could be heard clearly through her com when her attacker picked her up. She had lost a significant amount of blood. Getting shot was nothing like they show in the movies. The phrase "just a flesh wound" was misleading. A gunshot wound hurt like hell and no one ever fought back. One good bullet wound was enough to make even the strongest soldier beg for his mother. It took all Abby's willpower to hold on to consciousness through the pain.

"Easy does it, Abby," said the killer. "Don't want you dying before Jonas gets here." He smiled as he heard the heavy breathing of the man who had been chasing him for so long. "I'll take care of her 'til you get here, Jonas." There was no response.

Arriving at the slip with the cigarette boat, he placed Abby on the bow and began preparing to cast off. After a few minutes, he had done everything he needed to be ready to cast off and deal with the Interpol agent. He hoped Jonas would do the right thing. *I really want Abby to live a little longer.* All that remained was waiting for Lange to arrive. It was only two minutes later that the sound of tires skidding to a stop came from the parking lot.


Jonas kicked the gate open and sprinted down the gangway to the main dock. Turning the corner, he slowed and raised his Beretta. The Observer's trap was set for him. He could hear moaning from Abby through his com but nothing from his nemesis.

"What was the slip again?" asked Jonas, walking under the roof of the dock. There was no need to be quiet. Smythe knew he was there. "I'll follow the sound of the boat." He came upon the body of Michaelson. Seeing that there was little left of his face, Lange used his training to push his anger and sadness aside. Toward the far end of the dock was the boat with Abby on the bow. A noose was around her neck as she teetered, barely balanced. Any backward movement of the boat would leave her hanging in the air over the water.

"It is so nice to have the chance to talk in person, Jonas." The voice of his mortal enemy was quite charming. It was coming from the cockpit of the boat. "You know, I've watched you for a while. So what shall we discuss?" Jonas raised his gun toward the sound of the voice. "If you shoot me, I'll fall on the throttle and our dear little Abigail will be all choked up." There was a chuckle as the killer laughed at his own joke.

The rage Jonas had kept at bay since the death of Kristin was slowly rising to the surface. If he could kill this monster, he would be willing to sacrifice himself to do so. The thought of sacrificing Abby fleeted through his mind for a split second, but he knew he would never do it. Using all the control he could muster, he replied, "Were you able to catch a Blue Jays' game while you were here? They aren't doing too well; but how often do you get to see them play at home?" The German was trying to maneuver around to get a clean shot at the killer, while trying to keep any cover he could find between them.

"That's the Jonas I know and loathe," laughed the Observer. "So you have a choice. Abby is going to need medical attention. I'm pretty sure I didn't hit too many vital arteries. It's her arm and possibly the bone." His head showed through the glass of the boat. "Sorry about that Abby. I was trying to shoot the gun out of your hand." Abby's semi-conscious state cleared at the mention of her name. She and Jonas locked eyes, silently communicating what needed to be done. With a nod, Abby prepared herself.

Jonas made three quick shots at the Observer through the glass of the cigarette boat. Each ricocheted harmlessly away as the killer hit the throttle sending the boat racing backwards away from the dock. Jonas' next shot was not at the retreating boat but at the rafters where the rope was tied. The shot cut the rope before it could tighten around the neck of the profiler, leaving her free to plunge into the deep water of the bay.

Dropping his gun, Jonas leapt into the water reaching for his lover's sinking form. He caught her right arm, causing her to take in a mouth full of the disgusting water as the pain of the gunshot wound sent her body into spasms. Kicking to the surface, Jonas got Abby's head above water. Holding onto the side of the dock with one arm, he cleared her airway so she would take in the welcome taste of the oily, marina air.

Pulling himself onto the dock, Jonas hauled Abby out of the water as carefully as possible. Placing her weak form on the dock, he looked in her eyes. "You really need to be more careful. A girl can get hurt doing things like this," joked Lange.

"Tell me about it," grimaced the profiler. "Can you call an ambulance now? This hurts worse than it looks. I think I'm going to faint now."

"They're on their way," smiled Jonas.

A voice came from the water. "Hey, Jonas!"

Reaching for his gun, he spun around. The Beretta was not in its holster but on the dock. A shot rang out. Jonas turned to look at Abby, reaching up to his chest. Abby saw a hole in the German's jacket as he whispered, "Abby," and fell into the depths of the bay.

Abby passed out.

# Chapter Thirty

The Observer sped off through the darkness, smiling to himself. Jonas would not be tracking him anymore. It was a really good shot. A shot to take pride in. Right at the heart of the matter. The splash was epic. He would play that memory over and over in his mind for the rest of his life. If only he could have watched Jonas' eyes as he sank beneath the water. Well, you can't have everything. This was good enough.

Setting his course for Ontario Beach in Rochester, the killer opened up the throttle. Even at a fraction of its full power, this boat was amazing. He killed all the running lights so that he could travel invisibly in the darkness even though the engine could be heard for miles. To stay safe, he settled in at 60mph. Anyone chasing him would have a hard time keeping up. He would be on the shore of Rochester in a little over an hour. After that it would be a simple matter of sending the boat off to the north-east, giving them something to chase to wherever it ended up. Or maybe a slow fuse to the gas tank…

Sometimes the simplest plans were the best.

Abby heard voices. Pain shot through her arm. More voices shouted and fuzzy people entered and left her field of vision. She tried to speak, to tell what had happened. Some kind of new pain in her arm lasted an instant followed by warmth as the pain eased dramatically. She couldn't remember where she was. Abby would have sworn she was floating as the lights above her moved in pretty colors, followed by blissful nothingness.

Abby thought she saw someone in her room. She squinted at the man in the mask and she faded out. A shadow crossed in front of her, but she couldn't make it out. Words tumbled out of her mouth that made no sense to her. Finally, she managed one word. "Jonas?" There was something about Jonas, but she couldn't remember what it was. *It was something important. What was it?* Abby was adrift again in a sea of morphine.

Jonas was hurt. She remembered now. Her eyes shot open and she called him. "Jonas?!" There was a face above hers, but it was too blurry to see. "Jonas?" she asked the image.

"No, Abby. Not Jonas." The voice was familiar, but her drug addled brain couldn't place it. "You need to rest. You lost a lot of blood, but don't worry. You'll be fine." Even though the words were comforting, they didn't answer her question. She struggled to clear her vision but her eyes wouldn't cooperate. Then she was out again.

"… that, but when can she be moved back to the States?" The voice she had heard was talking to someone else. Who the hell was that? It wasn't Jonas. Was it Michaelson? Wait. Rupert. Something happened to him. *Oh my God! Rupert was dead!* The memories were starting to flood back.

Another voice sounded irritated. "Once she is awake and has a chance to talk to the authorities, then, and only then, can you take her wherever you want. She's out of danger, but she needs to rest."

"I think I've rested enough," slurred Abby. "Can someone turn down whatever is making me feel like I'm living a Pink Floyd album?"

"It a morphine drip, Agent Chilton. It is there to help you control your pain," the second voice said.

"If she wants it turned down, turn the damn thing down. She can't think like this." The first voice was almost recognizable. She started to drift off again.

Abby didn't know how long she was out; but when she woke up, her head was clearer and she could see Jeremy Mathis, sitting in a chair typing furiously on a laptop. "Those things don't move any faster when you beat on them according to Marcus," said Abby, startling the Special Agent In Charge.

"Welcome back to the land of the living, Abby. You had us worried for a while." Jeremy was being nice. That sent off alarms in her head. "Please take it slow. You've been out for a while."

"How long is a while?" asked Abby, alarmed. There were bits and pieces missing. She remembered the dock and Smythe shooting Rupert. She remembered getting shot in the arm and sitting on a boat. Then something happened that was still hazy.

"You were shot thirty-six hours ago," answered Mathis, calmly. "What else do you remember, Abby?"

Calling her Abby really made the profiler nervous. "I know Michaelson was shot. He died in front of me. Smythe shot me in the arm. He wanted to keep me alive. I remember being on the bow of a boat…" She struggled with the memory, like sifting through ashes to find a scrap of paper. Suddenly, it all hit her like a drink from a fire hose. "Oh my God!" gasped Abby. Looking at Jeremy with pleading in her eyes, she whispered, "Jonas?"

There was genuine sadness in her boss' eyes. "I'm sorry, Abby." That was all he needed to say. The notorious Abby Chilton's cold outer-shell shattered like a crystal chandelier crashing to the ground. Tears flowed without any noise escaping from Abby as if holding onto the sounds that would make him live. At last, a groan escaped that came from deep within her soul that morphed into a scream of agony. "Let it out, Abby. Let it out," was all Mathis could say, as he held her shaking, grieving body.

Neither one knew how long Abby cried. It didn't matter. All that mattered was that she was feeling the loss of the one she realized she had loved. *No, in love with. There's a difference.* She had finally let herself fall in love again, taken the chance to be vulnerable with another person. Something she never thought she could do again. And now – for the second time in her life – her love had been stolen. The sadness quickly morphed into anger at the one who had stolen this second chance at joy.

"What happened to Smythe? Where is that piece of shit?" whispered the outraged Abby. Mathis hesitated. Abby's mind was still clouded, but she knew when someone was not telling her something. "What is it, Jeremy?"

"The Coast Guard found the cigarette boat he stole. Well, they found what was left of it," said Jeremy. It was in the middle of Lake Ontario. It looks like a gas leak caught up with him. There wasn't a whole lot left."

Abby couldn't – no wouldn't - believe what she was hearing. That was impossible. This man could not possibly die like that. She rejected the explanation. "It's one of his tricks. He is trying to make us think he died so we won't chase him, Jeremy. You've got to see that!"

"We can talk about it later. You need to rest." Mathis made the mistake of trying to put off the profiler.

"Jeremy, you can't let this go!" demanded Abby. "I know this man. I'm inside his head. This is exactly the kind of shit he would do to make us stop looking for him! Are you really that blind, or are you that stupid?"

The SAC rose to his feet. "Chilton, you're injured and drugged, so I'm going to let that slide. I'm not closing the Observer case, but I am making it inactive. I am placing you on medical leave until you have healed and gone through the required psych evals even though we both know you can fake your way through them." Then, smiling, he said, "While you are on leave, you are not allowed to work on any ACTIVE cases. Do you understand?"

Abby hated to say it, but she really liked Mathis at that moment. "You have my word, sir. No active cases." As he was leaving, she asked, "When will my security credentials be flagged as being on leave?"

Mathis looked at his watch as he left the room. "It may take me a while to find that form when I get back. It could be days before that happens." Nodding toward the bed, he said. "Make sure you bring me that laptop I forgot when I was visiting you in the hospital." The door closed behind him.

Abby felt she would burst from the emotions welling up inside of her. Sadness was trying to force its way to the surface. Anger played hardball with sadness, shoving it aside. Something else was beginning to push both away. It was a feeling of euphoria. Abby looked up at the morphine pump that had given her a dose. Five seconds later she was out cold.


The Observer had briefly considered taking up the life he had painstaking created for himself in Rochester, New York. The furnished apartment was ready to occupy. Clothing was in the closets. Within hours, he could have high speed internet up and running. This was going to be his new home. But not yet.

Rochester was too close to the near miss he had with his nemeses in Toronto. He really didn't think anyone would be fooled by the Viking Funeral pyre he had made of the cigarette boat. Abby would never fall for that. Well, he hoped she didn't. It would be terribly disappointing if she did. She was damaged by Jonas' death, but she was not destroyed. Not yet. After meeting her, he could see it. *She is the one. Remove a few more obstacles and she will understand.*

The killer stayed at his apartment a day and a half. It was nice to sleep in a bed of his own. He knew that more than two days would be dangerous. As Abby was talking to Mathis, he was packing a bag with fresh clothing and supplies he would need for the next leg of his journey. Getting on the Suzuki Boulevard he had stored in Rochester, the killer headed to the airport.

*I understand Phoenix is nice this time of year.*


When Abby came around again, the first thing she did was remove the morphine drip. Pain she could manage. Passing out all the time, she could not. The laptop had been moved to a side table beyond her reach. Moving around to get to it, the profiler discovered that her right arm was numb. She reached with her left arm to try and make it work, but it was too heavily bandaged. She hit the nurse call button on the bed.

"Yes?" came a voice through the intercom.

"I'd like to speak to someone about my injuries. I'm a little in the dark right now." Abby was trying to be friendly. No point in irritating the nurses. Not yet, at least.

Within a few minutes, a woman with dark curly hair came in her room. Abby couldn't tell if she was in her forties or fifties. She had a face that was defiantly obscuring her age. Her thin frame told Abby that she was either gifted with a great metabolism or worked hard to maintain a lithe figure. It was probably both.

"Good to see you awake," began the nurse. Looking at the morphine drip, she asked, "You sure you want that out? It's gonna start hurting pretty soon." Abby was pleased that she had not tried to lecture her about removing the IV. The nurse explained that Abby had been given three units of blood and had surgery for a bullet wound in her arm. There was a chip out of her right humerus that would heal in time and eventually be stronger than the bone around it. Until then, there was a plate there to protect it.

The nurse took on a serious tone. "I have to call the Mounties now that you're awake. Sorry about that. They want to talk to you about what happened." There was something in the way she spoke that made Abby concerned. She raised an eyebrow. "Oh, don't worry. It's because you're an FBI agent and you got shot so I think there is a shit-load of paperwork they have to do." Abby wasn't buying it. "I'll get the doctor to change you over to something else for the pain. It'll still hurt, but you'll be able to think."

After the nurse left, Abby got on the computer and logged in to the FBI secure server. Before the screen had completely loaded, a video-call was ringing. Answering it, the face of Marcus filled a window.

"Abby! Thank God! You look like shit!" said Marcus, going from relieved to playful.

"It has been a rough couple days," she replied dryly. "Can you get Rikka on here? I need to tell her about Jonas." Simply saying his name was difficult.

Marcus looked confused. "Didn't you see her? She already knows. The last I heard from her she was in Toronto to identify… to get Jonas." He struggled with what to say. "She said she was going to see you while she was there. Let me try and call her." A phone rang from the doorway.

Abby looked up to see Rikka standing there. She was not what Abby expected. Even though Abby had seen her face on computer screens, it did not do her justice. Even though she was well past middle age, she still had the look of a woman who could hold her own in a bar brawl. Rikka was tall – nearly six feet. She was not thin, but certainly not fat. She looked like someone who spent hours a day at the gym staying fit and building lean muscle tone. It was the small, sad smile and steely gray eyes that made Abby think she could be the scariest woman she had ever met. It was easy to imagine her with a sniper rifle taking out a target or with a knife disemboweling a terrorist. Not thinking of her doing that would be a challenge.

She looked at the phone and didn't answer it. She walked over to the computer, turned it so Marcus could see her, and said, "I am 'ere. Abbee and I need to speak. She will call you back." Rikka killed the power on the computer and set it aside.

Abby held out her hand. Rikka looked at it and, after an internal debate, shook it firmly. *Okay. I'm not sure how this is going to go down. It would really suck to survive Smythe to have Rikka kill me with a spoon.*

Rikka sat and looked at Abby as if she were an insect she were considering stomping under her stiletto heels. "I want to know what happened on the dock," she said with no trace of the French accent she always used. She could have been from London based on her perfect pronunciation.

"You are full of surprises," began Abby, only to be cut off.

"Spare me the obvious. We both know I use the French accent to keep people off guard. Right now, I need you to understand me perfectly." Looking deep into Abby's eyes, she slowly repeated, "What happened on the dock?"

Abby shared the story as best she could remember. Jonas saving her from hanging and drowning were the high points. When she got to the part where Jonas was shot, Rikka stopped her.

"After that, you passed out. Correct?" asked the Interpol agent.

Abby knew Rikka was trying to intimidate her. It was pissing her off.

"Yes. I passed out. Blood loss and bullet wounds tend to do that to me. That whole hanging thing didn't help." Abby let her have it. "You don't have to be a stone cold bitch right now. I feel horrible that Jonas died. I blame myself and probably always will. The worst part for me, Rikka, is I let my guard down and fell in love with the bastard. That makes me feel even worse. So back off the queen of denial act and talk to me like a fucking human being."

A smile creased the Frenchwoman's face as a tear rolled down her cheek. "I know you did. So did I in a very different way. But I had to see how you reacted. He would want you to know, he loved you, too."

# Chapter Thirty-One

The Observer sat by his gate, looking at his files on Abby Chilton. It was not safe to check on her from the terminal. Public internet was too easy to track. He did find the Toronto news that listed a shooting at the marina with two dead and one seriously injured. *Good to know.* That meant that Abby had survived and would be available for playing soon. The Observer wondered if Abby got her looks from her mother. There were no photos of her mom online. Well, he would have to find out when he got to Phoenix. He double checked Roberta Chilton's address in Scottsdale, AZ.

Even though he had changed his appearance significantly, there were still some things that cameras could detect if they knew where to look. There was one camera that had taken a profile of the Observer as he had strolled along the short concourse. Computers in Lyon were processing even without their mistress watching over them.

Rikka had told Abby about Jonas' body being returned to Germany while she had been out. It was his family's wish. With his father exercising a great deal of influence in the German government, there was little that Rikka could do.

"His plane will be back this afternoon," explained Rikka. "He would have wanted you to head home in comfort. I'll make sure you get to Knoxville safely."

"His plane?" Abby was confused. "I thought it was a charter."

The lilting laughter of Rikka has a warming affect. "Abby, you are so cute. Jonas, used his own resources to accomplish his missions. That jet technically belongs to his family, but he used it more than the rest put together. He had a unique position at Interpol. He worked outside the international politics and bureaucracy. He didn't give a tinker's damn about moving up the ladder or any of the Interpol politics. We chose the missions he would work. He never failed. Well, until now." Rikka looked nostalgic for a moment. "For someone as gifted as you, there was much about him that you never saw. That is so adorable."

Abby shook her head in amazement. Truly, there was so much she hadn't known about that man and now she never would. She was about to ask another question when there was a knock at the door. Inspector Robert Gibson opened the door and peeked inside.

"Can I come in?" He entered without waiting for the response.

Rikka rose and touched Abby's hand. "We can talk later." Her thick French accent was back for the sake of the Mountie. She nodded to Gibson. "Inspector," she said. The temperature in the room dropped as she sent him her most cold-blooded stare.

He walked toward her bedside, looking over his shoulder at Rikka. Robert whispered, "That woman scares the bejesus out of me." Abby was surprised he admitted that. Turning to her, he said, "Abby, I'm sorry. I should have sent men sooner. I know that's not enough, but it's all I can say."

Abby wasn't letting him off the hook that easily. "Yes, you should have. I wouldn't want to be you when you told Kerri that her former brother-in-law died because you didn't send the cops we needed. Did you tell her before or after you told her that she hated the wrong one in that marriage?" Abby was venting her anger at the only person other than herself she could blame. Robert flinched at the words.

Gathering his composure, he was smart enough not to try the bullying he attempted before. "I need to get your statement, Abby. Would you rather have someone else take it? I can call someone else in." Back to being the professional.

Abby knew it would be easier for Gibson if someone else debriefed her. Jonas would have done the noble thing, letting him off the hook so he wouldn't feel worse. She wasn't that noble. "No. I want to tell you all the gory details, Robbie." It was going to be a long afternoon for the Mountie.

After an hour and a half of torturing the Inspector, Abby was left alone. She knew that she should probably rest, but she had rested enough for a week. She needed an update on the manhunt. Grabbing the laptop, she logged back in to the FBI server to find Marcus and Tina waiting for her. The split screen showed both analysts looking pensive.

"Abby!" screeched Tina. There was delight and sadness in the one word. Tina could communicate so much with so little.

"You do know that the speakers have limits, right?" said Abby. "It's good to see you, too."

Marcus joined the conversation. "You do know that we thought you were dead, don't you? Cut us some slack, Tiny."

"You thought I was what?" asked Abby, genuinely surprised.

The nodding image of Tina confirmed Marcus' words. "They said you had been shot and lost a lot of blood. Then we heard an FBI agent died and everyone assumed it was you." Her voice caught in her throat when she asked, "Did Rupert suffer?"

"He never knew what hit him," said Abby. "Jonas…" She began to tear up, but pulled herself together. "Jonas looked at me before he fell into the water. He said my name."

"Oh, Abby." Tina couldn't think of anything to add.

Pushing her sorrow aside, Abby took charge. "Okay. I'm on medical leave. Not allowed to touch any active cases. Mathis is making the Observer case inactive thanks to the burned boat. What else do you have for me? I'm checking myself out as soon as I can find my clothes. I don't know where to go from here."

Marcus looked at Abby like she said she was preparing to rocket to the moon on a flatulent manatee. "What?" asked the computer guru. "Are you serious?"

"Serious as a gunshot wound. Please talk to me. What do you have?"

Tina's image had lost most of its color. "Abby, you were just shot. Let someone else do this."

The sound of Abby's voice commanded obedience. "I am going after this fucker and I need your help. He killed Jonas right in front of me. I am going to find him and put a bullet in his brain. You can help me or stay the hell out of my way."

Marcus' looked at her as his fingers danced across the keyboard. "My best guess is he went to Rochester or Oswego, New York. My money's on Rochester. It is large enough for him to hide or he can catch a flight anywhere. If he went to Oswego, he would have to go to Syracuse to do any of that."

Abby could tell that Tina was still not on board with this plan, so she focused on Marcus. "Why don't you think he would go to someplace in Canada and lay low for a while?" Abby agreed with him, but was still not trusting herself. There were painkillers in her system.

Tina spoke up. "It doesn't fit his profile. He has become obsessed with you. He wants to hurt you, destroy you. Killing Jonas was big, but there is no way he could know you two were… involved."

Abby was impressed. Tina was thinking like a psychologist instead of an accountant. *There may be hope for her yet.* "Good point. I don't suppose anyone from the Buffalo field office has made any inquiries in Rochester, have they?"

"Two agents went and saw the wreckage of the boat. Other than that… Abby, it's an inactive case. Until we have proof that Smythe is still alive, the powers that be are going to let it rest." Marcus looked at her trying to decide if she was happy or sad about that.

Abby refused to let him see her pleasure, knowing that she could pursue this case without anyone looking over her shoulder. "Let me check with Rikka and see if she has any leads. Tina, check his paper trail. See if he has anything squirreled away in upstate New York. Marcus, work with Ronni and see if you two can dig up anything. Questions?" The authority she was assuming fit her well. Neither analyst had anything to add. "Thank you. I will call you when I'm out of this place."

Hitting the nurse call button, her curly-haired nurse entered a few minutes later. "Can I assume you are checking yourself out?" asked the woman, as if she were reading her mind. Abby, stunned, nodded. The nurse handed over a clipboard. "These are the standard 'it's your ass if you die' forms." Winking, she added, "Your French friend gave me a heads up."

After signing more forms than she signed when she bought her car, Abby thanked the nurse. Ten minutes and what felt like twenty pounds of bandages later, Rikka entered the room with a bag that had a new set of clothing. "I felt that you needed a new wardrobe. Nothing in your bags were items that suited you." Removing a blouse and black slacks, she handed them to Abby. They were nothing like anything she would ever wear, but they were beautiful. The blouse was a gold and silver print on black. The puffy sleeves would effectively hide the bandage on her right arm. She was not ashamed of her figure, but the blouse revealed more cleavage than she was accustomed to showing.

"Thanks, but I don't know why you want me to wear this. I'm going home." Abby was grateful, but confused.

"Often, how we look can make us feel better than we really do," replied Rikka. "It's a French thing. Humor me. It may help when the pain pills wear off."

Refusing the offered wheelchair, Abby left the hospital on her own two legs. Once seated in the waiting SUV, Abby collapsed. "I should've used the wheelchair." She looked around and realized that Rikka was driving Jonas' BMW. *How could I have had such strong feelings? I barely knew him.* She closed her eyes, hoping that Rikka would think it was from exhaustion. *Damn you, Jonas.*

"The plane is not here, yet. I think you need to eat something. I know a great restaurant on the way to the airport." Rikka was not asking as she took charge. Abby was grateful.

The small bistro was filled with divine smells of foods that Abby loved. Rikka, ordered a glass of wine for herself and a pomegranate infused water for Abby. They raised their glasses in a toast.

"To Jonas," said Rikka.

"Jonas," choked Abby. The glasses clinked together.

The waiter approached with an air of superiority that French waiters always had around Abby. A few quick phrases in fluid French and Rikka had ordered and dismissed the man before he spoke a syllable. Abby, as well versed as she was with food, had no idea what was in half of the food presented to her. All she knew was it was delicious. The cream sauces were perfect. The lamb was seared to perfection. There was even a kind of mushroom she had never even seen in one of the courses. She hoped it wasn't poisonous.

The sorbet was so light, Abby wasn't sure if it was flowing or floating across her tongue. A meal to mourn the passing of love was new concept for Abby. She found it oddly comforting. The presence of Rikka, with her enigmatic combination of caring aloofness was exactly what Abby needed. She spoke minimally, letting the food do the talking. Each word floating from her lips was the right thing to say at the right moment. Abby understood why Jonas had liked her so much.

Looking at her phone, Rikka's eyes widened. "IFTAS has fourteen possible sightings of Smythe." Reaching into her bag, Rikka produced a data tablet that looked too big to have come out of it. She smiled and showed Abby how it folded along the center. "Let's see who we have." Looking at a series of images on the screen, she frowned. "No. Not him. No. God, not even close! Perhaps. No. Too short. Hmmm. Look at this one, Abby."

Turning the screen to Abby, there was an image of a man walking through the concourse in Syracuse. He was wearing a hunter's hat and camouflage pants. There was something that looked wrong about the man, but he wasn't Smythe. Too thin. Tapping the screen, he began moving. There was a slight limp that became more pronounced the further he walked.

"He has something in his shoes. It's not our guy, but we need to tell TSA to stop him," said Abby, pulling out her phone.

Rikka placed her hand over Abby's. "I already did. Good job." Abby instantly knew what had happened. The Frenchwoman was testing her and Rikka could tell she knew. "When you get bored of playing by the FBI rules, I think I know a spot where you would fit in at Interpol."

Abby smiled. "Thanks, but I'm not ready to give up on the Bureau." With a smile, she added, "Not yet, anyway."

"I know. Now, look at this one. I think this could be him. Seventy-two percent probability." Rikka's statement caused Abby to raise an eyebrow. "Anything above sixty-five percent is a likely candidate. It's a new technology."

Abby took the tablet and carefully looked at the image. Putting it into motion, she watched him move through the airport. There was something that she couldn't quite articulate. As he turned, she saw it. He was looking everywhere while trying to make it look like he wasn't. The chair he took was positioned behind a pillar that would have meant he had no real view of others walking past; however, none of the people would notice him and cameras would not have good view of him either. She rewound the camera and watched him again. He stumbled once, like he was uncoordinated. She played it three times before she was sure.

"That's the son of a bitch." All the pain in her arm was forgotten. The meal she had savored was a distant memory. All that mattered was the man on the screen. She would find him. Smythe was hers. "Where is he?" she snarled.

Rikka was on her phone. "Ronni, where is number eight?"

The screen in her hand showed a new window over the previous one. He had taken a flight from Rochester to O'Hare. From there he had gone on to…

"Oh shit," whispered Abby. "Phoenix."

# Chapter Thirty-Two

As Abby and Rikka raced to the airport, the profiler considered calling Mathis. Her vengeance was not more important than the safety of her family. Both her mom and sister, Becca, were in the Phoenix area. There was no telling who he was going after. Rikka interrupted her train of thought.

"I have one Interpol agent, Enrique Rivalo, already in Phoenix. Another is on her way from Utah. Who do you want secured first? Roberta or Becca?" The no-nonsense, Interpol agent was back.

"Have them get to Becca first. She's probably at home. Mom should be at work. I'm guessing you don't need their addresses or phone numbers?" asked an impressed Abby.

Smiling a grim smile, Rikka replied, "No. We have all of that. But you could call them so they are not upset when an Interpol agent shows up."

Dialing her sister, the conversation was short and sweet. "Bec? It's Abby. You remember how I told you we may have problems because of what I do? It's happening. There will be someone there to get you from Interpol. I need you to go with them and stay off the computer."

Her sister's voice was shaky. "Oh, hell no! You better not be shitting me. I have too much going on right now to be..."

"Bluebonnet," interrupted Abby.

"Packing a bag now. Who is coming?" asked the sister.

"Agent Enrique Rivalo," replied Abby.

"If he looks like Enrique Iglesias I'll go anywhere with him. So, Interpol? What the hell have you done now, Abs?" There was concern in her sister's voice that Abby had been hearing since they were kids.

"Don't ask. Please stay safe. Gotta call mom now," and Abby clicked off without a "goodbye." Looking at Rikka, she explained, "Bluebonnet is our panic word."

"I figured that out," mused the Frenchwoman. "That's a good plan. It cuts through the bullshit in a crisis. You had better 'bluebonnet' your mother."

Abby had already hit speed dial. "Becca is excited. She has a thing for Latin men."

A chuckle escaped Rikka's lips. "In that event, I'd love to be… what's the American phrase? A fly on the ceiling?"

"A fly on the wall," corrected Abby.

"Yes, a fly on the wall when they meet. Enrique is not Hispanic. He is Spanish. From northern Spain. He is very European in appearance."

Abby laughed, too. "That'll be interesting." Her mother's phone was ringing.


Roberta was having a bad day. First, it was bad hair. Next, it had been bad traffic. Finally, she had the bad luck to have a patient that could have played both roles in *Grumpy Old Men*. She left the hospital and was heading to her car, thankful that census at the hospital said there were too many nurses for too few patients. Being the senior staff had its advantages. The walk through the covered parking lot was sweltering in the dry, Arizona heat. After a certain temperature, it really didn't matter to Roberta how dry it was. Hot is hot. Arriving at her car, she was not surprised to see that her luck had not gotten any better.

"Are you kidding me?" she asked aloud to no one, staring at the flat tire. "Perfect," she whined, tossing her purse in the passenger's seat. As she slammed the door, her phone began to vibrate from the depths of her Fossil satchel.

Roberta's late husband had made certain that every member of the family knew how to change a tire. Even though she was pushing sixty, there was no way she would call AAA for this. In the time it would take for them to get there, she would have it done and be home with a glass of wine. The trunk opened from the fob on her keychain to reveal clutter. She hated having too many things messing up the front of the car so the trunk became the catch-all for the things that needed to be hidden.

"Lovely," she muttered to herself.

"Sarcasm suits you," said a voice from behind her. She spun in alarm, reaching for the purse that wasn't there. She faced a man with green eyes and blonde hair. "Don't panic. Your daughter, Abby, sent me. There is a problem, I need to take you someplace safe." Holding up an ID, he said, "I'm with Interpol. My name is Jonas Lange. She may have mentioned me."

Looking wary and backing toward the car door where her purse and mace were resting, Roberta replied, "I'm sorry, Agent Lange, but I have never heard of you. You don't mind if I call Abby and confirm you are who you say you are." Tickles of sweat dripped down her face that had nothing to do with the heat of the day.

"Please do," replied the stranger. As Roberta reached for the door, she was seized with spasms through every cell of her body. Collapsing on the hot pavement, still quivering from the voltage of the stun gun, Roberta looked in the eyes of the Observer. He smiled the most malevolent leer she had ever seen. The next moment everything went dark as consciousness fled when his fist connected with her temple.

The Observer, looking around to make certain there was no one watching, tossed the blonde wig he had used into the driver's seat and carried Roberta to his rental car. After placing Abby's mother in the trunk, he left the grounds of the hospital heading to the address of Becca Chilton. It was time for the triple-play of the Chilton women.

Abby hung up her phone after leaving her mother a voicemail with the panic word and instructions to call her as soon as she got the message. Looking thoughtful, she dialed the main hospital number. "Yes," she began, "this is Agent Abigail Chilton with the FBI. I need to reach one of your nurses right away. Roberta Chilton." As the operator transferred her call, Abby asked Rikka, "How long to the airport?"

"Four minutes," replied the efficient Interpol agent. "But you can call her from the plane if you can't get through. Willis has the engines turning and we are cleared for priority takeoff. We will be in the air as soon as possible."

"Thanks," said Abby. "Yes, I need to speak with Roberta Chilton right away. It is urgent." There was a slight pause. "When?" asked Abby, with a little concern in her voice. "Okay. Thank you. I'll try there." Making a face that was somewhere between worry and frustration, she said, "Mom got off early. About ten minutes ago. She is probably driving and forgot to turn on the ringer, again." Dialing her mother's home number, Abby left the same message she had left on the cell phone. "I'll try again from the plane." Then, thinking it through, she said, "Can you send Rivalo to my mom's house as soon as he gets Becca? I have a funny feeling." Picking up her phone, Rikka made a call to tell her agent to move quickly as they drove up to the waiting plane.

"Hello there, Abby," came the Scottish brogue of Willis. "How're ya feelin'?" There was real concern in his voice.

"Been better, Andy. But right now, I'm worried about my family." Realizing he had lost a friend, too, she added, "I'm sorry about Jonas. I…" Her voice cracked.

"It's all right, sweetie. 'E died doing what 'e loved. Who could ask for more?" Gesturing and giving a slight bow, "Your chariot awaits, milady." His whole warrior death attitude would normally have irritated Abby as macho bullshit. With Willis it worked somehow.

Climbing up the stairs with a little help from the Scotsman, Abby sank heavily into the comfortable chairs. Rikka took a seat across from her while Willis secured the door and went into the cockpit. Abby could tell her color was ashen even without looking in a mirror. She was exhausted from the exertions of eating and getting to the plane. Perhaps a nap wouldn't hurt anything.

She was fast asleep in less than a minute. Abby never felt the plane jetting down the runway and into the air.


A knock at the door made Becca jump. She checked the keyhole and quickly stepped back. That did not look like an Enrique. With the warning from Abby, she was suspicious.

"Who is it," she called through the door, trying to sound friendly.

"Miss Chilton? I'm Enrique Rivalo. If you want to look through the keyhole again, I'll show you my credentials."

Becca had to admit that he sounded Spanish, even if he didn't look it. Checking again, she saw an ID that revealed he was who he claimed. Opening the door to the smiling agent, she asked, "So, Enrique, where are we going and what the hell is going on?"


Abby was startled awake by the voice of Rikka. She was speaking rapid French, sounding upset. Seeing Abby was awake, she ended the call. "We have a problem. You've only been asleep for thirty minutes. My agents can't find your mother."

There were no words to express the torrent of emotions raging through Abby. "How? Why? Where?" were the one word questions that came from her mouth.

Knowing how befuddled Abby was feeling, Rikka intervened. "Abby, I have two of my best agents in Phoenix. Rivalo picked up Becca and then went to your mother's home. She wasn't there. After getting your sister to a safe house, he traced the route she should have taken all the way back to the hospital. He found her car there with a flat tire." Rikka let all that sink in before continuing. "Abby, we found a blonde wig in the car." She didn't say anything further. Abby understood perfectly what that meant.

"But Becca is safe?" asked the rattled FBI agent.

"She is," replied Rikka. "I have Janet Dixon staying with her."

"Dixon? I've heard of her. I thought she was ATF."

If Rikka could have looked sheepish, she would have; but that was not in her nature. "She was. Now, she is Interpol. And she is damned good. I only recruit the best." Abby caught the not so subtle hint. "Rivalo is trying to track your mother's movements. The problem is Smythe changed his appearance on the plane so we have to search again to find him. *Merde*, he is a tricky bastard."

Abby grabbed the phone and dialed a number from memory. "Tina, don't ask any questions. I need your accountant magic. Smythe arrived in Phoenix three hours ago. Get Marcus and Ronni to help you snoop around the rental car companies. I need to know who rented cars between the time the flight landed and an hour ago."

"All right, Abby. But what's going on?" asked Tina.

"The son of a bitch has my mom," Abby clicked off without another word.

Rikka was looking at her, impressed. "Clever girl," she muttered. "There is nothing you can do until we find out what is happening. Rivalo will call me when he finds something."

Abby was shaking with rage. "If anything happens to her…"

The Observer was shaking with rage. There was a note on the door of Becca's apartment. "To whom it may concern: If you are in need of Miss Becca Chilton, please contact her sister, Agent Abby Chilton. She can be reached through the Phoenix field office of the FBI." *How the hell did she beat me here? Abby is even better than I thought. Excellent! She is almost perfect.*

Without waiting any longer, he returned to his car and headed to I-10 East. A triple-play of Chilton women would take a little longer. *This is so much fun! I can't wait to see Abby, again.*

An hour away from Phoenix, Abby's computer began beeping. Grabbing the notebook, she opened it to see a video call from Marcus coming through. The computer guru showed up on the computer monitor and the flat screen in the cabin.

"Abby, we have done some really difficult work here." The screen split into four windows. One each for Marcus, Ronni and Tina. One for another video feed.

Tina spoke up. "I narrowed it down to five possible debit cards that were being used to rent cars at three different rental agencies. Debit made more sense since credit cards could be easily traced."

Ronni added her contribution. "I did check all the credit cards used. None of them fit the profile, but I did look at all the videos to make sure. All credit cards were used by the right people. None of them were Smythe. While looking at the videos, there were two people who were not on my list to watch who could have been our guy. Marcus?"

The Korean was more serious than usual. "Ronni sent me links to vids of the men who looked like they could have been our guy. Both used debit cards with no name on them. Basic cash cards that you can buy anywhere across the country."

"So we're nowhere?" asked the perturbed profiler.

"Damn," swore Ronni.

"Told you," said Tina. "Never bet against me when it comes to Abby."

"What?" asked Abby, not understanding where this was going.

The Chilean hacker confessed, "I bet Tina you would wait and let us tell you everything before you said anything." Sighing, she muttered, "I hate shipping oranges."

Marcus rejoined the conversation. "As I was about to say, have a little faith in us, Abigail. We don't give up that easily. But," he took a breath, "this is gonna piss you off. One of the two guys used a fake I.D. The name of this man," the fourth screen showed a blonde man, smiling at the clerk, "is a Jonas Lange. The bastard is using Jonas' name. That is some sick shit."

Abby's face was crimson as her anger exploded. "I want to know where that motherfucker is right now! Track that goddamn car. Use GPS or lojack or whatever the hell you three have in your bags of tricks to find that car and shut it the fuck down!"

Rikka moved the computer so that the camera was on her instead of Abby. "Ronni, I need you to use the SAT8 to track the car. Reposition it to geosynchronous orbit centered on Phoenix. We need to know make, model, year and color. He is smart enough to have disabled any kind of tracking."

Marcus had been typing on his computer as Rikka had been speaking. "Am I the only one who thinks Rikka's English has improved radically since the last time we spoke?"

"Later, Marcus," said Abby. "What are those magic hands of yours doing? I know that look."

Marcus had a very self-satisfied look on his face as he announced, "The GPS tracker has our guy at a Holiday Inn in Scottsdale."

Tina was guarded. "We can't be that lucky. Why would he take Roberta there?"

Rikka was dialing the plane's phone. "I'm sending Rivalo there, now. Ronni, get the satellite in place in case this isn't him."

"Tell him if he shoots the bastard, I'll buy the beer," said Abby.

"I'm sure he'll take you up on that," replied Rikka.

# Chapter Thirty-Three

The plane was on final approach when the phone range. Abby reached for it but Rikka got there first. *"Si, Rivalo?"* The Interpol agent listened. *"Chingao!"* Turning to Abby, "The rental's GPS was wired into a '73 Beetle. This guy's sense of humor is pissing me off."

"Join the club," fumed Abby.

Rikka switched to English so Abby could understand better. "Enrique, continue investigating where he could have gone. Use all your contacts. We are landing so call my mobile." Listening, she replied, "No we didn't. Shut up and get to work." She was smiling in spite of herself. "He asked if we ran over anyone getting here."

Abby didn't laugh. Her sense of humor was missing in action until she found her mom. After the plane taxied to a private hanger, Willis appeared from the cockpit. "Awaiting your orders, ma'am."

Rikka stared at him, a tiny smile playing at the corners of her mouth. "You've never called me ma'am, Willis. Are you feeling well?"

The Scotsman had set her up. "I still haven't, darlin'. I was talkin' ta Abby." He laughed as he lowered the stairs. Rikka elbowed him as she deplaned. Willis winked at Abby and whispered, "I work for Jonas, not Interpol. Call me if ya need me. I want to get that bastard." He slipped Abby a card. "I will be fueled and ready to go anywhere in two hours."

"Thanks," said Abby. She really liked the Scotsman. It was hard not to.

The ever efficient Rikka had a car waiting for them. Getting in the Altima, Abby was content to ride. Rikka instructed, "We will be going to the safe house where your sister is being kept. It wouldn't hurt you to see her. There is an electronics command post there where I can see what they have done to IFTAS while I was away." Speeding off, Abby sat back and stared out the window, wondering where Smythe had taken her mom. Was she even still alive?

The Observer was tempted to kill Roberta right then and there. When she awakened in the trunk of the car, the feisty woman began screaming at the top of her lungs. *Some people need lessons on being a polite kidnap victim. That was unforgivably rude.* He tolerated it for over twenty miles of interstate highway driving, but enough was enough. Finding an exit that had no services, he got off and drove until he was far enough from the Interstate where no one would see them. The long stretch of road would give him ample warning if any vehicles headed his way.

Getting out, he walked around to the trunk and opened it to see the blinking form of Roberta trying to jump out at him. One quick punch to her solar plexus and she fell back, breathing out all her air. Roberta looked up into the eyes of the man. She wouldn't give him the satisfaction of begging, but she wasn't going to enrage him either. Biding her time was the plan of the hour.

"Roberta, we need to have a heart to heart. Now, I need you to behave yourself so I don't have to kill you. That would make it a bad day for both of us. Don't you think Abby would want you to stay alive so she can try some futile attempt to rescue you?" He spoke to her as if all this made perfect sense to anyone. *I can't believe I have to explain this. Abby definitely got her brains from Papa. Once this woman was dead, Abby could blossom into her full potential.*

"Now, if you keep screaming, we will have a problem. I could drug you, but I really don't know what kind of medicine a woman of your advanced age is currently taking. If you are on some kind of blood thinner, beating you into submission could be fatal. Or if you are taking some kind of beta blocker and I shoot you up with Thorazine, your blood pressure could drop and I'd be driving with a corpse in the trunk which would start stinking. The last time that happened, I couldn't get the cleaning deposit back on the rental. It was a nightmare.

"Now, are you going to stop yelling so I can drive in peace?" asked the Observer. Roberta was terrified of this man who could discuss all these horrendous things so calmly and peacefully. She was sure she was going to die. She only hoped it wasn't right that second. Roberta nodded to the man. "Excellent. Thank you so much for cooperating." With that, he took out his stun gun and zapped her again. "I know that was mean, but I have this feeling you are not going to behave." She passed out.

The Observer went and got an item out of his bag and returned to the unconscious woman in the trunk. Holding up a roll of duct tape, he said, "Look. I even got you the kind with cute little birds. You'll be adorable when Abby sees you."


Arriving at the safe house, Abby tried to rush in first; but the long legs of Rikka and her weakened state made the race a lost cause. As soon as she was inside, pain swept over her. Becca ambushed her, hugging and holding her, not knowing she was injured.

"Bec, stop it!" yelled Abby. Backing away, her sister was surprised. "Be gentle. I've got a booboo." The sisters carefully embraced and began to cry tears that were a combination of relief and fear. "I'm sorry," whispered Abby into her sister's ear. "I'm so, so sorry."

"Janet told me a little," sobbed the older Chilton sister. "You can't blame yourself when a psycho goes ape shit over you." Trying to make a joke, she added, "Still, he sounds better than most of the guys you dated in high school."

The sisters laughed briefly until the looming specter of their missing mother flashed back into their minds. "We're going to find Mom. Don't worry."

"Yeah, sure," said Becca. "You're a cop. You should be better at lying by now."

Rikka intruded on the moment. "Abbee, I need your 'elp," said the Frenchwoman, accent back in place.

Entering the tech room and closing the door for privacy, Abby asked, "Why do you fake that accent? Are you really that paranoid?"

Returning to the British resonance, the Interpol agent confessed, "Actually, that is my real accent, Abby. This one I use when I need others to take me more seriously. Or in your case, to make myself more easily understood. I'm really a lazy linguist if you want to know the truth." Pointing to the screen, she said, "Our dear Mr. Smythe rented a new, white Toyota Camry. I really hate that bastard right now."

"He knew that was the best-selling car and the most common car color in America. Hide in plain sight. I agree with you. He is easy to hate. What can your magic eye in the sky do with that?" inquired the psychologist.

"Well," began Rikka, "It would normally be difficult to locate one white Camry among so many cars in Phoenix. If the satellite had been in place when your mother was taken, I would already be sending someone to catch him. Ronni and Marcus are checking with your government to see if they can locate it through any of the American spy satellites up there." There was a ping on her computer. Rikka spun around and her hands moved gracefully across the keyboard, causing multiple screens to show up. "Merde! Have I mentioned how much I hate him?"

"What is it?" asked Abby, looking at the screen. There was a traffic cam that had focused on a license plate. It was on a white Honda Accord. "Let me guess. He swapped plates with that car."

Rikka nodded without saying a word. Her hands were still moving gracefully, but it was getting harder and harder to tell because they began to blur as they moved faster. A request went across the screen to the Phoenix Police Department to stop that car that with stolen plates.

"We need to know what plates he has now," explained Rikka. "Having the local law enforcement handle that leaves us free to try other things. I'll be busy for a while." It was clear that Rikka was dismissing Abby.

Returning to her sister, Abby took a few moments to check on her. She was talking animatedly with Agent Janet Dixon. The two were becoming fast friends. Abby caught her sister saying, "So, you had never met him until today? Well, he's hot for a Spaniard. Not as mocha as I usually like, but I'd make an exception for him."

Dixon looked up at Abby. "You do want some time with Becca, Agent Chilton?"

She had something else in mind. "No. And call me Abby. I need to rest a while. Is there a room where I can lie down?"

"Sure, Abby. Down the hall. The second door on your left. I'll call you if Agent Veilleux finds anything." Turning back to Becca, Dixon resumed the conversation. "I know what you mean. He has that 'I don't give a damn what you think' attitude about him."

Abby grabbed her bag and headed down the hall, leaving them to their girl talk. She was exhausted but too wired up to rest. She had not attempted this since she'd been shot. Opening her laptop, she went right to the chat room where she had first encountered the sociopath.

The Observer was cruising along at seventy-five miles per hour. It was only five over the posted speed limit, exactly like every other driver out there. Too slow or too fast would draw attention to himself. A little over two hours in and he was past Tucson. At this rate, he would be in New Mexico by nightfall.

The noise from the back had gone from a constant wailing to an occasional thump. There was too much duct tape on Roberta to allow her enough leverage to do much damage. Still, when he stopped for gas, it would be a good idea to check and make sure she was still breathing. He didn't want her dying quite yet. There was still so much to do. He would have so much fun with Abby, giving her a new defining moment. *She will be mine!*

The Observer became lost in his fantasy with Abby watching helplessly as her mother died at his hands. He would make her look in her mother's eyes as the life drained from them. They would be linked. She would finally know how he felt as he had watched all those people die. She would know how he felt when his mother had died in his eight-year-old arms, the victim of his father's drunken rage. *She will understand.*

His daydream was shattered as the red and blue lights flashed in his rear view mirror. Looking down at his speed, while lost in his thoughts he had taken his speed up to eighty-six. That was a little too far over the limit for the trooper to ignore. *Dammit.* He was prepared for this.

Pulling off at the next exit, he crossed over the road and stopped his car on the ramp that went back on to the Interstate. The road was cut into the rock so that no one traveling below would see what was happening on the ramp. Now he had to make sure that no one else was trying to get on the interstate while he spoke with the patrolman. He could see the trooper getting out of his car with a scowl. The cop was mad the Observer had not stopped on the shoulder.

Coming up to his window, hand on his holster, the Arizona State Highway Patrolman, barked at the Observer, "Boy, when you see those lights, you pull your ass over right then. Not on an exit or the other damn other side of the exit. You stop right there. Understand?"

"Understood," said the Observer, and used the stun gun on the man's neck. With no one getting on or off this exit, the Observer calmly got out of his car, took the gun from the officer, placed the barrel under his Kevlar, and sent a bullet into the man's heart. Carrying the cop back to his car, the killer placed him in the driver's seat and closed the door. As a car was passing, the Observer pretended to be talking to the trooper as the traveler ignored them, grateful he wasn't the one stopped by the cop. After the traffic had passed, the Observer opened the door, turned off the lights, and helped himself to the officer's mace, radio and extra clips.

Walking calmly back to his car, he pounded the trunk and yelled, "How are you doing in there?" A muffled sound told him she was still with him. "Great," he replied opening it. One quick spray of mace led to muffled cries. "Please be quiet now. I'm trying to drive." Getting back on the road, he heard a beep from his computer. He had a message. *It's about time, Abby/*


Abby began typing a message to the man who had her mother. {Sorry I missed you at the hospital. How is mom? I hope she is giving you a lecture on the error of your ways.}

After a long pause words appeared on her screen. {She is quiet right now. She was a little fussy at first, but we have come to an understanding. How is your arm?}

*Unbelievable!* {It will heal. Why don't we meet up and discuss it? Don't you think we should talk? You have someone I want. What do you want from me?} Abby was tempted to call Rikka and Dixon in. Some instinct deep within her gut told her to wait.

{You will know soon enough. How about we meet tomorrow? I promise dear Roberta will be safe for now. But I agree that a face to face without any gunshots is long overdue, Abby.}

Abby didn't like the "for now," but there was little she could do about it. {Where do you want to meet? I'm free right now.}

{LOL. I'm sure you are but I'm a little busy. So much to prepare and so little time. I'll call you in the morning. Get some rest. I'm sure that arm is hurting.}

{Wait a second, Smythe. Let's talk some more.} Abby tried to keep him on the line. She needed more information.

{Good night, Abby. And please, call me Darrell.} She could see he had logged out of the chat room.

"Dammit!" muttered the profiler. This was going to be a long night. Sleep was not an option.

# Chapter Thirty-Four

Abby dozed fitfully in a chair next to her sister. Each time the profiler woke she glared at the computer screen, willing a message to be there. Around four, lit only by the light of the monitor, Abby looked at the shadowed form of her sibling and heard a sob escape from Becca.

"Bec?" called Abby, reaching a hand out to touch her sister's shoulder. The older sister jolted awake.

"What's wrong? Is it Mom?" asked Becca, alert instantly.

"No, sis. You were making a noise while…" The lights were turned on, blinding them, as Rikka entered the room with a sense of urgency.

"An officer of the Arizona Highway Patrol was found dead an hour ago. Dixon is on her way to check it out." Rikka could see the confusion on their faces. "He called in that he was pulling over a white Camry about an hour away from New Mexico. The tag matched the tag which was stolen off a different Camry in Phoenix. He switched them twice before he even left town."

"What does that mean?" asked Becca.

"It means he has a gun and is not afraid to use it," said Abby. "How long ago did he stop the car?" Something didn't quite add up.

Rikka looked at Abby as if she were sizing up a thoroughbred horse. "He was stopped a little after seven. A few minutes later, the officer called in saying he had a family emergency. It wasn't until his wife called to check they realized he was missing. Smythe has his radio.

"I have our satellite searching New Mexico, but in the dark it is more challenging to find a specific car. Rivalo is on the ground in El Paso, working his way back toward Arizona. Abby, any idea what he wants in New Mexico? This makes no sense." The woman from Interpol looked tired and frustrated.

"No clue, Rikka. He is so far off profile now that I can't even guess. Something happened in Toronto that made him devolve. It may have been killing the woman so soon after the last, or maybe killing Jonas sent him over the edge." Abby began reworking her profile as her mental agility recalled all the details. "He seems fixated on me like he was on Jonas for a while. After killing Kristin, Jonas was changed. Now, he has taken my Mom to mess with me. The strange thing is that he is being reckless. That's what I don't understand. Even when he killed Kristin, he remained controlled. Now he's flying off the rails."

Rikka agreed. "Something is sending him into a spiral. Whatever it is that you do to him, it is taking him down a path that..." A tech called to Rikka from the electronics room. She left without finishing her thought.

Becca looked at her sister with pity. "This is what your life is like? Who is the therapist for the therapist?"

"Good question," replied Abby. *I'm going to need one when this over.* Her computer beeped. Abby jumped and dashed to the table with her sister following. There were words on the screen that made Abby's pulse quicken.

{You really should be sleeping, Abby.}

Abby's flinched as she typed. *Damn that arm.* {Well I have a lot on my mind. So where are you this morning? I'm ready for that face to face.}

{LOL. I'm sure you are. Here's the deal. You and Becca. Alone. No FBI. No Interpol. You can bring your favorite gun if it makes you feel better. Anyone but you two, bye-bye Mommy. If it's just you, bye-bye Mommy. Any questions?}

Abby looked at her sister. "This is really dangerous, sis. He wants to hurt me and kill people I care about. There will be a target right there." she tapped her sister's forehead. "If you can't do this, I'll try to find another way."

"Try and stop me. I may only be an online customer service rep, but I'm not letting that son of a bitch hurt Mom because I was chicken shit." There was fire in her eyes Abby hadn't seen since they were fighting over a boy in high school.

{Deal. Where are you? We will be there.} typed Abby.

{I thought it should be someplace Divine. LOL.} The connection was severed.

Becca looked at her sister who was in shock. "Abs? What's wrong? You look like someone walked over your grave?"

"I think Smythe just did. Divine, Texas is where I was shot two years ago. It's where Phil died." Anger welled up within her. "He's waiting there with Mom. That's the son of a bitch's game. He's in my head." She took out the card that Willis had given her and dialed the number. "Wake up, Andy. Warm up the jet. We're going to San Antonio."

Abby's phone rang three times as the sisters drove to the airport. She ignored the calls, certain it was Rikka. She would call her once they were in Texas. With Becca behind the wheel, the thirty minute drive to small Phoenix Deer Valley Airport only took twenty minutes. The car was filled by an awkward silence. There were no words either woman could say that would make things any easier.

Willis was standing by the jet, looking wide awake in spite of the early hour. "Abby, why the hell are we goin' to Texas? And who is the lovely lady with you?" He kissed Becca's hand as he had kissed Abby's the first time he greeted her.

"Let's go, flyboy. Hands off my sister. Becca, meet Andy Willis. Hands off the pilot." She moved up the stairs, welcoming his assistance. "The bastard is there. Use the turbo or afterburner or whatever the hell you use to get us there fast."

"Can I assume we're not working with Interpol on this little trip?" asked the pilot.

"That would be a safe assumption," replied Abby, unsure of the reason for the question.

Pulling the hatch closed behind them, Willis explained. "Without Rikka's Interpol clout, I have to play by the rules. We will be on the ground in about an hour and forty-five minutes. Maybe thirty if I can charm me way into the queue." He disappeared into the cockpit.

"He's nice," said Becca. Looking around the Gulfstream, she whistled. "When I grow up I want to be a Fed. Nice plane."

"It belonged to a friend of mine. He's … gone. But Andy is helping me get that bastard. I'll tell you all about it later. Right now, I need to rest."

The plane was in the air five minutes later.

Darrell Smythe was sitting happily in the homely house. The place where Abby had lost so much had seen its better days. No one had lived in it since "the day of the FBI shootout," as the locals liked to call it. The sun was starting to brighten the sky, but you couldn't tell from within. A propane lantern lit the room, casting dancing shadows all around. The boarded up window panes looked like rotten teeth which were ready to fall out. All the glass was long gone, broken by the kids who had been dared to go up to the "haunted house." Debris was scattered around as he imagined it. Everything was perfect.

Seated on a table above it all, he and Roberta were royalty surveying the crumbling ruins around them. He looked to her, smiled and said, "This is where your little girl got shot. Did you ever meet Phil? He was her partner." Roberta was barely awake. She was cramped from being stuffed in a trunk and severe dehydration. It was hard for her to focus on the words coming from his mouth. She knew was she was going to die. There was a rope with one end around her neck and the other end tied to a rafter. If he knocked her off the chair, she would fall backwards and die a slow, strangled death.

"It's true. This is the place. Your little girl lost her baby and her ability to have her own little girl right in this room." Seeing her eyes widen, he continued. "I'm thinking that Phil was the baby daddy. Did she ever tell you?" Tears tried to well up in the eldest Chilton's eyes as Smythe leaned her chair teasingly back. "Abby, why didn't you tell your Mommy you were knocked up?"

Abby and Becca walked out of the shadows by the doorway. What they saw was right out of their worst nightmares. The killer welcomed them warmly. "So glad you could both make it. We've been expecting you, right Roberta?" Pointing a gun at Becca, he said, "Abby, I really think you should put your gun on the floor. We both know you can't aim with your good arm, and are a really bad shot with your left. You wouldn't want to miss and hit Mom, would you?"

The gun she had gotten from Willis was placed on the ground. "If it's me you want, let's make a deal, Darrell. Stop tipping mom backwards and we can talk."

An evil smile crept onto his face. "We can talk perfectly like this. But if Becca reaches one more inch behind her for the gun she has, I'll shoot her where she stands. Turn and use two fingers please, Miss Chilton." Becca, exhaled in frustration.

"Shit," she muttered. She spun and removed her gun as instructed.

"Why, Darrell?" inquired the counselor, trying to buy some time. "Explain it to me." Abby took a few steps forward, placing herself between the killer and her sister. Becca remained defiantly in place, refusing to bolt to safety. "Help me understand why you are who you are. Was I right about your father?"

The look in Smythe's eyes was filled with manic rage at the memory. "He killed my mom! She wanted to take me to grandma and grandpa's to live for a while." He was traveling back into his memory, digressing into the eight-year-old he had once been. "He hit mommy over and over and over. I held mommy. She looked at me and I looked at her. She kept looking at me, but didn't see me anymore."

*Oh my God!* Abby had to pull him back to today. "Darrell, it's okay. You are safe now. He's not here. I can help you."

The childlike digression disappeared and the killer was back. "Abby, Abby, Abby. I know he's not here. I made sure he wouldn't hurt anyone else ever again that night. Watching the light go out of his eyes wasn't the same as Mom." He looked nostalgic. "Nothing ever was. But, you are the one who can bring that back. You will see."

*Watching the light go out in his Mom's eyes and killing his Dad for causing it. Take those ingredients, stir, and add to a pressure cooker. The perfect recipe for a serial killer.* Abby needed to keep him talking. "Why me? I'm only a profiler. I'm a shrink."

"You are the only one who gets me," replied Darrell. He said it like it was so obvious a kindergartener could see it. "No one else understands; but you do. We are so much alike, Abby. It's not like the game with Jonas. He was a distraction for both of us. He really needed to go. Can't you see that? We need each other. I'm going to make you perfect."

Abby understood. He needed someone to fill the void. Killing was his only form of intimacy. "You don't have to do anything to make me understand. I get you. You need a partner. Let me be that." Abby was horrified at the words coming from her mouth. *Dammit Willis! Where the hell is the backup?*

For the first time since childhood, Darrell Dalton Smythe smiled a real smile of joy. "Yes, it's time. As soon as we get rid of everyone who is in the way." He tilted Roberta's chair backwards and raised his gun toward Becca.

A shot shattered the slow motion horror playing itself out as Abby watched helplessly, rooted to the spot. The amazing phenomenon of adrenaline rush created the illusion of slow motion during times of stress. Abby processed the impossible. Instead of dangling, kicking her feet as she struggled to breathe, Roberta crashed to the floor in a tangle of rope and the remains of the chair. A second shot rang out, but not from the killer's gun. From far behind him, the bullet caught Smythe and sent him sprawling forward off the table. He landed on the floor in front of Abby, wounded in the shoulder, the gun skidding to a stop at the profiler's foot.

Abby looked for the source of the shots. There was a room in the back of the house where the previous occupant had hidden and tortured those whom he had molested. From those ominous shadows, a shadowy figure floated forward, smoking gun in hand.

"What is it with you Chilton women and ropes?" said a smiling Jonas Lange.

Abby was sure she was seeing a ghost. This was not happening. She gawked, wanting to believe her eyes, but her mind refused the evidence of her eyes. She saw him die. He got shot. He fell in the water. He called her name.

Becca dashed to check her mother. Looking at the man emerging from the shadows she called "Enrique? How did you get here?"

Jonas, keeping his gun on the killer, walked toward Abby. "Actually, it's not Enrique. My name is Jonas Lange. I'm a friend of your sister." Turning to Abby, he said, "At least I hope I still am."

"You're dead," gasped Smythe, in a pool of his own blood.

"The reports of my death have been greatly… well… wrong," replied the Interpol agent. He kicked the killer over on his back causing him to cry out in pain. "It was a really good shot though."

The sound of a slide cocking a pistol made a click as loud as gunfire in the silence between them. Abby's left hand was holding the gun that had landed at her feet. Jonas looked at her to see where the pistol was pointed. She walked up, stood with one foot squarely on the crotch of Smythe, and pointed the gun right between the killer's eyes. He squirmed from the pain in his shoulder wound, the agony of the grinding foot of Abby, and the fear of looking down the barrel of a gun.

"You killed hundreds of people. I watched you blow Rupert's brains all over that dock. You shot me. I thought you killed Jonas." She glanced at the German with relief and anger in her eyes. "You kidnapped my Mom and tried to kill my sister to make me like you. You are too fucking sick to live."

"Abby, don't do it." At first she thought it was her sister speaking, but quickly realized it wasn't. Jonas' words were the most calming thing she had ever heard. "He wanted to destroy you, but he didn't. You beat him. But if you pull that trigger, he wins. You are not a killer. This isn't self-defense. It's an execution. That is not you. Abby, look at me." He waited until she met his loving, green eyes. "Please... don't."

Abby let the gun drop to her side. "So he goes to jail." Her voice was filled with regret. "A nice comfy jail cell. Or even worse, a nut house. It's not fair." She stepped back, removing her foot from the killer.

"You're right, Abby. Jail isn't fair for this monster." Jonas looked at the beaten man on the floor. "You're not a killer, Abby." Pointing his gun between the terrified eyes of Darrell Dalton Smythe, the Interpol agent said. "But I have no problem with it."

There was genuine terror as the killer's eyes pleaded with Jonas, begging him for life. Jonas managed a malevolent smirk. "You deserve to die." The two locked eyes, neither one flinching until Smythe closed his eyes in defeat. "I'm just messing with you, Darrell. But it was fun watching you piss your pants," said Jonas, winking at Abby.

The eyes of the killer popped opened and morphed from defeat into rage. Smythe kicked out with all his might, catching Lange in the shin, causing him to fall back. Twisting around, the fallen

Observer scrambled to his knees as he grappled for the gun in Abby's hand.

Falling back, Jonas rolled into a backwards somersault, ending with one knee and one foot each on the ground. In a perfect shooter's crouch, the bullets exploded from the barrel of his Beretta, once again shattered the quiet of the crumbling domicile. The nine-millimeter rounds all found their target as Jonas emptied his clip into the chest of Darrell Dalton Smythe. He was dead before his body hit the ground.

Walking over to the still form of the killer, Jonas looked down and said, "Bad move."

# Chapter Thirty-Five

Abby stared at the body lying at her feet. The killer of countless people would never kill again. She was shaking from Smythe's attack, the shock of his death, and the realization that Jonas was standing right in front of her. She took half a step toward the man she had thought was dead, wrapped her arms around him and kissed him long, hard and passionately.

Becca had managed to sort out her mother from the remains of the chair and removed much of the duct tape that had kept her muted and immobilized. Looking at her sister kissing the man who had kept her from the hands of a killer, she muttered, "I think they've met before today." Looking back at her mother, she continued the cleanup. "Something tells me I won't be getting my shot at Enrique or whatever the hell his name is." Her mother nodded her agreement, too dehydrated to speak.

After kissing him with all the love in her soul, Abby pulled back. "That is for not being dead." Then, without hesitation, she slapped him across the face. "And that is for not being dead, too!"

Becca looked up at the sound of hand against face, "Hmm, maybe I will."

Jonas smiled in spite of the pain and the red imprint of a hand on his right cheek. "I deserved that. Abby, you had to think that so Smythe would believe it. Do you understand?"

Abby's mind played out a series of possibilities. Had she known Jonas was alive, what would she have done? Jonas would have stayed in Toronto with her. Smythe would have gotten both her Mom and Becca. When she saw the killer, she wouldn't have been as desperate. He would have seen through that. As sick and twisted as he was, he had still managed to get inside her head. Smythe would have killed Becca and her Mom on the spot to destroy her instead of bantering with her.

"How did you know to go to Phoenix? I didn't see that coming." Abby needed more information before she passed judgment.

"It was simple, really. Smythe didn't really know how close we were for certain. He wanted to destroy you. To be honest, I had no clue about him wanting you to be his partner. That was a shock. But, I figured he would go after those closest to you. Rikka had Mathis keep Marcus and Tina at the FBI building, keeping them safe. Going after them really wasn't his style anyway. But, going after your family would be the next thing he would do. I'm not a genius profiler, but I do have good instincts."

Abby understood. "So you went to get Bec and Mom someplace safe."

The German nodded. "Well, not right away. I think you saw me once in the hospital. I had on a surgical mask when you opened your eyes. After you were out of danger, I headed down there. Sorry I didn't get to your Mom fast enough." The two approached the two other Chilton women. Jonas produced a bottle of water from his pack. "Drink this, Mrs. Chilton. But slowly. Help is on the way." Looking to Becca, he said, "Sorry about using an alias. Enrique Rivalo is one of my favorites. I'm really an Interpol Agent but my name is Jonas. I have worked this case with Abby."

"Yeah, I kind of figured out you two knew each other from the lip lock," replied Becca. "So, you were dead? Cool trick. May I say you look very healthy and handsome for a corpse?"

"Down girl," interjected Abby.

"Well, I did get shot. At least my phone did." Jonas reached into his jacket pocket and produced the remains of his beloved mobile phone. "Mine has a Kevlar cover. It comes in handy when it is dropped, run over or shot. I always keep my phone right here." He put his hand over his heart, right where he'd been shot. "It never stopped a bullet until now. But it does knock the wind out of you. It's like getting punched really hard in the chest." Pulling his shirt aside, it showed a bruise that was roughly phone-shaped. "I'm glad it was there, but I'd rather not do that again. I almost drowned when I lost my balance." Becca looked confused. "I fell in Lake Ontario. It's worse than it sounds."

The conversation was interrupted by police and paramedics arriving on the scene with Willis bringing up the rear. He walked up and shook Jonas' hand. Abby watched the Scot carefully and put one and one together quickly.

"You haggis-eating, sheep-blowing, son of bitch. You knew!" yelled Abby at Willis.

Willis took the outburst in stride. He reached into his pocket and handed Jonas a five dollar bill. "I really didn't think she'd mention haggis." To the profiler he said, "Abby, how did ya think Jonas got to Phoenix? He doesn't have a rocket in his arse."

Turning on Jonas once again, "Who else knew? Mathis? Tina? Marcus?" Thinking for a second she said, "Dammit, Rikka! That bitch knew, didn't she?" Willis handed another five to Jonas and walked off shaking his head. "You'd better stop betting on me or I am going to shoot your dick off!"

"My dick? Really?" asked Jonas. Roberta was being loaded onto a stretcher. Becca looked Jonas up and down, raising an eyebrow with an expression that reminded him of her sister. "Well, it is a big target." He winked at Becca while Abby fumed. "Willis and Rikka were the only ones who knew. We had to keep it with those who needed to know. That's why I was Enrique."

"That's a dumbass alias," muttered Abby.

Jonas took charge. "Be mad at me later. Right now you need to take a ride with your mother. Becca, can follow in the car." He showed his I.D. to the paramedics. "This woman is Special Agent Abby Chilton with the FBI. She was injured and is in need of medical attention. Please take her with you."

"Now wait a goddam second," began Abby.

The paramedics were trying to get her attention, but she wasn't having any of it. Jonas whispered in her ear. "Look at your Mom. She looks hurt and terrified. You can yell at me all you want later. Right now, she needs you and I have to take care of this mess and do all kinds of paperwork for a shooting.

Abby acquiesced and went with the medics. Becca was impressed. "I have never see Abs listen to anyone like that. Impressive." She was really looking him up and down, staying focused on the down. "Hmmmm…"

Jonas was amused. "Sorry, Becca. I'm not on the market. I'm in a relationship."

"Does Abby know that?" asked the older sister, playfully.

"I pretty sure she does. I don't think she wants to admit it, yet. She'll come around eventually." Jonas was using all his charm, hoping that Becca could be a help in the matter.

Taking a pen from one of the nearby cops, she took his hand and wrote her number. "If she doesn't come around, there are other Chilton fish in the sea." Becca strode off to follow the ambulance, putting a little extra shake in her walk.

Jonas looked at the number on his hand, turning to one the officer in charge. "Do you have anything that can wash ink off a hand?"


Two weeks later, Abby walked into the Knoxville FBI field office to cheers and applause. Her office was decorated with balloons and a welcome back sign that looked like it had been done by fourth graders. *It's the thought that counts.*

She had only been back in town for three days and only cleared to return for light duty yesterday. Marcus and Tina had picked her up from the airport, grilling her for all the details of the end of the case. The FBI had classified the case so there was more rumor and innuendo than facts flying around the office.

Marcus had discovered Smythe's file on his computer, listing his kills. It would be months before all the victims could be confirmed, but each one they had tracked so far turned out to be accurate. There was even an abandoned quarry north of the city that held almost as many bodies as the nearby church cemetery. Ronni was coordinating with Marcus on the international victims. With two-hundred and seventy victims to find, it was all they could do to keep up.

Keeping a lid on this case was going to be challenging. Already there had been leaks about a serial killer who was shot by police in Texas. There had been no mention of Interpol or FBI, yet. That is how both organizations wanted it. A killer this prolific would become a cult anti-hero with fans and groupies claiming he was still alive and well, killing anyone who showed up on a missing person's report.

Abby had spent the majority of the last two weeks recovering from her wounds. It helped that, although he had an apartment in

Lyon, Jonas' home was someplace much warmer than his native land. The Caribbean island of Martinique made for a rather peaceful place to recuperate. Between basking in the sun to swimming in the Caribbean Sea, it had made the idea of sitting still much more bearable. Jonas' home was very secluded allowing her to tan without tan lines. It also allowed them to swim without fear of being interrupted. They did manage to scare the hell out of a lot fish and give the dolphins an eye full.

The only visitor had been Rikka toward the end of her stay. There was an initial tension between the two women when the Interpol agent arrived. Rikka was still upset that Abby had been stupid enough to take her sister to face the killer alone. That kind of off the wall, outside the rules, make-it-up-as-you-go attitude is the kind of thing that made Rikka want to file an official complaint with the FBI to get her fired, so she could come to work for Interpol. She would be the perfect addition to Jonas' team.

Soon, Abby and Jonas knew that it would be time to return to their lives. Even though she was still a little irked at Jonas for not telling her the plan, she had forgiven him about the third day into their island holiday. Between the rum, the sun, the water, and his knowledge of g-spots, there was no way any woman could stay mad. The FBI wanted her back and Rikka had a list of new assignments for Jonas to peruse.

"So what are we going to do now?" asked Abby, on their last night in paradise. "Do we say good-bye? Or are we going to try and make this work?" Abby knew what she wanted more than anything else. It was so hard to tell what Jonas wanted beneath the façade of handsome civility and those amazing green eyes which captivated Abby every time she saw them.

"Well, it will be complicated," said the German, trying to sound like it wasn't tenable. "But, what the hell, I like complicated. The rest of my life is so uneventful, I can use some excitement in my love-life." They came to an understanding. Neither one expected total fidelity until the day they could be together permanently. But neither one would allow anyone else to come between them when that day arrived.

When Tina asked for details, Abby, for once, was an open book. She shared everything she could remember and even made up a few stories to keep her hooked. When Marcus asked about using Jonas house to meet Ronni next month, she promised to talk to Lange.

As soon as she had made herself comfortable behind her desk, there was a knock at the door. Jeremy Mathis came in and sat down. Placing a steaming cup of coffee on her desk for her, he asked, "So, Chilton, how are you feeling?" He was starting off nice with a cup of coffee, making her nervous.

"It was touch and go there for a while, but I think I'll be peachy. How have you been while I've been gone? Don't tell me you missed me?" teased the profiler.

With a mischievous look, he asked, "Touch and go? Chilton, I don't want to know about Barbados or wherever it was you and Lange disappeared to." She laughed a genuine laugh at Mathis' jest. "Are you ready to get back to work?"

"I suppose so," sighed Abby. "I guess it's time to start working on the annual psych evals, isn't it?"

Smiling, Jeremy replied, "Yes it is. Hanna is already bitching about having to do all of them." Abby first looked confused and then suspicious. "I figured that you have some experience we need to use on some other cases. Unless you want to be stuck over there by the couch listening to agents bitch and moan about having to do their psych evals?"

Abby's smile was as wide as her face. "Well, I guess it would be a poor use of resources to put me on the bitch and moan cases. What did you have in mind?"

"Well, there is one case that Jenks has discovered," began the agent. "Do you think it's odd that four people from the same high school class have all died of mysterious strokes in different cities and three states?" The penny was in the air.

Abby raised an eyebrow. "It's statistically unlikely, but not impossible."

"What if I told you that none of them had anything in their medical files indicating they were at risk?" asked Mathis, letting the penny drop.

Abby felt guilty for the excitement that was welling up inside. "It sounds like you need a profiler to look into a serial killer. Let me see what I can do."

# After Words

A special thank you to all who had the honesty to tell me where the first edition needed to be edited. It takes courage to speak the truth and not worrying about a temperamental writer taking offense.

www.ingramcontent.com/pod-product-compliance
Lightning Source LLC
Chambersburg PA
CBHW072218170626
46813CB00003B/992